My Better Half

By Jerome Griffin

To a true inspiration – Orna Ross. Some people get to the heart of the matter. Others hit the nail on the head.
Orna splits the atom!

Jerome Griffin has been published on numerous occasions in the marketing and advertising trade press in the UK. He has also had travel pieces published in Real Travel magazine and written business related articles specifically for translation into Russian language publications. Jerome is 42 and lives in London with his wife, Elaine.

Follow me on Twitter @jeromegriffin2

Find me on Facebook: Jerome Griffin or my page: My Better Half

Check out my blog: www.jeromegriffin.wordpress.com

ACKNOWLEDGEMENTS AND THANKS

In 2008 I enrolled in a six month creative writing course in Dublin called Get It Written, the aim of which was to get the first draft of a novel completed by the end of the six months. I got exactly what I needed from that course, so thanks to Orna Ross for running such a brilliant programme.

Thanks also go to my fellow students on Get It Written for their support, encouragement and feedback, as well as the shared fun and experiences. In particular I would like to mention the contemporary fiction group, Tara Smith, Geraldine Creed, Samantha Ryan and Simon Boylan.

Thanks also go to a few close friends who helped with feedback as the novel progressed – Fergal O'Donnell, Charlotte Yapp, Simon Boylan and my wonderful wife, Elaine.

Elaine also came up with the original concept for the jacket cover and her initial sketches were eerie enough, but then Ben Yates got Alex Borg on board to finish the design, which sent a chill through my veins – thanks so much guys – couldn't have asked for more.

A few very good friends always enquired about progress with the book whenever I met them, so Aoife Fitzsimons, Hayley Brace and Dulcie McLerie, thank you all so much for your unwavering interest and encouragement.

I count myself extremely lucky to have a great many fabulous friends as well as an incredibly supportive family who are always there – thank you all so much!

Finally, thanks to my wife, Elaine, for better or worse.

Satan's Whore

We used to wait for God to fix our lives. Now we wait for the Lottery. Same shit, different deity.

"Lord, please help me get the job," has become, "If I won the Lottery I'd never work again."

I want! I want! I want! It's the ultimate letter to Santa Claus. In so many ways we're always eight years old.

Thing is, when we are eight years old, we seem to have life figured out better. We know exactly what we're going to do. Exactly who we're going to be.

I was going to be an astronaut and go to Mars. I was going to be an explorer and discover lost cities. I was going to be Bob Geldof and fix the world. Every goal I scored in the playground was the winner in the FA Cup Final. Every ace I served won Wimbledon. Every putt I holed, the Ryder Cup.

But I'm none of those people. I did none of those things. Instead I'm a…well, how do I explain what I am? Who I am? It doesn't make sense to me so how can I even begin to make you understand?

OK, let's try this.

Take a perfect vacuum. I'm not talking about a domestic cleaner, a Hoover or a Dyson or anything like that. Not anything man-made. Nothing natural either. Not a black hole. Not even Space itself, but a perfect vacuum where nothing exists.

Nothing will ever exist.

Nothing can exist.

Take this perfect vacuum, multiply it by a million and you're still nowhere near understanding how empty it feels to work in advertising.

So there it is. I'm an account director for an ad agency.

My job is to con people into buying products they neither need nor want. I'm a carpet bagger selling junk to native Americans. I'm a bogus doctor selling the elixir of life to ignorant hicks. A used car salesman. A walking oil slick. Society's cancer. Satan's whore.

Home is London, although my roots, like 750,000 others in this city, are Irish. So, like most people living in London now, I'm a blow-in. The thing is it has always been like that. The city has lured people into its web for centuries with the promise of work and riches to follow. Go back a few generations and every family tree comes from somewhere else. There's no such thing as a dyed-in-the-wool, genuine Londoner. Just seven million people looking to get by and maybe a little better. Seven million people driving the relentless beast, but nobody steering.

It takes a lot of effort being Satan's whore. Every day turns into a late night. On the odd occasion you do leave the office at a reasonable hour you get looks. Your colleagues and peers, other teams and departments, the management, even the computers stare at you and ask 'where are you going, part-timer?' The EU can talk all it likes about a thirty-seven and a half hour week, but MEPs have never worked in the ad industry. Anything under sixty is a light week. And that's just in the office. Then there's the work you do on the Tube and at home. It's not a weekend unless you're chucking back a bottle of red on Sunday night while working on a pitch that's already running late.

After a while there's nothing else. You no longer play sports. The West End might be your back garden, but when was the last time you went to the theatre? Or a museum? Or even the cinema. Nowadays the cinema is something that happens to other people.

The things you used to do at the weekend, well now you work instead.

But then, you can see the point. After all, it's probably a big important pitch - the kind of pitch that will change the world. Maybe a certain soft drink company is launching a new flavour cola. They've already got vanilla, lemon, cherry and a host of others as well as the original. And now they're launching peach. And it's really important that it's a success so that the company can make more billions and obesity levels can rise. Or maybe a certain sports clothing company has lost 0.03% of its market share and needs a new campaign to redress the balance and calm the rising shareholder panic. Or maybe £9bn profit isn't enough for a certain high street bank who needs a campaign to explain to its customers that bank charges have to rise by 25% for the sake of 'sustainability'.

Yep, it's bound to be a big important pitch. But it's good to know that you're making a difference. That all the sacrifices have been worth it. Who wants to play sports when you can get an advert on TV instead? At least you're leaving your stamp on the world. Then again, so did Stalin.

So all you've got outside of work is your partner. But even that relationship has been fake for longer than you can remember. But it's all you've got left. And then, one day, even that's gone.

What then?

'I just don't feel the way I used to,' says Helen. 'I still love you. I just love you more like a best friend now. I would never do anything to hurt you.'

It can't be hurt I'm feeling then.

So is that it? Are the ten years we have been together now over? Is a seven year-old marriage finished? I stare hard at nothing. I can't focus. I've never felt so alone.

'Did you suddenly feel this way or has it been developing over time?' I hear myself asking.

'I think it's been happening for a while, but I only realised recently,' she says.

'Is it something I've done?' I ask.

'No.'

'Are you in love with someone else?'

'No.'

'Do you fancy someone else?'

'No.'

'Then what has changed?' I ask.

With venom.

'I don't know,' says Helen and bursts into tears. She's crying. She tells me it's over, my insides turn to mulch, but she's the one who's crying.

I'm too numb to cry. I want to comfort her. I want to hug her and kiss her and tell her it will be ok like I always do, but I don't know if she wants that. I don't know what she wants. She doesn't know what she wants, so how am I supposed to know? Ten years and this is the first time I don't know what to say or do in her company since our very first date. Jesus, I never expected a break-up to be as awkward as a first date. Does everything eventually come full circle?

And when the circle is complete, where do you go? This is the lives of two people that will never again be the same. Until this point every step we took together as a couple was just natural progression. The next logical move.

First date. Second date. First shag. First post-shag date. Christ, I remember that was awkward. But at least it was still natural progression.

Being an item. Letting friends know. Meeting parents. Falling in love. Predictable. Following the herd. Natural progression.

Weekends away and holidays. Moving in together. Getting engaged. Natural progression.

Buying our first home together. Joint bank accounts. The inevitable – getting married.

Moving again. Bigger mortgage. Pensions.

Then falling out of love.

It just doesn't fit. The next step was supposed to be growing old together. Then dying together. Natural progression. Falling out of love was not how it was supposed to go.

For the first time in my life I feel like an adult. Everything before this was easy. Everything was fun. Even the frustrations and annoyances and bad times. All those late nights lining the pockets of rich bosses who would not have thought twice about firing me? A piece of piss. It was all fun. All a game. But this? This is serious. This is real life.

I should be thinking about saving my marriage. I'm in my thirties and my marriage is over. We were supposed to die together. That was the deal. Fall in love, be lovers and best friends for the rest of our lives and then die together. Gently farting maybe. I should be persuading my wife to give it another go. But I'm not. If I'm honest, I don't feel the same either. If I'm honest, I've been going through the motions too. Natural progression has left the building.

So, this is a failed marriage. This is the spectre that haunts society, destroys families and finances law firms. This is the terror I was certain would never visit us. Any second now I should see my soul float out of my mouth never to return. If I was to die this instant and they were to cut out my heart, it would be black. No doubt the legal teams will arrive soon with a huge chainsaw to cut the house into pieces and split the possessions. We should really have our bank accounts ready to hand over.

Still though, there must be a reason for the break-up. Something real. Solid. Tangible.

'It can't be that simple, Hels,' I say softly, 'you must have some insight into why you want to break-up with me.'

She nods and snuffles back sobs. She blows her nose and steadies herself. I give her time. She takes a few deep breaths before beginning with: 'I don't think you're happy with much in life anymore...'

'Well, considering how shit everything is that's hardly a surprise, is it?' I say, cutting across her. Mistake. I should have let her continue. I should have let her finish. Suddenly I'm the villain again. She has called an end to our marriage and I'm the villain. The world is a fucked up place.

'Sorry,' I offer, 'what were you going to say?'

She gathers herself again. Wipes her eyes. Blows her nose. Takes a few deep breaths.

'I've tried to help you but you seem to be on an ever increasing downward spiral. You're never in a good mood anymore. You used to be fun all the time. I've suggested counselling, which you just scoff at and dismiss outright. I think you're severely depressed and you are refusing help,' she says.

'OK, I admit I'm a little down at the moment,' I say. 'But the reason I'm down is because everything is shit! Talking to a shrink won't help that!'

'Fine! Do what you like! Or don't do what you like, more to the point! But I can't go on like this. And I won't,' says Helen trying to blink back tears. It doesn't work. The dams burst and the tears roll down her face. She looks away and gulps down a sob. She looks back at me, straight into my eyes and through to my soul.

'I don't know you anymore,' she whispers.

There's no answer to that. I'm paralysed, blow to the kidney style.

For a long time neither of us says anything. We gather thoughts. I think of arguments against breaking up. I think of insults and words to hurt. But it all seems a bit pointless right now. When Helen makes up her mind it stays made.

'So, what happens now?' I ask eventually.

'Well, I'm going to go and stay with mum,' says Helen. Her mum. El Dragon. On forty fags a day she even breathes fire. 'Maybe after a few days, once we've both had a chance to think through our options, I'll give you a call and we can decide what's best for us.'

Simple as that. Have a think and then we'll dismantle the marriage. A new plan.

'What are you going to do?' Helen asks me.

'Do I have a fucking choice?' I bark. I hate myself immediately. I'm being unfair. She's just trying to make things as easy as possible.

'I'm sorry, that was uncalled for,' I say.

She nods but doesn't say anything. She's trying to hold back tears.

'Are you sure you want to go to your mum's?' I ask.

'It's for the best,' she says.

'I could always go to Claire's,' I say. My sister. Sometimes you know what you're saying is stupid before you finish saying it. And, reliable as Halley's Comet, Helen jumps on my mistake before I can even begin to swallow the words.

'Are you mad?' says Helen, 'the kids will drive you insane in minutes and you'll be arguing with Claire before you even get there!'

I know she's right but telling me what I already know doesn't help right now. Besides, considering the conversation we've just had, I don't think she has much right to tell me what's what anymore. Still, I decide to swallow it and not snap back. Old habits die hard.

'El dragon will do the same to you,' I say softly.

She smiles.

'Yeah, but at least I've got my old room for refuge. You'll have nowhere else to go,' she says. Fair point.

'True,' I say.

I let go a mammoth sigh.

'I suppose I'll stay here then. Maybe I'll take a few days off work to get my head round things.'

'Yeah,' she says, 'me too.' Then there's silence. We never have nothing to say to each other. It feels weird. Then again, we've never broken up before either.

'I think I'll pack a few things and go,' she says.

'OK,' I say. I smile at her and walk out of the room. On my second step I hear her start to cry again.

Therapy – bloke style

I tell him I'm not in the mood. I told him on the phone earlier and I tell him again when he comes round to the house. But he won't take no for an answer. And he's incredibly persuasive.

'I'm not up for it, Gary,' I say 'I'd much prefer to stay here and watch the footie in the comfort of my own home.'

'So you want to listen to the moronic opinions of Andy Gray and Richard Keys then?' he asks.

It's a fair point but I'm not giving in this time.

'They might be moronic but at least they're not hypocrites like that Gooner crowd down there,' I say. 'One minute they're advocating tight defence and one-nil to the Arsenal, the next they're wittering relentlessly about the Beautiful Game as though they fucking invented it.'

'I know,' he says and sighs. 'But we always watch the England games down there. Anyway, if anyone needs a good piss-up, it's you.'

Therapy, bloke style – a piss-up cures everything. Your team gets relegated – go on the piss. You lose your job – go on the piss. Your marriage is over – go on the piss. The piss-up is this season's magic sponge.

'Come on, Rodney,' he says in his best Del Boy, 'you know it makes sense my son.'

'No,' I say firmly. 'I'm staying here. You can stay too if you like, but I'm not going anywhere.'

I take a slug of beer. It's supposed to be defiance, but even I know it just looks like a pouting sulk.

'Suit yourself then,' he says, 'I'll just use your bog and then I'll be off.'

I hear him head upstairs. A few moments later the doorbell rings. I get up and answer it. The door slams into me as I get it open and I'm buried beneath a scrum of bodies as three of my mates burst in on me. I'm pinned to the floor by my three mates and Gary stands above me on the stairs.

'You've got a choice,' says Gary, 'you can get yourself ready. Or we can strip you, shower you and get you ready ourselves. Who knows, we might even shave you too!'

This last part he says holding an imaginary penis out of the way with one hand while completing a shaving action with the other.

Like I said, he's incredibly persuasive.

So I find myself down the pub on Saturday night – the night after Helen and I split up – watching England beat Moldova with four mates. One match and six pints later I was up for anything. It's amazing what a victory for your country can do for your mood. It's amazing how a World Cup more than twelve months away can whet the anticipation. It's amazing how much quicker you drink when you're watching football.

As soon as the match ends the transmission gets shut down in the pub, the big screen retracts and the jukebox kicks back into life. The alcohol-fuelled euphoria celebrating a mediocre and predictable victory against inferior opposition is quenched in a heartbeat. Normality returns to the pub like nothing has happened. Further proof, if it were ever needed, that the English don't know how to celebrate.

With the football over the pub empties to a few groups scattered throughout. The atmosphere that pumped with animal energy a few short moments before is gone. Now it has all the energy of a morgue.

'What shall we do now?' asks John.

'We can go back to my house,' I say, 'I got beers in earlier for the footie and we can get a take-away. Anyone fancy a curry?'

My suggestion meets a chorus of negativity. Something's not right here. The lads turning down a curry, well, there's more chance of Bill Clinton turning down a blow-job.

'How about,' says Gary, 'we have a couple more here and then hit the Venus Club?'

'I'm up for that,' says John.

'Yeah, I could go for that,' says Dave.

'A fine plan,' says Vince.

We never go to lap dancing clubs. This is obviously for my benefit. Again, this is therapy bloke style. Right now I'd rather peel my buttocks and sit in vinegar. How come blokes always get it so wrong?

The thing is though, they're really only trying to help and I can't let the side down.

'You lot planned this all along,' I say.

'Course we did,' says Gary putting his arm around me and administering a bear hug. 'What better medicine to get your mind off Helen than different pussy?' he says.

Better medicine? Maybe stick needles in my eyes. Maybe boil my penis. Maybe run a hot bath, put on some Radiohead and let the blade do the rest.

Maybe a night alone.

Definitely not someone else.

But hey, like I say, I can't let the side down. I tell myself that if I protest they will drag me along anyway. But if I'm honest, there's a part of me that wants to go right now. If I'm honest, there's a part of me that wants to fuck someone right here, right now. Someone. Anyone. Anyone at all would do.

In equal measure my thoughts disgust and delight me. Going to a lap dancing club is the last thing I want and it's the only thing I want.

I want nothing more than to just be with my wife. But I'm not.

And the thing is, you can't flick a switch and turn off a million years of genetic engineering.

Nothing reflects the ugliness of man better than a lap dancing club. There's a damned fine reason the lights are always down low in places like this, but I'm not sure whose ugliness the darkness is hiding.

I'm not attracted to any of the girls. None of them own what you would call natural beauty. There are no stunning faces. Elle McPherson bodies are conspicuous by their absence.

Thighs and arses ripple not with lithe muscle, but with orange peel cellulite. Industrial quantities of peroxide, mousse, and other products mean the girls are all suffering disastrous hair days. Make-up has been applied thick as a Van Gogh original obliterating their features the way napalm did the Vietnam countryside. Proof, if ever it were needed, that these girls don't have any true friends.

But that's ok. It's not like I'm looking for love. And I'm no Brad Pitt. I don't see any lurking in the shadows either.

Even though there is nothing attractive about the girls or the place, the senses are enflamed nonetheless. Sex is available by the flesh on show. Sex is available by the erotic music and low moans. The very air tastes of sex. Tits brush up against me with a promise. But the strongest sensory assault is on the nose. Accompanying the stale smoke and stale booze is that distinctive aroma of sex. On one level it's enough to make me heave, but on another level, the animal level, it couldn't be more arousing.

Sex is within touching distance. And not the kind of sex for which you have to respect her in the morning. This is the opposite of that. No respect. No responsibility. This is dump your load and walk away sex.

I know what's coming but I have to wait for it to start. I don't have to wait too long. Gary begins the process.

'Which one do you fancy?' he asks.

Like everything else, there's a protocol to be observed. Certain things have to happen in a certain order.

'None of them,' I reply, 'they're all mingers.'

'We've all chipped in and we're buying you one tonight.'

'I don't want one,' I say. There, I said it. The lie. I'm not with Helen and I can't change that. In the absence of Helen, of course I want one, but I'm not going to let on. There are rules to this game. I have standards to uphold. But as long as I'm forced into it, it's ok. I'm exonerated from blame. Gotta love peer pressure.

'Well if you don't pick one, we will,' he says, 'and believe me you don't want that.'

I sigh.

'Alright,' I say with resignation, 'I'll have that blonde over there.'

Gary nods approvingly.

'You have chosen wisely,' he says.

He walks away with a nonchalant confidence that I wouldn't manage if I took lessons for years and passed all the exams. His is a walk that says he can do anything he wants any time he wants. He speaks to the girl briefly and she glances over in my direction. I take a nervous slurp from my drink. She smiles, nods and follows him over to me.

'Let's go somewhere a little more private,' she says taking my hand and leading me away from my cheering, laughing mates, past the tables of sweaty, fat businessmen and downstairs to a tiny cubicle only big enough for an armchair for the guest and a little carpet space for the girl. She sits me down in the armchair while erotic music pipes into our cubicle. She starts to dance provocatively, flashing a coy smile. She gently takes my right hand and lifts it to her mouth. Slowly she sucks on each of my fingers.

'You don't know where I've been,' I say smiling with my sap rising.

'That's true,' she says, 'but I know where I've been and I know where I'm taking you.'

She drops my hand and begins to strip. She's wearing a black mini dress that has tie-ups at the shoulders. In a sleek movement she unties them and holds the dress to her chest coyly before allowing it to slide slowly down her body. She steps out of it and clamps a stiletto to my chest pinning me to the chair. I start to take off her shoe but she slaps my hand away playfully.

'Ah, ah, ah,' she admonishes me with a wagging finger, 'no touching.'

She then somehow manages to lose her shoe without seeming to move her foot at all. She keeps her foot on my chest as she slowly rolls her stocking down her leg. The lower she gets the closer she moves to me until her cleavage is only a few inches from my face. Then she pulls back with her stocking dangling from her blood red fingernails taking the promised tits from me. I'm so distracted by them I don't realise she's finished taking off her stocking which now flutters to the floor. She then does the same with her other stocking and all the while the sap rises within me.

I can see through her g-string that she has a tidy v. No Brazilian, no Hollywood, not even a little triangle, but a tidy, manicured v. Manicured doesn't seem the right word. Manicure is hands, pedicure is feet, so is her v a vagicure? Sounds like an ointment for an embarrassing condition. A nicer term might be lady garden topiary. I wonder if the v is supposed to be Venus. More like for venereal.

She's gyrating provocatively and it's only when I look up from her g-string that I realise she has removed her bra exposing a pair of pert, firm breasts. She turns around and eyes me seductively over her shoulder and she wiggles her arse in my face with the promise of pleasure under the bend.

I reach out to stroke her arse but she moves just out of range and wags her finger again.

'No touching you naughty boy,' she says smiling. 'Am I going to have to punish you?' she asks playfully and then bites her lower lip on one side before slowly releasing it again. I've never seen anything so erotic. I'm completely lost in the moment. That little bite of her lip reduces me to her slave. Right now she could make me do anything.

And now I'm transfixed. Up until that point I was taking in her entire performance. Now I can't take my eyes off her mouth. I don't even notice she's removed her g-string. I couldn't tell you a thing about the last couple of minutes of her routine and it's not because I didn't watch. And it's not because I can't remember, but because her mouth was my universe.

Then suddenly her mouth is saying something.

'Sorry,' I say, 'I didn't hear you. What did you say?'

'That's it honey,' she says, 'my show's over.'

'Oh right,' I say, 'thanks. Now what?'

'What do you mean?' she asks.

'Well, what happens now?' I ask.

She lets go a little giggle.

'Well, you go back to your friends,' she says resting her palm on my chest gently, 'and I go back to work,' she says taking her palm off my chest and placing it on her own which is now back in her bra and dress. I didn't see her get dressed and I realise I'm still completely zoned in on her mouth.

'Unless,' she says putting her hand back on my chest walking her fingers slowly upwards, 'you want more?' she says.

'Definitely,' I blurt and even I can hear my own desperation.

'OK,' she says, 'you sit back down, give me the cash and I'll give it to my manager and be back in a minute to continue.'

'Er, is there anywhere more private?' I ask looking around.

She giggles again.

'Why?' she asks coyly, 'are you embarrassed all of a sudden?'

'Well, no,' I say, 'but if we're going to do more...'

It's suddenly Arctic.

'I don't think I know what you mean,' she says enunciating every word the way a parent does to a naughty child.

'Would you care to explain?' she asks and her coy, seductive look has been replaced by granite.

Now is the time to cut the losses. Now is the time to make apologies and walk away. Now is the time to move on. Unfortunately, now is also the time I'm already pissed and not in control of my thought processes.

'I don't mind paying,' I say.

'For sex,' I say.

She turns her head just long enough to flick a nod. I look over in the direction of her nod and a bouncer the size of Texas suddenly appears. I never noticed him before. He must have been part of the wall. No, scratch that, he must have been the wall. He rolls over to us languidly but with an amazing turn of speed. He owns the biggest neck I've ever seen and his shoulders, well, God doesn't make tectonic plates that size.

'There a problem, Maxine?' he asks.

It might sound like he asked the question of her, but his eyes haven't left mine since he started walking towards us and he was definitely addressing me.

'No...' I begin, but the fair Maxine beats me to the punch.

14

'You could say that, Patsy' she says.

'This…gentleman,' she spits, 'has just offered me money for sex.'

'This is not that kind of establishment,' she sneers.

Two minutes ago she was thrusting her well manicured v into the face of a stranger, but it seems I'm the one with the low standards. The bouncer reaches down and takes my arm.

'Come with me, sir,' he commands.

'Pervy scumbag,' princess Maxine screams.

I'm too flabbergasted to speak as the man mountain leads me out. We head back upstairs and I see the lads over the other side enjoying the dancers on stage. I make to go over to them but my chaperone's grip nearly crushes my elbow.

'I need to get my jacket,' I protest.

'You can pick it up in the morning,' he says staring straight ahead. I haven't seen his head move once. Maybe that's what happens when you build up your neck that big. Then again, if my name were Patsy I'd beef up too.

I decide not to protest too much because even in my drunken state I can sense that Patsy is just waiting for me to give him an excuse to dance on me. Strike that, he's not waiting, he's hoping. Praying even.

We reach a door which I realise is not the front door and I start to panic. Patsy's going to give me a kicking anyway. I start to struggle but I'm a fly in a spider's web. Another bouncer opens the door and Patsy bundles me through it and throws me down to the ground. I curl up in the foetal position ready for the kicks to start.

One.

Two.

Three.

Four I count. I realise I'm holding my breath. Nothing happens. I open my eyes and slowly move my arms away from my head. Standing above me is Patsy and two other bouncers looking down at me like they've never seen anything so pathetic in their lives.

'Don't show your face around here again,' warns Patsy and he closes the door.

I'm in an alley around the back of the club. Clearly they don't like the idea of throwing someone out the front. I'm just thinking through my options when the lads appear through the same door manhandled by bouncers amid feeble protests. The door closes and it all goes quiet. Then Gary sees me.

'What the fuck did you do?' he asks laughing.

'Nothing,' I say, 'why?'

'They said you had caused a disturbance and we're all barred,' he says.

'I only asked for sex,' I say, 'I was willing to pay.'

The lads burst into hysterics.

'What?' I ask.

'You muppet,' says Gary, 'it's not a brothel. Just as well too,' he says. 'That dance just cost us £40. Imagine what sex would have cost?'

Even I'm laughing now.

'Christ, £40?' I say, 'Just buy me a beer next time boys,' I say.

'I don't fucking believe it,' says Vince slapping his forehead.

'I signed up for life membership earlier. Then I get barred straight away. That's a hundred quid down the drain. Bollocks.'

There's a moment's pause before we all erupt into hysterics again.

Me time

If this were a movie I would open one eye first. Very tentatively. Then the other eye. And I'd do it all very slowly in micro-movements. Almost like the way you imagine the bomb squad would try to defuse a device. My shoulders would be hunched up around my ears with my head trying to disappear into my ribcage the way a tortoise retracts its head into its shell. Then I'd smack my Sahara dry lips together a few times giving the impression of extreme thirst. I might even half groan before realising I don't need to.

But it's not a movie. So instead I get out of bed and make it halfway down the landing before my eyes open fully. I'm mid-pee before I realise I'm not hungover. I should be. Christ I should be. But I'm not.

In fact, I feel great. And it's only 8am.

I'm pretty sure it was gone three when I eventually made it into my bed and by then I'd had a kebab. Proof, if ever it were needed, that I was pissed.

Less than five hours sleep, drunk as a proverbial Lord and fighting fit. In such circumstances I could be forgiven for thinking that it doesn't get any better than that.

No plans for the day. But I'll soon change that. And the first thing I'm going to do is go for a run.

An early morning run does many things. It gets the blood pumping and the adrenaline flowing. It invigorates and energises you for the day ahead. It allows you room to think and space to breathe. It gives you the chance to organise your thoughts. At least, that's the theory. My theory.

And it gives you an opportunity to gain perspective.

Gaining perspective is easier when you're a practical, pragmatic thinker. Like me.

I start running as soon as I leave the house to my local park less than a minute's jog away. The easy rhythm takes form quickly and my feet pound concrete path and my thoughts pick up the beat and follow the same time.

I tell myself that it's over with Helen and nothing is going to change that. I may as well accept it and move on. Sure, it hurts, but I know it's the right decision. The marriage had come to an end. It's that simple.

I tell myself that a lot of people think I've already won the lottery with a career in advertising. Thousands study every year to break into the industry. To them I'm living the dream.

I tell myself lots of things.

I haven't got it so bad. I've got a lot for which to be thankful. I've got a beautiful home. I've got a dream career. I've got mates who care about me and rally round in my time of need. I've got family who love me and who will always be there for me. I'm young, fit and healthy. Cop on and stop moping about the place. Just get on with your life. There's plenty more fish in the sea. The reason proverbs like that exist is because they're true.

Like I say, gaining perspective is much easier when you're a practical, pragmatic thinker like me.

I tell myself that starting from now I must get a grip and shake my life up. I've become lazy and lost my drive. I've gone stale.

I tell myself that work is life and work is who you become.

I've got a message for myself – just get on with it.

I tell myself lots of things and I think about mistakes I've made at work. I tell myself how I would do things differently next time round.

I tell myself I will bring more focus to my work. I tell myself I won't play games and browse the internet and mess around in the office. I tell myself that I will work when I go to work and anything that doesn't matter will be left alone. I will make an impression.

This is the new, determined, focused me.

After my run while I'm showering I get a flashback. Did I really offer her money for sex? Am I really that depraved? The heat of embarrassment rises rapidly from my neck steadily up my face to the top of my crown. I don't need a mirror to know how flushed I look. Oh well, these things happen I suppose. Then again, it's never happened before.

And it never will again. Not with me being the new me anyway. The new determined, focused me.

In market research focus groups we ask things like: if this new cereal were a car, what kind of car would it be?

If this new mobile phone were a supermarket chain, what supermarket chain would it be?

If my agency were a celebrity, what celebrity would it be?

Well, if the new me were a professional footballer, I'd be Roy Keane: determined, focused, winner, leader.

But I won't get to play the role of Roy for a few days yet. After Helen and I decided to split I phoned my boss to take a few days off and get my head straight. A few days might seem optimistic. I certainly didn't think I'd manage it during one morning run.

But I did and I feel fine. Better than that, I feel great. I'm ready to take on anything. I could run a marathon right now. But I won't. Now it's time to relax with a nice Sunday lunch and a couple of Sunday papers over a few Sunday beers. I've earned my leisure. I've gone for my run and organised my life. The way I feel now I could go back into work tomorrow, but I won't.

There are plenty of decent pubs and bars in my area that do a decent Sunday lunch, but today is about me and I don't want to bump into anyone I know who can spoil my 'me time'. Or at least, I want to reduce the possibility of that happening, so I'm going down to Richmond. Plenty of nice bars along the river. Plenty of space and fresh air. Perfect.

Outside a pub on the river I find a spot. My spot. Chatter in tongues buzzes all around me and floating over that The Kinks sing Waterloo Sunset from the jukebox. The Kinks were right – it is a dirty old river, but I wouldn't swap it for the world right now. The sun warms my face, my arms, my legs, my flip-flopped feet. I sit with my eyes closed and soak it up. Cheshire Cats don't grin this wide. Perfect.

Every now and again I take a leisurely sip from my pint. My newspapers rest on my table unmolested. I talk to nobody and nobody talks to me. Surrounded by people but all alone. Perfect.

'Would you like to order some food?' she asks. I hadn't noticed her approach but here she is right in front of me.

'Yes please,' I reply automatically. Then I realise I haven't even looked at the menu.

'What do you recommend?' I ask.

Initially she's completely thrown by my question. Then her frown is replaced by a friendly smile.

'I am sorry,' she says, 'my English is not so good. I had to think about what you said.'

She picks up the menu and points to a dish.

'I had this chicken stuffed with feta and peppers yesterday,' she says, 'and it was very good. Very tasty.' She smacks her lips together. 'Yummy,' she says.

I laugh.

'Sold!' I say. 'I'll have that please.'

'OK,' she says, 'you would like something more to drink?'

'Oh, I didn't realise it was table service for drinks too,' I say.

'Is no problem,' she says.

'Great. Yes please. Fosters,' I say.

She smiles and wanders back inside. Perfect.

This is the life. A lazy lunch by the river in the summertime with nobody to answer to but myself. Perfect.

Life is good. If I were one of the seven dwarves I'd be Happy.

I pick up my newspapers. The thing about the Sunday newspapers is they render the usual demographics redundant. There are people more liberal than Gandhi who read the Sunday

20

Times and on the flip-side there are those who could give Thatcher a run on the conservative front who read the Independent or Observer. It's almost like each week Sunday is the newspapers' day off from their jobs too. I suppose the reality is that people tend to read the supplements and magazines which aren't necessarily singing the same song as the rest of the publication. Whatever the reason, whenever I've got a few hours on a Sunday I tend to pick up the Independent and Times. This is what Sundays were made for. When God made it a rest day this is what He meant.

In between reading the newspapers the waitress brings me my lunch and drinks as and when I order them. We chat and exchange pleasantries and even flirt a little. And that is virtually all the human contact I have during the day. Perfect.

Four hours and eight pints later I'm sitting at the same table struggling with the Sudoku. The numbers dance across my vision so I give up and put it to one side. Sudoku is the kind of thing you should do sober. I decide I've had enough and need to go home. I get up from my seat, leave my half finished pint on my table and wander out to the street and hail a cab.

In the cab I get a second wind and decide to stop off in my local. Well, I call it my local. It's the closest pub to me but it's not the one I drink in with the lads. Not surprisingly there's nobody there I know. I have two more pints alone before wandering home. Home to nobody. My empty home.

With no work in the morning it seems crazy going to bed at 9pm. This is logical thinking when you're drunk. Clearly, the thing to do is crack open a bottle of red and tuck into that.

I boot up my laptop and check my emails. I check the sports news. I check other news. Neither news has anything new to offer. More like checking the olds.

I dial into my work email and quickly scan for any that look important. Only one sticks out and that's because of the subject – Frames. This is one of the pitches I've been working on. We win this, it'll mean big bucks for the company. We lose this, it'll be three in a row we've lost. Big blow to morale and all that. I open it and start to read. I read the first two sentences three times and they still make no sense to me. Christ, I must be pissed. I give up and close it. Doesn't matter anyway as I won't be at work for a few days.

I sit there for a few minutes staring at the blank screen. I drain my glass and re-fill it. I sit there some more.

No work tomorrow. New me. Master of my destiny.

Life is good. The perfect day.

All alone. Just me. Nobody pestering me. Nobody to answer to.

Nobody sharing my time. My newspapers. My thoughts. My life.

No Helen.

Yep, I tell myself that life is good as tears roll down my face.

I open Word and start to type.

"Hey baby, I miss you so much…" I begin.

I stare at the blank screen and pick up my glass. I drain and re-fill it again. I start typing again gaining momentum by the word until my fingers move furiously across the keyboard. I type and I type and I type. And I sob and I sob and I sob.

Yep, if I were a state of mind, I'd be denial.

If I were a state of heart, I'd be broken.

People talk in clichés. And people in the ad industry have their own clichéd language. Then again, in such a creative environment it's essential that people think outside the box while they get their ducks in a row if they're going to push the envelope and deliver a holistic approach in order to maximize the potential of Project Blue Sky's USPs. After all, it *is* rocket science you know.

It is brain surgery.

It is the b and the end of all

If art reflects life and life reflects art, then the same is true of advertising. More true in fact, dahlinks!

If the show must go on, then so must advertising. Nothing in this world is more important. The only thing that matters in life is your current campaign.

This might sound a little melodramatic but after a while in the industry you get to realise there's nothing melodramatic about it. In Adworld it's all true.

The best lie-in is on Monday morning when everyone else you know is at work. Maybe you've got holiday to use up. Or maybe you've got a day off in lieu. Or maybe you have a doctor's appointment later in the morning. Whatever the reason, it's the best lie-in – no question. It feels naughty. I get robbed of that luxury by my mobile phone ringing at 8am. I had set my alarm for nine and there's no way I'll get back to sleep for that hour. I pick up the phone and see it's my boss's number.

'Hi Amanda,' I croak, 'what's up?'

'Hiya mate,' she oils, 'how are you feeling?' Uh-oh! She wants something. Something big I'm guessing. It's the only time she ever calls anyone mate. Immediately, my defences are deployed. Well, deployed as well as can be expected with a stabbing eye hangover. My left eye waters uncontrollably. My head thumps and my guts churn.

'Yeah,' I begin and try to clear my cloyed mouth with its red wine-induced, super-sized tongue. The kind of tongue Jamie Oliver owns.

'I'm fine,' I say, 'how are you?'

'Good, good, good,' she rattles the words off machine-gun rapid and with as much emotion. 'Glad to hear you're well,' she says.

Uh-oh.

'Listen, I hate to ask, mate,' she says, 'but the brown stuff has collided with the oscillating thing and I fantastically need a fabulous favour.'

Oh how ad fab.

She waits for me to say something.

I wait for her.

The gestation period for a basking shark is about three and a half years. This pregnant pause feels longer.

And all the while my left eye waters uncontrollably, my head thumps and my guts churn.

Eventually she sighs deeply and concedes defeat in the waiting game.

'I need you to come in today, mate,' she says.

'To work?' I ask.

'Yeah,' she says, 'I'm really sorry. You know I wouldn't ask if I didn't have to,' she says.

I try to count to ten. I make it to two.

'Amanda!' I snap, 'you know what happened!'

'I know and I'm really sorry, mate,' she croons, 'I honestly wouldn't ask if I had an alternative.'

'You said you'd cover it,' I say, 'you said it would be no problem! You know my head's all over the place,' I say.

'I know, I know, I know, and I'm really, truly super sorry,' she says, 'I will make it up to you. You'll really be pulling me out of the fire.'

There's that pause again.

I breathe. I sigh.

'What's the deal?' I ask.

'Les grande fromages want to see the story for the "Frames" campaign,' she says. 'I thought I'd be able to get someone in to pick it up later today but that's not an option anymore.'

'How long do you need me?' I ask.

'Once the "Frames" campaign is done you'll be free to go,' she says. 'We've got the meeting with the Group Board at twelve and then we may need to tweak it ready to present to the client for Wednesday. I reckon you'll be done by three. Tops.' she says.

What if I were killed? What would they do then? The decent thing, possibly. But they won't do that if you're already dead but still able to walk. Strike that, you don't need to be able to walk as long as you can work.

'I don't think it's a good idea, Amanda,' I say, 'I'm really not focused. I've got too much personal shit right now.'

'Puh-lease!' She actually enunciates it like a six year old begging for ice cream.

Then there's silence again. I'm about to tell her I can't. I'm about to tell her I wouldn't be doing her or myself any favours by being there. I'm about to tell her I think I should stay away from people for the moment. But she beats me to it and speaks first.

'Help me Obi Wan Kenobi,' she says.

'You're my only hope!' she says.

I sigh again.

'OK,' I sigh.

'Ta muchly sweetie,' she syrups, 'you're a star!'

Click, she hangs up.

I could kick myself. I'm such a sucker for Star Wars.

Two hours later I'm racing to reach a deadline that didn't exist before I woke this morning. I've got a stabbing eye hangover and my head thumps and my guts churn.

The office is a blur of bodies running around being busy. Looking busy. Same same but different. A constant cacophony washes over everything. Different radio stations playing different music combine with the white noise of office equipment which combines with telephones ringing which combines with outside traffic combines with drawers crashing combines with doors slamming, with people talking, people chatting, more doors slamming, police sirens, telephones ringringringing, drawers crashing, fucking idiotic ringtones, people singing, laughing, shouting, screaming, braying... making noise for the sake of making noise.

And all the while my left eye waters uncontrollably, my head thumps and my guts churn.

I have to stop a moment or my head will fall off. Here I am carrying on as normal. I've split up from my wife and life will never again be the same. But I'm carrying on as normal. I look up from my desk around the office at my colleagues. I mean I really look.

Not the usual glance at people getting on with their work. Not the everyday look at the guy with the face I could never tire of punching. Not the routine look at my boss through her office window frustrated at having to deal with morons above and below her. Not the normal admiring glance at a passing bum. I ask myself – are they carrying on as normal too? I ask myself – what are they dealing with right now? What shit are they having to suffer? How's life at home?

And then I ask myself – why am I asking myself when I really don't give a shit? I know nothing about these people and they know nothing about me. And they're some of the closest people in my life. How the fuck did that happen? Where have all my real friends gone? Did I ever have any?

In a city of seven million people carrying on as normal, we are all alone.

25

I gather my head and gulp back the Solpadeine that's dissolved and ready to join the other four I've already had this morning.

My team is pulling out all the stops to get the story boards printed and mounted even though we'll probably conduct the whole thing on a laptop and projector. My PA is desperately trying to hijack a meeting room and get it set up in time. In the meantime she needs to organize lunch for a dozen people too. How hard can that be? Surely you send someone down to M&S for a platter of sarnies and some fruit? Or get the local café to deliver? Well yeah, that's how easy it should be. But this is Ad World dahlink! The local café? M&S sandwiches? Are you quite mad? What's the point in Harrod's Food Halls if you don't use them?

And all the while my left eye waters uncontrollably, my head thumps and my guts churn.

Long story short, people are now ready to kill. You might look at the news in disbelief when someone in America turns up at work and offs everyone. I don't. Not anymore. Now there are days when I could happily do the same.

And the reason for this bedlam? The big boys want to see their toys. Plain and simple. They want to see the gimmick that will sell millions of their client's products across the globe. Products made in sweatshops by underprivileged kids. Products that will stick around on the market place for as long as the latest fourth-placed contestant in X Factor before being discarded in a green field where they will stick around for about 500 million years.

But hey, that's the modern world for you.

The Group Board Directors turn up and people who were ready to rip off heads with their bare hands are now sweet as pie. Kissing arse is an art form and nobody does it better than an ad pro.

I know I'm a director but really I'm not. I'm just an account director, which is a bigged-up manager. Inflating titles is another thing the ad industry specializes in. It's just a shame inflated salaries don't always go with them. No, these directors are real directors who run the company. No inflated titles this time, just inflated egos and inflated stomachs.

The Chairman takes pride of place at the head of the table, the Group Creative Director sits to his right and the Group Managing Director sits to his left. Lesser mortals line the cheap seats.

'Are you ready to go?' demands the Chairman looking at his watch.

Before I can say anything he steamrollers on.

'Because I've only got twenty minutes. I've got lunch at the Ivy with Branson and you know how that can drag. And I forgot about that Guinness Book of World Records thing tonight and I have to go to that as I'm presenting the award. And I've got an awful lot of work to do in between, so chop chop, let's get on with it.'

Oh God, he's in one of his moods. This isn't going to be pretty.

I wonder what Freud would make of his name-dropping and insecurities? I was at the meeting where he virtually begged our client at Guinness Book of World Records to be allowed to present an award. And it is *an* award. Not *the* award. It's no doubt one of the lesser efforts sandwiched in between World's Longest Nasal Hair and Strongest Halitosis. If he forgot about this awards ceremony then maybe peace in the Middle-East is possible. But I don't see that happening either.

I bet he's got a really big car.

Half an hour later a metaphorical tornado has ripped through the office and left our campaign, our morale, our team in tatters. The Group Board Directors have gone. My boss is trying to pick up the pieces. And all the while my left eye waters uncontrollably, my head thumps and my guts churn.

They hated it. They hated the concept. They hated the story. They hated the execution. They hated the design. They hated everything about it. We've got to start from scratch.

Thing is, a few weeks ago I mentioned the Frames concept to the Group MD and he loved it. Amanda had spoken to the Group Creative Director and he thought it was "sensational". Get them in a room together with the Chairman though and they wait for him to decide. And everyone knows it's all dependent on his mood. And his mood wasn't good today. Nothing would have impressed him. Today we could have presented the Guinness domino ad and he would have rejected it.

So it's back to the drawing board. So much for being done by three. Tops.

Libra

Sometimes bigger numbers have less impact. Thousands die in an earthquake somewhere ending in stan and it barely registers on our own personal Richter Scale. Hundreds of thousands die of malaria every year in developing countries but that's ok because we've got our tabs. Tens of thousands die of starvation every month in sub-Saharan Africa as we throw stale food out of our refrigerators and cupboards to make room for new food to go stale.

But one junior minister gets killed in a terrorist attack and immediately the country is up in arms. Outrage and revenge are the order of the day and it makes me wonder if it's a peculiarly British thing that as a nation we love to fight. To go to war. To trample an enemy.

This unadulterated blood lust.

This need to kill.

This eye for an eye mentality.

The irony is that the terrorist attack was the real act of vengeance. Libra said so in his tape to the press. He might have nicked the idea of sending tapes to the press from Bin Laden, but his execution is so much better. Less rhetoric, more slick propaganda. And that voice. That spooky, eerie, hypnotic voice that makes you listen. The loudest pub falls silent when that voice starts talking. It must be doctored somehow.

Distorted.

Corrupted.

Mangled.

Brando's voice in Apocalypse Now had nothing on Libra.

It's difficult to achieve notoriety. More so than it is to become famous. You want your fifteen minutes of fame, act like an arsehole and get on Big Brother. You want notoriety you have to go further. You see it's all been done before. The worst acts you could possibly imagine have already happened.

And it's no good just talking the game. In a world inundated with idle chatter nobody hears a threat.

But you take real action and suddenly the world's nads are in your palm and all you have to do is squeeze.

Nobody had heard of Libra or his movement, The Scales of Justice, until he assassinated that junior minister. Now you can You Tube his entire back catalogue of spooky tapes.

He's been sending these tapes for months to TV and radio stations, printed press, government ministers, armed forces – everyone and anyone he thought needed to be warned. And they all ignored him. They dismissed him as a joker. A spoof. A kid with too much time on his hands. Even though the tapes became more threatening and sinister with each one. People hoped that if they ignored him, he would go away. He even took action but nobody knew. Acts of sabotage to make the world hear his pleas.

That raid on the army barracks months ago when a stack of rifles was replaced with olive branches – that was Libra and The Scales of Justice. That high street clothing fashion chain whose advertising posters were stamped with the words: Sponsored by Sweatshops – that was Libra and The Scales of Justice.

Now everyone knows him. Now everyone knows he's serious.

Yes, it's difficult to achieve notoriety, but he has it now with the assassination of the junior minister. That junior minister is how everyone refers to him. Nobody can remember his name but everyone now knows Libra. And the reason for the assassination? It turns out that the junior minister secretly owned a chain of sweatshops in south-east Asia as well as a number of overcrowded slums in London. One report suggested there were seventeen illegal immigrants forced to share a broken down one bed flat. It also turns out that Libra had sent him a tape personally. And the junior minister was worried enough to alert the police. And they told him there was nothing they could do.

He could have done something personally though. But he didn't. And now he never will.

The bar is dormouse quiet. No jukebox, no TV, no mind pureeing shrill squeaks from game machines. No banter. Just a few sad, lonely punters nursing their drinks and wondering what happened to their lives. That includes the barman, Jack. Jack's one of those guys who always has it worse. You've got a cold, Jack has flu. Some little chav keyed your car, Jack's motor was totalled. A bet you didn't make came in, Jack's numbers came up in the lottery but he didn't do it. You get cancer, Jack's already dead.

Aptly named The Tombstone, it was once a gothic pub and is still adorned with graveyard memorabilia. This graveyard bar, well, hermits' diaries get more activity. It's where I come for a quiet drink and I know nobody will bother me. I generally sit and read in a corner. My corner.

And tonight I need to be left alone. What a week. So much for taking a few days off to get my head together. So much for being done by three. Tops. The earliest I left the office all week was nine o'clock, after starting at seven each morning.

Most of the agency are on the piss in town tonight for a leaving do. I stayed for the speeches then disappeared. Just enough to show my face. The week I've had, if I were on the piss with the rest of the agency tonight I'd get myself in trouble. Best to stay away. Especially after we didn't win that account. We're all under pressure now and there's talk of redundancies.

Flashback to Monday. A nightmare. A full blown disaster. After the meeting with the Group Board, Amanda holds a brainstorm and tells us that we're going to run with the best idea – no matter how bad – to come out of it.

No matter how bad. How to instil confidence in your team – one easy lesson. Problem is, you use negative language like that,

31

well, it grants people licence to under-perform. But Amanda wants us to come up with something effective, contemporary and fresh.

Everyone in ad world owns a white elephant. Everyone has got their bad idea that they love and everyone else hates. And they always get recycled at times like this.

Nik reincarnates his bionic mouse. Sarah's weeping willow brings tears. Again.

For some reason Once in a Lifetime by Talking Heads loops through my mind and David Byrne sings "Same as it ever was" over and over again.

James inevitably breathes new life into his macho gladiator.

Same as it ever was.

It takes us an hour to get through half a dozen of these.

Same as it ever was.

'For fuck's sake,' Amanda snaps, 'we're in the shit here and we need something new. Something fresh.

'Now if I hear one more of your fucking abortions, that person can consider themselves fired. You're all paid a lot of money to deliver creative ideas. Stop wanking your egos and give me something new.'

She's gone from ad luvvie to playground bully in under three seconds. She didn't even change gear. That's pretty good going even by her high standards. Possibly even a record.

For a while after that everyone is too afraid to say anything.

Then Nik stands up and starts singing. Well, rapping. The Real Slim Shady to be precise. At first, I think he's flipped. To be honest, everyone thinks the same. Then the penny drops. The products lie sprawled on the table, and Nik is standing them up one by one as he sings:

"Would the real Slim Shapey please stand up?

Please stand up?

Please stand up?"

Nik doesn't need to tell us how the rap fits for the client's low fat products. It's self-explanatory.

It's effective.

It's contemporary.

It's fresh.

All around the room colleagues tell him how the idea is so original.

For some reason I think of Coca-Cola, the *Real Thing*. I think of McCoy's crisps, the *Real McCoy*.

And now we're giving birth to the *Real Slim Shapey*.

Amanda's nodding and smiling. She likes it. Ladies and gentlemen, we have a winner.

It's effective.

It's contemporary.

It's fresh.

It's certainly not original.

But it's all we've got.

We've got our new concept and we run with it. For the next two days we shape the Slim Shapey idea into a workable pitch and on Wednesday we present it to the prospective client.

No matter how bad. The words come back to haunt. Same as it ever was.

The client hates it. They are about to launch a series of low-fat, convenient, healthy products to appeal to middle-class professionals and we've decided to align their aspirations with a foul-mouthed, drug-taking, controversial chav. As own goals go it's pretty spectacular.

After that Amanda insists I work on a new pitch that came in the same day. We're in the shit, she tells me. We're looking at redundancies, she tells me. Don't give them a reason to fire me, she warns me. Strike that, that was no warning, but a full on threat.

I've had better weeks.

So on Friday night I find myself in The Tombstone. Alone. Just how I want it.

I'm nearly finished my first pint and half way through the first chapter of a book when the temperature in the bar drops a further degree and the distinctive hybrid aroma of sunscreen & hash wafts on the air.

Clive.

My twin.

'Hey bro,' he says in his customary greeting, 'wassup?'

He says "wassup?" all the time but it's never a question. I stand up and we hug.

'Dude, I heard your news,' he says, 'I'm sorry man.'

'Yeah, I know,' I reply, 'what can you do? These things happen.'

'Yeah,' he says and sighs.

'Heineken?' he asks pointing at my glass.

'Yeah,' I say and he goes to the bar.

It's funny. Most twins know which one of them was born first. Not me and Clive. We don't know, nor do we care. As far as we're concerned we arrived together. When we were kids we used to say that we arrived together, we'll always be together and we'll die together. Then I guess we grew up.

Thing is, even though we don't know who arrived first, Clive was always the older, wiser one. It's like he arrived years before me. He was always the strong one, the decision maker. And sometimes when I was having it tough he'd bail me out. At times it was even like he was my protector.

The rest of the family don't see Clive. They don't speak to him. They don't even speak *of* him. Some time ago there was an "incident" and they never even mention the "incident". It's the taboo of all taboos.

It doesn't bother me though. I'll see Clive no matter what. He's part of me and I'm part of him. It's a twin thing. Like he always says, we're not joined *at* the hip, we're joined *in* the hip.

He puts my pint in front of me and sits opposite. We clink glasses and drink.

'So, tell me what happened, dude,' he says.

And I tell him everything. Clive's the only one I can tell everything to – the whole story. I might see the rest of our family more often than Clive, but I'm still nowhere near as close to them. It's a twin thing. I can't even remember the last time we met up. The thing is Clive disappears for weeks, months, sometimes years on end. And then he's back for a while before vanishing again. Clive is an eagle soaring. I'm a budgie in a cage. He's a lion on the prowl. I'm a hamster in a wheel. He's out there busily living his life. I'm busily saving a pension for mine. Still though, we've got more in common than meets the eye. We share the same wavelength. When he's back in town he doesn't even call. But I know he's around. Like I said, it's a twin thing.

'That's way fucked up, dude,' he tells me when I finish wittering on about my shit existence.

'Yeah, I know,' I say, 'but hey, that's the way the mop flops.'

I laugh. I laugh until I cry again.

'Let it out, man,' says Clive. 'You'll feel better, bro. And then you'll be ready for some advice'.

Clive always has the best advice. I'm not sure if it's because he doesn't subscribe to modern life and so can be more objective or if it comes from a deeper wisdom or something, but he can always cut straight through the bullology and solve any problem.

Some people get to the heart of the matter.

Some people hit the nail on the head.

Clive splits the atom.

The guy's a guru, no question. I wipe my eyes and blow my nose and ready myself for Clive's solution. If anyone can help me it's Clive.

'You ready?' he asks.

I nod.

'ARE. YOU. READY?' he asks again.

'Yes,' I say.

'Right,' he begins, 'to sum up: You and Helen have split up, you hate your career, you hate your life and you no longer believe in yourself,' he says.

I remain silent.

His look is waiting for an answer.

'That's about it,' I say.

'Well then bro, your life as you know it is over and it's time to end it,' he says.

He smiles.

He winks.

He laughs.

'Relax bro,' he says, 'Jeez man, you would swear I just told you to kill yourself or something,' he says and laughs.

'Well, didn't you?' I ask.

'Nah man,' he says. 'I merely told you what you knew already – your current life is over. And you just need a new one'.

I exhale audibly and it's only then I realise I've been holding my breath.

'A new plan is what you need, that's all. And if the entire Middle-East and North Africa can be transformed with the Arab Spring, then it's easy for one man to change his own life,' he says. 'So how about we get pissed and discuss your options?'

Relief.

'That sounds like a fine plan to me,' I sigh.

'Great! I'm off to the bog, your round!' he says.

And so the pendulum swings. I'm on the way home after a night out with Clive and all my worries have melted away. Miserable and depressed to euphoric and elated in a lightning strike.

After we finished our pints in the Tombstone we moved onto an underground club that had a couple of live bands on the bill. Clive has been coming to this club for months and I can see why. I've never heard music like this before. It's a new movement – so new it doesn't even have a name yet. Even the bands don't have names. It makes punk and grunge look like Disney productions. And just like punk and grunge it's the antidote to what went beforehand.

Before punk we had the Osmonds, Shawaddywaddy and the Bay City Rollers. Before grunge we had Kylie, Jason, Rick and the rest of the Stock, Aitken and Waterman stable of thoroughdeads. And now at last we have the antidote to Cowell and Walsh. To Sharon and Cheryl. Danni and David. This new movement will put the ex into X Factor and the rest of the TV karaoke genre.

And so the pendulum swings.

This is big. It's the start of something huge and it is gaining momentum. When previous generations reminisce about being at Woodstock or Live Aid or the Cavern, this is what they're talking about.

This is chaos. This is emotion. This is passion. This is alive.

It doesn't have a name.

The bands don't have names.

The songs don't have names.
Nobody owns it.
Nobody controls it.
Nobody understands it.
But everybody wants it.
Everybody gets it.
And it…well, it just is.

That eerie voice draws you in. It chills your spine. The hair rises on the back of your neck higher and higher with each word. But you can't stop listening. More than that, you can't stop agreeing. Then again maybe you can't stop agreeing because he makes so much sense. Maybe Libra is this season's King David.

Martin Luther King.

Nelson Mandela.

'We've got to stop replacing our fears with yet more fears,' says Libra. 'Communism became nuclear annihilation became global freezing became acid rain became the hole in the ozone layer became global warming.'

I look around the pub and see silent heads nodding. And I realise I'm nodding too. Apart from Libra's doctored, even tones there isn't another sound in the pub. Nobody chats. Nobody orders drinks. Nobody plays pool or the slot machines. The barman watches the TV screen with everyone else as the evening news plays the latest audio tape. On the screen is the shadow emblem that has come to represent Libra and the Scales of Justice – a faceless silhouette with a warped, tilted scales in the foreground.

Libra has not been out of the news since the Scales of Justice assassinated that junior minister. Scotland Yard vowed to find him and bring him to justice. They still don't have a single lead. The PM and various ministers condemned the assassination outright and vowed to end terror and advocated the use of diplomatic means to air grievances. More blah and more blah and more blah. The public were initially horrified. But the more tapes we hear the more sense he makes.

'Aids replaced by Ebola replaced by SARS replaced by MRSA replaced by bird flu replaced by swine flu,' says Libra. 'Colonel Gadaffi morphed into Saddam Hussein morphed into

Osama Bin Laden morphed into Kim Jong Il. It's just a different face on the same problem. All these fears have gone away but the problems still exist. The biggest problem though is that they were never the bigger problems to begin with. The bigger problems are always our leaders. The people with wealth and power.'

All around me heads nod. Yeah, initially there was public outrage at the assassination. But that didn't stick around for long. And soon enough the government panicked and tried to get Libra censored. They rushed through legislation to stop his tapes being aired. For a week the networks were banned from playing the tapes. But they were easily available on-line. And everyone listened. So the government tried to ban them on-line. While at the same time they condemned China's censorship of Google. Then the government relented and lifted the ban but tried to get the voice dubbed the way they used to do with Gerry Adams. Because it worked so well first time round clearly! Sometimes it seems we're incapable of learning from our own history.

'All the problems they give us, well they're just smoke and mirrors to hide the real problems,' says Libra. Everyone knew Saddam Hussein had nothing to do with 9/11. Everyone knew he had no arsenal of WMD. But we invaded Iraq and deposed him anyway because of those false fears. Those false rumours. Those lies. Excuses. Everyone also knows that it had nothing to do with those excuses. It was all about wealth and power.'

In the pub all eyes are fixed on the screen. On that faceless silhouette. Those warped, tilted scales.

Nobody really knows anything about Libra yet. Everything is rumour. Urban myth. A friend of a friend told my mum's cousin's cat…that kind of thing. One thing is for sure though – he's not alone. Nobody knows how big the Scales of Justice is. Could be hundreds, thousands, who knows? But it certainly extends beyond Britain. And it seems more recruits are added daily. And nobody knows how. Most people believe he uses the internet to recruit, which sounds plausible. I mean, if a bunch of idiotic, looting thugs can organise riots that bring Britain to its knees, surely a leader with vision can achieve so much more with the same means. Other people say Libra doesn't recruit, but his followers find him. However he's doing it, it's successful.

'Everyone knows the banks caused the global recession with their greed and flagrant abuse of the regulatory system,' says Libra on the TV. 'Lessons we were supposed to learn from Barings and Enron and Polly Peck and The Mirror Group and other scandals, well it turns out we didn't learn them. Legislation like Sarbanes Oxley is about as much use as a condom to a eunuch. The politicians and bankers make the right noises and deliver the nice soundbites and tell us there are new procedures in place which will ensure these scandals never happen again. And the global media does its bit by giving us something else to worry about. They give us swine flu which is going to become a pandemic. Nothing can prevent that from happening. Then suddenly there's a vaccine that the government spends millions producing to fight the pandemic. And even though less than 3% of the population is vaccinated the pandemic never arrives. And normal flu kills more people than swine flu in the winter. So it must be a miracle or something. Or maybe it was just never the threat we were led to believe it to be. Maybe it was built up that way so the public had something else to worry about besides the economy and banking crisis. Smoke and mirrors,' says Libra preaching to the converted.

Libra is this season's Robin Hood.

Zorro.

Batman.

He is the man of the people but he's an elusive shadow. Nobody sees him. Yet a lot of people claim to know him. Some say he is a disgruntled soldier. Some say he's a member of the royal family. Others that he's the second coming. Some believe he's more than one person, a committee if you like. I've even heard one person claim he's Keyser Sose. And the myths multiply and grow more exaggerated through the grapevine of Chinese whispers until they become completely ridiculous. Then again, considering what he has done, how ridiculous are these rumours?

'And this is nothing new,' says Libra. 'This has been happening since the dawn of time. For the Crusades protecting Christianity, read extending our wealth and power. For World War I protecting the rights of small nations, read protecting our empire and extending our wealth and power.

It's just new smoke and new mirrors. And it's time it stopped.'

Therapy – girl style

It's a way of coping. When two people break up it can be like a bereavement. Everybody has a different programme for moving on. Helen went back to her mum's. Back to familiarity. Back to the family home. Home for a while to suck her thumb. It's just a way of coping.

Helen calls me on my mobile. She tells me she's spent most of the week with her sisters and girlfriends. It's a regular pukefest of nostalgia. She tells me that every story begins with 'Do you remember when…' This is how people speak when they no longer have anything in common. The curse of old friends is that it's all in the past. They rally round to offer support, but you know it won't last. You go home to suck your thumb and reminisce old times, but deep down you're thinking about the future. Worrying about the future. Afraid of the unknown. When you were with your partner it was all mapped out. Now it's a blank canvas and it scares you to your core.

Your friends rally round, but they can't do that forever. They have their own lives, their own problems, their own fears. And every minute spent comforting you is a minute less looking after their future. You see them sneaking quick glances at their watches. And you wonder: are they here because they care or are they here out of duty? Do they want to be here or do they have to be? Or even worse, are they here because they're afraid that one day they will need you too?

Helen thinks these things and so do I. Well, at least we grew cynical together. In spite of this, Helen's enjoying her support group.

The night I made an arse out of myself with my mates at The Venus Club, she went out with her mates too. Maybe our programmes for moving on aren't so different after all.

All her girlfriends went round to her mother's place to get ready. Getting ready means four hours washing hair, applying make-up, nail polish, mousse, ad infinitum. Getting ready means listening to cheese – the Grease soundtrack, Dirty Dancing, girl power numbers. You get the idea. At some point I have no doubt Gloria Gaynor would have assured them she would survive. It's just a way of coping.

The first step in the programme is to surround yourself with friends and re-live old times, so you don't have to think about your ex. That way, when it comes to time to think about your ex, it will be so far down the line that it won't hurt. That's the theory. Like I say, it's just a way of coping.

When they left her mum's house they were already pissed. Getting ready also means downing gallons of wine. They went to a couple of bars before moving onto a club. This is all part of the ritual. A pub crawl is a must to see who is around and more importantly, be seen around. A gang of girls on the loose and out for fun. Would blokes figure in this fun? Hard to tell right now. The eternal conflict. Wanting to be sexy but not a sex object. Of course, the average bloke who has had a gutful of alcohol on a Saturday night can always spot the difference.

But the girls were having fun and nothing was going to spoil that. Or at least, that was the plan.

It was later in the club it happened. All night with her friends she hadn't thought of me once. Well, except when they were singing feminist anthems early in the evening, but that was fun because I was only mentioned in jokes. But then this guy comes up to her in the club and asks her to dance. She says no and bursts into tears. The guy reminds her of me. No, scratch that, the guy reminds her she's alone. And she bursts into tears. She runs from the club a hysterical mess and her girls follow. They find a bench and Helen sits in the middle sobbing and her girls comfort her.

Helen needs to be the centre of attention because she's special.

She's broken up with her husband and she's special.

She's all alone and she's special.

She needs to be the centre of attention because nobody else feels the way she does.

She's all alone, just like everyone else.

But she's fine now she tells me. After all, you can't spend ten years with someone without missing them sometimes, she tells me. It's only natural, she tells me.

Preaching to the converted.

So Helen is enjoying her support group. I wish I could say the same.

Although, that's not entirely fair. The lads have been great. Well, at least they've done their best. We've gone on the piss. We've watched football together. We've done lads things. The thing is, I can't remember a single conversation. It's a bloke thing. We don't chat. We don't share problems. We don't do understanding. That's just what girls do. But the fairer sex goes too far. They analyse it to death. Every word has a hidden meaning. Every act is a window to the soul. They try to go beyond understanding. At least the lads have done their best.

It's my female support group that's doing my head in.

Flashback to a few days before. Mum greets me at her front door with a big hug and smile to match. The smile may be big but it's plastic as Vegas. If she were an act she would be a brave face. By the same token, there are no tears so a few days getting used to my news must have helped.

'Hi love,' she says, 'you're looking well.'

'You too,' I say kissing her cheek.

She heads straight to the living room which is unusual. It might be called the living room but in my parents' house all the living is done in the kitchen.

'Look who popped in to say hello,' she says opening the door. I don't know if she's talking to me or Father McGuinness who is getting up from the sofa.

'How's it going, fella?' he says shaking my hand.

'I'll just make a pot of tea,' says Mum sloping away. She couldn't look more guilty if she were wearing a striped jumper, a mask and carrying a bag labelled SWAG.

I'm left alone in the living room with Father McGuinness. Anyone else would be preferable.

Myra Hyndley would be preferable.

Or the Kray twins.

Hell, even George Bush.

For maybe fifteen seconds there's silence. Uncomfortable silence.

Don't get me wrong, I'm comfortable with it. But Father McGuinness clearly isn't. He's sitting on the sofa leaning forward, elbows resting on his thighs, hands clasped together and he's rocking and nodding. He smiles up at me. If Mum's plastic smile was Vegas, his is Disneyland. He blows through puffed up cheeks Louis Armstrong style. He rubs the back of his neck.

This is not how it's supposed to go. He's a priest. The norm dictates that people approach him when they've got a problem. They do it themselves. But I didn't arrange this. Mum did. I know it and he knows it.

I wait.

He'll speak soon enough and in the meantime I'll enjoy the silence. The awkward silence. Awkward seconds. Seconds so long acorns could become great oaks and die.

'I hear you're in a spot of bother,' he says.

I remain silent. An ice age thaws.

'I understand things aren't so good at home,' he says.

I remain silent. Planets form.

'Your ma tells me you're thinking of splitting up with your wife,' he says.

I remain silent. The never ending story...ends.

'She's worried about you, your ma,' he says.

I remain silent. And all the while my eyes haven't left his. I'm wearing my best poker face.

44

He looks away. He rubs the back of his neck. He gets up and walks around the room blowing through his puffed up cheeks Louis Armstrong style.

I'm alone with Father McGuinness. He sits back down. I remain standing by the window. My eyes remain fixed on him. I remain silent.

A carriage clock my mother has had for about 150 million years sits on the mantel piece and clunks out seconds the way a kango hammer would on low battery. It's the only sound in the double-glazed room.

Mum must be baking the biscuits for the tea.

He glances at his watch. He turns back to face me.

'You should work at your marriage,' he says.

'You should give it another go,' he says.

'You have made a promise to God,' he says.

Marriage counselling, church style. Catholic church style. I'm getting advice on my marriage from a guy who has never been married. A guy who is not allowed to marry. A guy who has never lived with a woman. A guy who is supposedly celibate and has never had sex. A guy who sometimes wears a dress in public.

I'm thinking he's not qualified. I'm thinking if I want marriage guidance I'll speak with Helen first and we'll go together. And I'm thinking we wouldn't go to a Catholic priest.

'Thanks for the advice, Father,' I say. 'From a man of your experience it means a lot'.

He throws me a look. My face says butter wouldn't melt.

'Thank you,' he says uncertainly.

'Ever been married, Father?' I ask.

'To the Church, yes,' he says. And he means it.

And all the while my eyes are locked on his. He looks away again. He blows through his puffed up cheeks Louis Armstrong style. He turns back and smiles.

'So you'll give it another go, then?' he asks.

'With, em…' he stumbles, 'your, em, wife,' he finishes.

'You mean Helen?' I say.

'That's right, Helen,' he says and smiles again and nods. He nods for a few seconds until he realises he's doing it and stops.

He looks away.

Again.

'You'll never guess who I bumped into the other day, Father,' I say laughing.

He turns back to me with a smile. The mood has lifted. I'm suddenly in jovial spirits and he's more than happy to join me. Clearly my marriage must be fixed again. A chat with a priest is this season's magic sponge. The miracle cure.

'Who?' he asks.

'John Sweeney,' I say.

'John Sweeney? Little Johnny Sweeney?' he asks. 'Lord, I haven't seen little Johnny Sweeney for years. How is he?' he asks.

'Oh very well,' I say.

'Good, good. Glad to hear it,' he says, 'Johnny Sweeney eh?' he chuckles.

'Yeah, John's good,' I say.

'Well, as good as can be expected I suppose,' I say. And for the first time since I walked into the room I look away from the priest. I gaze at nothing in particular. More a glaze than a gaze.

'How do you mean?' Father McGuinness asks.

'Oh well, he's had it tough, Father,' I say. 'You know he did time?'

'Well, yes, now you mention it I did hear that,' he says. 'He seemed to go off the rails for a while during his teenage years.'

'Teenage years,' I parrot. 'Yeah, that was probably it,' I say. 'A lot can be blamed on the teenage years eh?'

'True, true,' he says.

'But the good news, Father,' I say lifting the spirits again, 'is that he's on the straight and narrow now,' I say.

'That is good news,' he says.

'And he's getting help to sort out his problems,' I say.

'Problems?'

'Yes, problems. Mainly emotional. Well, psychological maybe,' I say.

'Oh, that's sad to hear he has troubles. But at least he's getting help,' he says.

'Yes,' I say. 'It is good he's getting help. And it seems progress is being made. He was telling me it seems his self-destructive tendencies stem from a self-loathing situation experienced at a young age.'

'Oh really,' he says. The smile evaporates from his face.

'Yes, apparently it's textbook,' I say. 'Self-loathing brought about by embarrassment and humiliation,' I say.

'Right,' says the priest. He clears his throat. He looks away. He rubs the back of his neck. He blows through his cheeks puffed up Louis Armstrong style.

'Fascinating stuff,' I say. 'And do you know they have even pinpointed the kind of embarrassments and humiliations that can cause that kind of self-loathing and self-destructive behaviour?' I say.

'Really?' says the priest in a quiet voice. The kind of voice you expect a mouse would have. If there were a scale for voices with Paul Robeson being a ten and the kid who played Oliver! being a zero, the priest's voice would come in at four.

'Yes,' I say.

'It might be bullying...but then I don't remember John ever being bullied,' I say. 'Or it might be parental ridicule. Or some other kind of emotional or mental or even physical abuse.'

'Really?' says the priest in a two, 'that's interesting.'

'Yeah,' I say. 'And the really good news is that John's therapist thinks they're close to fingering the root cause of the problem,' I say.

The priest loosens his collar.

'John's therapist is even considering hypnotherapy,' I say.

The priest dabs his forehead with his hankie.

'Are you ok, Father?' I ask, concern etched on my face.

'Er, not feeling too good actually,' he says, 'I think I should go. Er, say thanks to your mother,' says the priest as he walks slowly past me.

'Bye Father,' I say.

The front door closes and within miliseconds the living room door opens and my mother sees me alone.

'Is Father McGuinness gone?' she asks.

I nod.

'Oh,' she says, 'I thought he was going to stay for tea,' she says. 'Did you have a nice chat?' she asks.

I nod.

'What did you talk about?' she asks.

'Actions and their consequences,' I say and I walk out towards the kitchen.

Mum makes a pot of tea and before she manages to pour it my sister Claire arrives. The three of us sit at the kitchen table with our tea and biscuits. Dad's out doing a private job but should be home any time soon. That'll be a relief. The inevitable subject of my break-up hangs over us guillotine style. But we ignore it. Instead, we engage in small talk. Filling space. Saying nothing. Wilful distraction.

It can't last forever though.

'I knew something wasn't right at Christmas,' begins Claire.

'Helen didn't play in the games and she didn't sit next to you all night,' she says.

'She got pissed out of her head and went to bed early,' she says.

As recoveries go this is spectacular. If she were a biblical character she would be Lazarus.

I sigh. I breathe. I count to ten but only make it to two. Does counting to ten ever work?

'Claire,' I begin, 'when I phoned you with my news last weekend it was a total shock to you. You found it so difficult to believe that you told me to fuck off three times, started crying and hung up,' I say. 'But a few days later you saw it coming? Give me a break. This is difficult and painful enough already without you suddenly being Mystic Meg.'

'I know how I reacted,' she snaps. 'But when I thought things through it was so obvious. I could see there were problems because you two looked so happy all the time. That's not natural. And I did think things were odd at Christmas but I just dismissed it. I'm sorry. I should have warned you that things weren't right.'

This must be that female intuition I hear so much about. It's probably always at its most potent in retrospect.

'For fuck's sake,' I say, 'you're sorry you didn't warn me? Claire, get over yourself,' I say, 'you're not some sort of relationship guru.'

I get up to leave. Claire gets set to launch her retaliation. Neither happens.

'Shutup the pair of you!' shouts Mum, 'and sit down! Arguing with each other won't solve anything,' she says.

Claire and I both sit again.

Silence reigns.

Until the doorbell rings.

If I were religious I'd pray that it's my Dad at the door. If there is a God, He didn't answer my unsaid prayer. If anything, it's the exact opposite of my Dad arriving home. Instead it's three of my Mum's sisters. All they need now is a cauldron.

Irish mothers must receive special training. I can't imagine they're born like that. Here they are en masse to help me through my "crisis".

Later, after everyone leaves, Mum will tell me that they're just concerned. It shows they care about me.

They're just offering support.

They only want to help.

In my head I translate these sentiments. They want their gossip to be first hand.

They want ring-side seats.

They want to be at the front-line.

They're just being human.

We all talk a great game about wanting the right things. World peace, an end to poverty, clean water for all, ad infinitum. In some respects we're all just overgrown prom queens. But nothing commands our attention more than seeing that plane crash through the second tower.

The spectacle.

The drama.

The excitement.

It's just being human.

Mum makes another pot of tea and we sit in the kitchen chatting. Catching up. We talk about work. We talk about holidays planned. We talk about relatives. We engage in small talk.

Again.

People with nothing to say, saying it too loudly. Filling space. Saying nothing. Wilful distraction.

Small talk will be the death of language.

For a while we avoid the real reason everyone is here. For a while it's even nice. But I knew it wasn't going to last. And it didn't. Eventually the clichés and proverbs get thrown around confetti style.

'Plenty more fish in the sea.'

'Time is a great healer.'

'Absence makes the heart grow fonder.'

Thing is I remember the days when flowers made her heart grow fonder. And chocolates. And surprise trips to the continent. And that fucking huge diamond.

But hey, like the Murphy's, I'm not bitter.

And why are the proverbs written in stone? Why isn't it plenty more birds in the sky? Or plenty more flowers in the field? Surely they are more apt for the sentiment.

'Time is a great healer.'

Yeah, so is Preparation H. Maybe I could use some now. I've got four pains in the arse dispensing unwanted advice.

Still, even the overused, predictable clichés are better than what comes next.

'I know why your marriage failed,' says my aunt Brenda.

I remain silent. Everyone watches me expecting me to ask for her advice. I remain silent.

'Do you?' my mother says eventually. She throws a scowl at me for good measure.

'As a matter of fact I do,' says Brenda.

I remain silent. The whole room is waiting for me to ask for her wisdom regarding my marriage. I won't give her the satisfaction. I don't want to hear it. Even more, I don't need to hear it. But she's waiting for me to ask her why my marriage failed. They are all waiting for me to ask. Pure voyeurism. They're not here to help, they're here to witness. Better than reality tv. Plenty more parasites in the cess-pool.

I remain silent.

She's aching to tell me, but that's not how the game is played. I have to ask. I'm enjoying her pain. Maybe I'm more like them than I thought. I shudder trying to shake that thought from my mind.

I remain silent.

There's a protocol that needs to be followed. A family elder has offered an insight beyond my powers and I'm supposed to plead for the knowledge. Beg. Grovel.

My arms are on the table, my chin is on my arms and my mouth is staying resolutely shut.

I remain silent.

'What do you think the problem was?' my mother asks and she treats me to a more severe scowl.

'I'll tell you,' says Brenda through a pinched mouth clearly annoyed that I didn't follow the correct protocol. In fact, her whole face is pinched. Probably from the faces she pulls when she reads the Daily Mail from her holier than thou throne.

'It's because you didn't have any children,' she says. 'Deep down every woman wants children of her own. Maybe not all men do. But if Helen kept telling you that she didn't want children she was lying.'

'True,' says one of the other crone clones.

'Definitely,' says the third.

They all nod sagely.

'Sure, a marriage isn't a marriage without children,' says Brenda.

'It's genetic, you see,' says Claire aiming at a wise look but hitting constipated.

I sigh and get up to leave.

'Well?' challenges Brenda the wisdom imparter.

'Well, what?' I reply irritably.

'What do you think of what I've just said?' she asks triumphantly. This is her theory to end all theories. She has surpassed all thinking – every woman wants children of her own. QED. Who the Hell is Einstein?

'Does it matter what I think?' I say. 'It's all black and white to you. You've been talking out of your arse for years, so I can't expect you to change the habit of a lifetime,' I say.

'Well, I must say there's no need for that!' she says. 'I'm just trying to help! I've never been so insulted in all my life!' she says.

All the others flock around her cooing and calming. My mother throws me a look that almost disowns me. Unfortunately, it's only almost.

'You've never been so insulted in all your life?' I say.
'Well, you've been bloody lucky then,' I say.

Libra Calling

'There is no such thing as a religious war,' says Libra, 'and there never was. There is no such thing as an idealistic war and there never was. There is no such thing as a good war and there never was.

Every war that has ever been fought has been for power and wealth. Religion has been guilty of allowing itself to be used to further the struggle for power and wealth but it has never been the root cause. The same is true for idealism and good.

Make no mistake about it, when war is declared it is never for anything as noble as the rights of the people or the protection of liberty, it is only ever for the pursuit of power and wealth. In time, you would think that at least the propaganda would become slicker, but Blair's 45 minute warning put paid to that. We all know why we are in Iraq and Afghanistan – oil. Power and wealth, my friends, power and wealth.'

The phenomenon of Libra has only been with us for a couple of weeks and already it is out of hand. He has been getting fan mail. His adoring army of fans have been sending letters, emails, text messages, gifts…all sorts of things to the TV stations in the hope of reaching him. Of course, nobody knows the location of his bat cave, so the TV stations were the most logical option.

As well as that, campaigns are springing up all over the place begging for him to run in elections, to take over the country, to lead the world.

'When we go to war with North Korea and Iran, as we inevitably will,' says Libra, 'it will be for exactly the same reasons. Power and wealth. We are told almost on a daily basis that both countries are developing nuclear weapons. Ahmedinejad and Kim Jong Il are painted as James Bond style villains hiding in sophisticated underground lairs. And we believe this. We believe this from the same people who told us incessantly that Saddam Hussein had an arsenal of weapons of mass destruction. The same people who promise so much in elections, then fail to deliver so much more. The same people who claim outrageous false expenses thereby stealing money from our pockets. People who regularly cheat on their partners. Who manipulate official statistics to suit their own needs.'

It's not just one way though. As well as the letters of support and gifts and what not, he has also been getting requests. People want his autograph. People want his photo. People want him to sing a song for them in his mangled voice. They want his wisdom. His sperm. His holy powers to cure them. They want favours that they can't do for themselves. Like tickets to the Champions League Final. And changes in legislation. And to kill personal enemies.

Libra is this season's Jim'll Fix It!

'These people cannot be trusted with the simplest things,' says Libra. 'Yet we believe them and trust them with our national security. We doubt their words, actions and motives with the day to day things, but we trust them implicitly with our lives.

Well, we vote them in, we pay the price.

But we can change that too. We elected them. Their jobs are to represent our interests. So I have a challenge for the people of Britain.'

Thing about Libra is, he thinks outside the box. I know that's such an adworld cliché, but he really does. Like nobody else. He has no physical assets but he doesn't need any. He uses the latest technologies to his advantage. He uses his strengths and attacks his enemies' weaknesses. He is this season's David to the government's Goliath. He is this season's Michael O'Leary.

'The PM says that violence is unacceptable and that change must be brought about by diplomatic means. He says the people of Britain have elected him and his party to do a job and that they will do it. He says that he will not give in to violence.

That's fine. The Scales of Justice will play by his rules. Each week for the foreseeable future the Scales of Justice will hold a referendum. From midnight tonight until midnight tomorrow the people of Britain can vote in the first referendum. The question is: Should British armed forces be withdrawn from Iraq and Afghanistan? Text yes or no to 51999. This is a free service, but please only send one text. Duplicate phone numbers will only be counted once. People of Britain, let your voices be heard!'

London calling

I go to the bar and get the round in. It's crowded but I only see two other guys waiting to get served. Everyone else stands at the bar drinking. Nobody lets me in. On the jukebox, the Kaiser Chiefs sing I Predict a Riot.

Behind the bar one guy pours a pint of lager and this takes up all his concentration. When the pint glass fills to the top he turns off the tap and places the glass on the counter. He reaches up, takes another empty glass from the shelf and starts to fill it from the same lager tap. This takes up all his concentration. Again. Clearly multi-tasking is something that happens to other people.

At least he's serving someone though. The other two, it seems, are paid to discuss the merits of last night's TV. Getting their attention, well, there's more chance of finding an honest politician. London has many things to be proud of, but its bar staff isn't one of them.

Eventually the barman spots me and serves me through a crowd of blokes. I pay him, take my change and go back to the lads with the drinks. I make eye contact with nobody. This is one of the rules of drinking in London. Around the world you make eye contact, you nod, you smile, you might even say 'hi' and chat. In the wrong pub in London, you make eye contact it means you want a fight. And there will be plenty to take up the offer.

Another rule is you apologise for an accidental bump even if it wasn't your fault. Another rule is that even if you obey all the other rules, it doesn't mean you won't end up in a fight. It doesn't mean you won't get a pint glass pushed into your face until it shatters and splinters and makes fountains of your blood. It doesn't mean you won't get bottles smashed over your head and then stabbed in your kidneys. It doesn't mean you won't get your cheek slashed with a Stanley knife. And if that's not bad enough, it could be a Stanley knife sporting two blades so the wound can't be stitched. It doesn't mean that even if you obey all the rules you won't get jumped by a gang and kicked relentlessly by Doc Martens with razor blades sewn into the soles. These things probably won't happen. But one of them only has to happen once to put a serious crimp in your outlook.

I'm out up town with the lads. We've only had a couple and already I think it's a mistake. My own stupid fault though. I would have agreed to anything rather than sit alone in my home without Helen. And then Gary phoned.

Another London rule is the pub you drink in after work on a school night isn't the same pub on a Saturday night. And right now the Rhapsody is not full of marketeers speaking adlish, but Essex boys and girls speaking chavish. When they're not speaking chavish, they're speaking cockney rhyming slang. Even worse.

Cockney rhyming slang is one of London's peculiarities. One of its exceptions. In London everything gets shortened whenever possible. Names for example.

Derek becomes Del.

Sharon becomes Shaz.

Jonathan becomes Jon.

People too busy or too lazy to say the full thing.

Everything gets shortened except for the working week and cockney rhyming slang. Both of those just get longer.

Pearly queens and cheeky chappies who can't keep still for a second. Ducking and diving. Bit of this, bit of that. Perpetual motion.

Mate becomes China plate.

Look becomes butcher's hook.

Stairs becomes apples and pears.

Cockney rhyming slang – proof, if ever it were needed, that morons are alive and well and living in London.

On the jukebox the track changes to Baggy Trousers by Madness. Around the pub twenty-somethings start skanking Suggs style. None of them were even born when the song originally hit the charts. Parents used to teach their kids the waltz. Then the Charlston. Then the Jive. Now it's Skanking and Vogue. Some things never change, the rest remains the same.

Essex, a county made up of ex-Londoners who moved to the country and took the city with them. Seeing them here in this pub on a Saturday night, these Essex boys and girls, it's like they've come home to roost. To breed. Maybe they have.

Either they're in uniform or else it rains Ben Sherman & Tommy Hilfiger gear in Essex. Standing still they manage to swagger and roll their shoulders boxer style. So much cash is flashed I'm tempted to check the news to see which bank has been robbed. And the jewellery on show, well, Fort Knox doesn't hold this much gold.

The Rhapsody during the week is one of our pubs. Right now though, a divorce lawyer would be more welcome in the Vatican. Standing there with Gary, Vince and Dave, I get bumped from behind and beer slops over my hand and down my arm. No apology. No recognition of any foul. Just laughter, braying donkey style.

'Let's finish these and move on,' I say.

'This is painful,' I say.

'It's going to kick off,' I say.

Vince nods, relieved that someone else has said it. Someone else has offered the coward's way out. His bunched up shoulders visibly relax.

Nothing about Gary changes. Daddy Cool. Always.

'You big gay bear!' says Dave. 'They're just a bit boisterous. You're not scared of a few kids, are you?'

He stands poised.

Ready to go in a fraction of a nanosecond.

Giving it the big 'un.

Again.

Dave always gives the impression he loves a rumble. Still, I've never seen him in a fight.

'A few?' I say. 'There's eleventy million of them! And they're hardly kids.'

Dave turns his face away disgusted at my yellow streak.

'You're right,' says Gary. 'It feels nasty here. Besides, I'm a lover not a fighter,' says Gary and he smiles and winks.

Once again Daddy Cool has diffused the tension.

Some things can't be bettered. Some things are just perfect the way they are. Friday nights in Soho during the summer for example. You finish work like everyone else. You head to a bar with your workmates like everyone else. You stand on the street drinking, soaking up the glorious sun like everyone else. You spot slebs like everyone else. Marketeers drinking with actors drinking with designers drinking with musicians drinking with dotcomers drinking with writers drinking with IT guys drinking with dancers drinking with everyone drinking with anyone. Free to be individuals. Free to be yourself. Free to be different. Choosing to be the same.

Friday nights during the summer in Soho are unique. Tonight's not like that.

The next bar, The X Bar, is the same as The Rhapsody. Weekenders giddy with the prospect of a night out in town stand drinking at the bar getting in the way. They stand in the walkways normally kept free of traffic by the mid-week regulars. Swaggering kids bump into us like their shoulders are too wide or they've got too many elbows.

This was not the plan. This night out was supposed to melt away the week of work. This was supposed to be a massage for the soul. To untangle all those internal knots and bunched up muscles.

Instead, my body is a collapsing star. My muscles condensing themselves under pressure so extreme they're in danger of becoming diamonds.

Boiling my head would be more fun.

And then it hits me. It's not just that the bars are different at the weekend. It's just that I've been out a few times with Clive to

Foe gigs. That's the name given to the new music movement. I don't know why it's called Foe. Nobody does. The point is that, compared to a Foe gig, anything else seems insipid.

Wet.

Boring.

Dead.

It's a bit of a chicken and egg conundrum – which came first, Foe or the Scales of Justice? On this one everyone's an expert and everyone knows the truth. Problem is, the truth varies. Violently.

Some say Libra was inspired by Foe. Some say Libra started as the leader of the original Foe band. Problem there is that nobody can agree on the original Foe band. It might be Kyoto Double Cross. Or Third World Sweatshop. Or maybe it was The Eton Rifles or Up The Junction or Pretty Vacant. It might even have been The Tards or The Spas.

Others say that Foe was spawned from Libra's on-line recruitment.

Anyhow, it doesn't matter which one came first. The point is they are both inextricably linked. And a Foe gig makes any other night out seem dull.

'I've had enough,' I say, 'this is crap. I'm going home.'

Dave rolls his eyes heavenwards.

'Lightweight,' he says and turns away.

'Piss off, Dave!' I say.

'Leave it out, Dave,' says Gary. 'He's right, this is shit. We'll go somewhere else.'

'It's the same everywhere!' I say. 'Look around! I'm going home.'

Dave turns back and glares at me.

'How come you're such a boring, moody bastard these days?' he says.

'Oi! I said leave it out,' says Gary. 'He's just split up with Helen. Give him a break.'

'He's been like this for months,' says Dave. 'No wonder Helen left him.'

'Fuck you, you wanker!' I scream and I launch at him.

Time to move on

Glasses fall and smash. Beer spills and floods. The four of us grapple and struggle. Then bouncers grapple and struggle. Once we're on the street the bouncers leave the four of us to grapple and struggle on our own again. They stand back at the door watching. Waiting. If needed they'll be there, but otherwise it's no longer their problem.

Vince and Gary separate us. Dave's nose is bloody. I don't know if I caught him with a punch. Or my shoulder. Or my head. Or if it was even me. I'm not sure if he hit me. The four of us and the bouncers grappled for a bit and that was it really. This is how real fights happen. The punch ups in the movies, they're real in the same way that extra-terrestrials are cute with huge blue eyes and Duracell powered index fingers. Real people don't want to get hurt so they hold onto their opponent and when you do that you can't swing punches.

Vince talks to Dave, calming him down. Gary's with me.

'Mate, come on,' says Gary. 'Dave didn't mean it. You know he can be a bit hot-headed and suffers from foot and mouth.'

I taste bile in my throat and my entire body shakes. I'm ready to rip his head off. I'm ready to gouge out his eyes. I'm ready to kick and punch and scream. I remain silent.

'You're going through a bad spot right now and we just want to cheer you up, that's all,' says Gary. 'We just want to take your mind off it for a while. Have a few beers, have a few laughs, that kind of thing,' says Gary.

My head pounds white hot with pressure. My eyes bulge obese with tears. I could happily dance on his head. I could happily slice off his scrotum. I could happily tear off his fingernails. I remain silent.

'Come on, mate,' says Gary. 'Let's ditch Soho and head over to Hoxton. Have the craic eh?' says Gary.

My teeth scrum together. My breath floods my elastic chest. I want to cause damage.

Then suddenly I'm fine. The anger does a Keyser Sozé and, like that, whoosh, it's gone.

'OK,' I say calm as Gandhi.

'Let's go,' I say.

I make to move away but Gary doesn't let go.

'You OK, mate?' he asks, his face etched with concern. Or fear.

'Yeah, I'm fine,' I say and smile.

I walk over to Vince and Dave who watch my every move. Behind me I feel Gary watch me too. And the bouncers.

'Sorry Dave,' I say. 'For hitting you, I mean.'

He wipes his bloody nose with a tissue and looks at it.

'No harm done, mate,' he says. 'I shouldn't have said what I did. I'm sorry too.'

We hug.

'So, do you reckon we're barred?' I ask smiling. The three boys chuckle. Gary hails a cab.

Hoxton is the new place to be. Acting as a buffer to keep the east end at arm's length from the city, its regeneration into a trendy neighbourhood has seen prices rise threefold from coffee to property. Then again, that always happens wherever a coffee becomes a skinny latte and a flat becomes a des res apartment.

The bar we're in has no name and they don't serve draft beer. Instead, you get a bottle of Brahma Brazilian lager at £6 a pop. I think it's that price because it comes with a black straw.

The DJ spins a backbeat behind every track and every track is ultra cool and ultra new. Everyone moves to the music in some fashion, but nobody is really dancing. We have to raise our voices to be heard and even though the vibe beats through us we can still hear clearly. The levels are pitched perfect catalysing the smootheness of the atmosphere.

Everyone is cool. Everyone is chic. Everyone is trendy, funky, crisp. This is more like it. So this is where our crowd hangs out at weekends. It's so long since I've been out up town on a Saturday night that I'm completely out of touch. This is the spot to spot and be spotted. If that's what you're after.

'See anything you like, sir?' asks Gary.

I roll my eyes.

'Mate, I'm not ready!' I say. 'It's the last thing on my mind! I've just split up with my wife!'

'Exactly,' says Gary smiling. 'You're a free man! You have been granted the license!'

'For Christ's sake!' I say. 'Gary, you're such a cock sometimes! Don't you have any idea of how I feel right now?' I ask.

'Of course I do,' says Gary. 'And the best thing you could do is get out there as quickly as possible. Besides, it didn't stop you last weekend,' he says.

'That's unfair,' I say. 'Last weekend was a mistake. And I don't want to make another one. I'm not ready,' I repeat.

I turn and face the bar and peel the label off my bottle of Brahma.

'Fine,' says Gary.

'Suit yourself,' he says and wanders off.

Vince and Dave are chatting with two girls so I stay on my own at the bar. I came out for a few beers, not to go on the pull. Clearly I was alone with that view. Fair enough. I'll finish this beer and head home.

I turn away from the bar to face the crowded room. Smiling faces. Happy faces. Laughing faces. Chatting faces. Kissing faces. No misery, no pain, no suffering. It's like the fucking Mickey Mouse Club.

Familiar face. Gary wanders back grinning with two girls in tow. After the briefest of introductions he zones in on his target leaving me to chat with the other girl.

Bastard.

'So Gary tells me you're an advertising director,' she says smiling. She tosses her hair and then plays with it with her right hand.

'Yeah,' I say.

'Cool,' she says. She sips her wine.

Silence.

'So, like, what adverts would I have seen?' she asks. 'That are, like, yours?' she qualifies.

'Oh, I dunno,' I say. 'I don't have much on TV right now.'

'Oh,' she says and stops playing with her hair. She looks away. She couldn't look more bored if she were adjudicating a paint-drying watching competition.

Silence.

I drain my beer.

'Listen,' I say, 'I'm sorry but there's been some mistake here. I'm going home now,' I say and I walk away.

I don't say goodbye to my mates. My mates. One of them I've known for eight years and I couldn't tell you a thing about him. I punched another one earlier this evening and the last thinks everything is cured by going on the pull.

How can they be my mates when I don't know them? How can they be mates when they don't know me?

Wilful distraction

People keep asking me if I saw it coming. People keep asking me if we were having problems. If there were outside factors. If there was another party. Not necessarily an affair. Work maybe. Or an interfering sibling. That kind of thing.

Over time we develop stock answers for every occasion. We come back from holiday with a pre-recorded review ready to fall from our lips. For our favourite author we have a list of reasons why he or she is the greatest. The same is true of favourite bands.

And actors.

And sports stars.

Ad infinitum.

Well, let me tell you now, from experience, it's the same when your marriage breaks down. The arse falls out of your world and you deal with it by launching automatic pilot. You draw up your list of replies for every eventuality. Your clever little soundbites. Rehearsed so well they don't seem rehearsed.

If I were a TV programme, I'd be Blue Peter. Here's one I prepared earlier.

Thing is though, deep down in that secret wardrobe housing all your rattling skeletons, you know it's a lie. All of it. All of those carefully crafted politicians' answers are big, fat fibs. Or at very best they're just excuses.

We drifted apart.

We don't feel the way we used to.

We love each other more like friends now.

Thing is, right from the very beginning there were problems. But we ignored them. We hoped they would go away. And every relationship is the same.

Early on you justify this by saying it is good that we challenge each other. Thing is, when does it stop being a challenge? Yeah, it's ok that he doesn't like soaps and she hates football, but what about the stuff that matters? What about the decisions for the future? Like when one of them wants to launch a business but the other wants the security of a state pension? Or when one wants to live and work abroad for a few years but the other doesn't want to be away from family? How do you reconcile those differences? How do you refrain from wondering what if? And then how do you prevent that regret from becoming bitterness?

Yeah, like all couples we brushed it under the carpet and ignored the issues.

If we were a colour, we'd be yellow.

Instead, we focused on other stuff. Fun stuff. And you can see the point. I mean, who wants confrontation when you can have a barbecue instead?

Wilful distraction.

But the problems build and build and build and then one day a stray spark ignites the whole pile, and whoosh, it's an inferno.

Maybe things would be different now if I had confronted issues as they arose. Maybe those endearing little qualities wouldn't have become annoying little habits. And maybe Helen could say the same. Scratch that, Helen could definitely say the same.

And maybe I'd still be sick with love instead of, well, just sick.

Mankind's biggest problem is lack of focus. We could achieve so much. But we don't. All the things that matter, all the things we should do, well, we always find something else to do first.

We check our emails before beginning work. We have a coffee before cleaning the house. We shop on-line before paying our bills.

Wilful distraction.

And it's the same in every walk of life.

An election in Nothing Backwater gets rigged, but you skip onto the latest Britney trauma. Or another suicide bombing kills 20, including three British peace-keepers, in Unimportantsville, but you really need to catch up on the footie scores. Or a refugee camp is now home to a million refugees in the middle of Nowhere Central, but clearly you need to check out the latest designer clothing range which those same refugees should be manufacturing in sweatshops.

And then one day three Tube trains and one bus get attacked killings scores and you wonder how it happened. Why would people do that? What pissed them off so much?

I'm not religious but you reap what you sow.

Wilful distraction.

I suppose the point is eventually reality catches up. You can't keep running away. It will get you in the end. And when it does you will know pain.

Once that door is open there's no closing it. It's a bulkhead on a sinking ship. And all of those issues you've been avoiding, all of those problems you were going to get around to one day, all of those things that weren't real priorities, well, they become priorities pretty damn quick. The pile grows and grows Jack's beanstalk style into your very own reality monster.

When the cold hard facts of reality won't quit stacking up against you, you can really see the appeal of a life as a junkie. It suddenly becomes a life choice. A career path. Zoned out zombie beats stressed out realist any day of the week and twice on Sunday.

Maybe the addiction to unreality starts young and never truly leaves. Maybe we just graduate to stronger influences. As a kid all you needed to escape reality was your imagination. Perhaps with the help of a fairy tale or Disney movie. It's not long though before you've outgrown those stimuli and you're on video games. Then you graduate to alcohol. Then pot. Then your nose becomes a hoover. And before you know it the term cooking has different connotations for you and your belt has another use.

Then again, what can you expect when every little girl is convinced by her parents that she's a fairy princess who will marry a knight in shining armour and every boy is destined to play football for his country? When reality strikes after that the only way is down.

'I want a permanent separation,' Helen tells me on the phone. We've done the small talk, the hellos and how are yous and what have you been up tos, and now it's:

'I want a permanent separation.'

I thought I had thought of it as permanent. Somehow Helen saying it makes it more real. You know when you get a whack in a kidney and you can't catch your breath? This is worse.

'Do you mean a divorce?' I ask. That's not fair. She has raised the issue but I'm the one who had to say the D word. Permanent separation doesn't sound as harsh.

'Well, yeah, I suppose so,' says Helen.

'Why?' I ask. The question sounds hollow. No substance. Redundant.

'Well, because it's over,' says Helen. 'No matter how hard this is now it's the right decision. We both know that.'

'But…' I say.

'But…' I say again.

And the rest of it won't come out. I want to tell her I love her. I want to tell her we can work things out. I want to tell her what she means to me. Everything. I want to tell her that we're perfect together and that this is just a phase. I'll try harder. I'll change things around. We can go to counselling. We can make this work.

But it all sounds so clichéd in my head. They're the kind of things actors say in crap American movies. Coming from me they would just sound false.

'You know it's the right decision,' she says. 'The only decision. We haven't been right together for a long time, and that's not going to change.'

'Can I take some time to think about it?' I ask. Although, let's face it, it would be pretty difficult to keep the marriage going on my own.

'Of course you can,' she says. 'This isn't easy for either of us. So take as much time as you need.'

'OK,' I say. 'Thanks.' My heart has been ripped out and I'm thanking the ripper. This must be what it's like when a hostage defends their captor.

'But I think we should do a couple of things,' she says.

'Like what?' I ask.

'Well, I think we should put the house on the market for starters,' she says. 'And I think you should see someone. A therapist. Now that we've been apart I can see that you've been depressed for some time.'

'What?' I ask. 'Who fucking died and made you Frasier?' I say.

She sighs and takes a moment. We might be speaking on the phone but I can see her putting her hand to her forehead and fighting back tears.

'It's just a thought,' she says. 'I'm only trying to help. I don't think you're enjoying much in life anymore.'

'And us splitting up is going to help that, is it?' I ask.

'Well, staying together certainly didn't!' she says.

As retaliation goes it's a good one. Touché. I swallow the rising rage and find a level tone.

'Right,' I say. 'Well, thanks for the advice. I'll consider it,' I say. If I were a temperature, I'd be Kelvin.

'Don't be like that,' she says. 'You know I'm just trying to help. So much in our lives has been getting you down over the past few months. Work, family, friends…me…everything.'

Her voice is concern. I soften.

'I know,' I say. 'I'll think about it. Honestly,' I say.

We say our goodbyes and hang up.

So I can take as much time as I like to think about a divorce but in the meantime we'll just go ahead and sell the house and continue to dismantle the marriage. I can think about the divorce but it's going to happen anyway. For some reason Nirvana's Come as You Are plays in my head.

How did we get here? To the place where we are splitting up forever? I try to think through the gradual slide to this state of affairs but it just doesn't seem to exist. One minute we were happy together, the next we're signing divorce papers. I try to conjure up bad images of us together but the memory banks are only holding the good stuff. Our first date. Our moving in day. Holidays. Engagement. Wedding. Birthdays. Helen's 30th in particular. That was special. And then it hits me. That was probably the last special time.

It helped that we were now working for different agencies. It was easier to arrange everything by phone without arousing suspicion. Helen was still working at MCH and I knew her boss well. So well that I had her mobile and home phone numbers. I called her a few weeks before to arrange for Helen to have the time off. Just a long weekend which helped to keep Helen's diary free.

Well, the original plan was to keep Helen's diary completely free on the Friday and Monday, but then one of her clients arranged a meeting for 10am on the Friday. It might not have been a problem as it would probably have been finished in plenty time but I couldn't risk it. Helen's boss stepped in and explained everything to the client who then phoned Helen and re-arranged it for the following Wednesday.

After that little scare Helen's boss quickly filled the diary with phantom meetings for both days. The piece de resistance was her boss putting in a 12.30 birthday lunch on the Friday. A lunch that was never going to happen because I was going to turn up and take her to the station.

I started the treasure hunt on the first. Helen came out of the bathroom, a big towel wrapped around her body while she was drying her hair with another towel. She stopped dead in her tracks when she saw the A1 map of Europe on the wall and me standing there with a sheet of coloured stickers in one hand and a wrapped present in the other.

'Happy birth month, honey,' I said and I walked over and kissed her.

She let go a suspicious, nervous, little chuckle.

'What's going on?' she said.

'Well, my gorgeous wife, you are thirty in ten days time so this is the first day of your birth month. And each day you will receive a present from a different European country. But before you are allowed to open it you must guess the country of origin with a game of twenty questions. I can only answer yes or no and you can only guess the country three times.'

'Okaaay,' she drawled. 'And what happens if I don't guess it correctly?'

'Then you don't get the present!'

She pouted. Fake pouted. As though I were being deliberately mean. But she knew as well as I did that I would give her all the presents anyway. I just wanted to make it a little more fun.

'Yeah well, what will you do with the presents then if you don't give them to me?'

'Take them back to the shops.'

She treated herself to a sharp intake of breath at that answer.

'You wouldn't dare!' she said all mock confrontational.

'Try me,' I said.

'Huh!' she said and threw me a filthy look with a grin attached.

She dropped her hair towel, took the coloured stickers from my hand and snogged me. Then she chuckled and grinned.

'I love you so much,' she said and hugged me tightly.

She looked at the map and I looked at her. Cheshire cats don't grin this big. God, I loved making her smile. I loved making her happy.

'Is it in Scandinavia?' she asked.

'No,' I replied, 'nineteen.'

'Hmm, is it an island?'

'Nope, eighteen.'

She paused a moment to study the map.

'Is it in two continents?'

'No, seventeen,' I replied. 'I'll give you a hint though you're being way too specific too early.'

'How do you mean?' asked Helen.

'Well, that last question only rules out Russia and Turkey, and prior to that you got rid of Scandinavia, Britain, Ireland and a few islands in the Med...'

'And Greenland and Iceland,' she blurted and stuck her tongue out at me and turned away all aloof.

'Cheeky bitch!' I said as I laughed and hugged her. She was laughing too.

'OK,' she said, 'fair point well made. Right then, is it in the former Eastern Bloc?'

'Good question! No though. Sixteen.'

She stared at the map for a few seconds and thought about her next question.

'Does it have a coastline?'

'Brilliant! Yes, fifteen.'

'Is the coastline in the Med?'

'No, fourteen.'

'The North Sea?'

'Yes, thirteen.'

'A Benelux country?'

'Yes, twelve.'

'Holland?'

'No, eleven.'

'Belgium?'

'Yay!' I said and I hugged her and kissed her.

''I love you,' I said.

'I love you too,' she replied, 'now give me my pressie!'

And so for breakfast that morning before work we shared a tray of Belgian chocolates and had the other tray that night.

The next morning Helen opened a voucher I had made up entitling her to a romantic meal for two at her favourite Tapas restaurant and we went that night. The next day was a voucher to a Turkish spa. The next, a bottle of Champagne. And each day began with a present from another European country.

On the Friday morning she opened a Venetian mask. The scene was set.

We travelled into work together on the Tube and Helen told me of her hectic schedule for both today and Monday and how she really should have managed her diary better for her birthday weekend. At least she was having a birthday lunch courtesy of work today. And she kept probing me about the next night and what I had planned. And I played it coy.

I walked her to her office building like I did every morning and kept going in the direction of my own office but at Tottenham Court Road Tube Station I went underground and home to pack for our weekend away.

At 12.30 Helen was getting ready to go to lunch with her work colleagues after they had just enjoyed some celebratory bubbles and cake, which surprised her as she thought they would have waited until after lunch for that.

She was even more surprised to see me walk through the door pulling a wheelie case in one hand and holding a wrapped present in the other.

'What's going on?' she asked.

'You have to open a present,' I replied and got the map out and put it on the wall complete with the coloured stickers of places she had already guessed. All of her colleagues knew about the little game each morning and so knew what to expect now.

'Ok,' said Helen, 'does it have a coastline?'

'Yes,' said everyone, 'nineteen!'

Helen burst into a fit of giggles.

'Is it in the Med?'

'Yes, eighteen!'

'Is it in the Balkans?'

'No, seventeen!'

At this stage everyone was laughing and Helen had to regain control before each question.

'Is it an island?'

'No, sixteen!'

'OK, well I've already had presents from Spain, France and Italy. Am I going back to one of those countries?

'Yes, fifteen!'

'Spain?'

'No, fourteen!'

'France?'

'No, thirteen!'

'Italy?'

'Yes!' said everyone and followed it with a round of applause and yet more laughter.

'We're going to Italy?' Helen asked me.

'Well, why don't you open your present and find out,' I replied.

And she opened a guide book to Venice and two tickets on the Orient Express.

She gasped and burst into tears. I hugged her and kissed her and told her I loved her. So very, very much.

And everyone else awwed and cheered and clapped and wished us a wonderful weekend away and a happy birthday to Helen.

And she did have a happy birthday.

And that was probably the last time our relationship was perfect.

All change

'So the Prime Minister is adamant that the actions of the Scales of Justice will not force the British people to change our way of life,' says Libra, 'even though it is the British people who are asking for the change.'

When Libra talks the world stops. Everyone tunes in to the news for the next tape. When there isn't one, there's a feeling of disappointment. A sense of loss.

So far there have been three referendums. For each one a different method has been applied. The first was a text message. The second was via Facebook. The third via Twitter. Who knows where he will go next. Or she. The latest rumours suggest Libra is a woman. The voice is so distorted on the tapes it's more than possible.

For each referendum an independent party was used to announce the results. The text message poll was controlled by the BBC and over 80% of mobile phones in the country submitted a vote. It was a landslide. 84% want the forces out of Iraq and Afghanistan.

The government dismissed the vote as a gimmick. They said it was too black and white. It didn't lend itself to the reality of the situation and that it was too complicated to be resolved on a yes or no voting mechanism.

'I remember similar empty bravado just before the introduction of the extra restrictions in airports,' says Libra. 'And the Patriot Act in the US. And the anti-terrorist laws that make it a criminal offence for certain people to own a London A-Z or to protest within 500 metres of parliament.'

The second referendum focussed on civil liberties and Britain's colonial heritage. It was in the form of a questionnaire on Facebook and offered a range of values from 1-5 in the usual manner of questionnaires. You know the kind of thing – 1 if you feel very strongly about a certain subject, 5 if you don't feel very strongly, and the varying degrees represented by 2-4 in between. Over thirty million people took part in the survey. Actually, that's a lie. Almost 600 million people took part in the survey but only 30 million were from the UK so only their votes counted. Again, the responses suggested overwhelmingly that reform was wanted and needed in the system.

This time round the government line was that it was too vague and not representative of enough of the population. Which takes some gall considering less than 27 million people voted in the general election.

'On another note I also remember when Britain was crippled by strikes,' says Libra. 'The cities were infested with rats because rubbish had not been collected for weeks. We endured power cuts every night. This was our way of life then and we were not happy with it so we forced change. The politicians of this country are elected by us to serve us. How dare the Prime Minister suggest he will not give the people what we want! What we need! How dare he suggest he will not listen to us!

The third referendum opted for a middle ground between the previous two polls. It asked one question but offered a number of potential outcomes. The question was: On a scale of 1 to 5, with 1 being very good and 5 being very poor, how would you rate the government's overall performance? This survey was conducted on Twitter and a massive 41 million people in the UK took part. Of the 41 million, 86% chose either 4 or 5. Any other scores are pretty much immaterial in the face of that overwhelming statistic. That was two days ago. The government has yet to comment. But Libra had a word or two on the matter.

'The people of Britain did not want these illegal wars,' says Libra. 'We did not want to invade Iraq and Afghanistan. We are annoyed and frustrated by the Big Brother restrictions imposed by this government. We feel let down by this government. The majority of the public is embarrassed by our colonial past. And we want to put things right,' says Libra.

I may be watching this at home, but I can sense the nodding heads around the country. Around the world. Libra is in tune with the people. If Libra were a God, he would be Minerva, Goddess of Wisdom.

'We have played by the government's rules and voiced our discontent by diplomatic means,' says Libra. 'We have held three referendums in the last three weeks which have demonstrated the public's feelings,' says Libra.

'The people have spoken,' says Libra.

'We were given three weeks to prove our point. We will now give the Prime Minister and the government three weeks to respond,' says Libra.

'Now the Prime Minister needs to start listening to the people who elected him to his lofty position. Or else he won't be there for much longer.'

It's a big important pitch. Not world changing. Not a huge brand. Not even that much money. But it's a big important pitch. It's big because we're going head to head against Amanda's old agency. It's important because we haven't won anything new for a while. The last three pitches went down quicker than Tommies in no man's land.

We need this for morale, Amanda tells me.

This could save our year, Amanda tells me.

If we don't win it jobs will be lost, Amanda tells me.

No pressure then.

People get twitchy when you're on a losing streak. It's only natural. Not our Financial Director though. Nothing fazes Bill the Bull. Bill doesn't do twitchy. Bill doesn't panic or worry. Bill calculates.

He knows we've got enough in the locker to keep us safe. To keep us ticking. No, scratch that. It's better than safe, better than ticking. We're in a strong healthy position. It's a vibrant company. Profitable. Efficient. Lean.

Yeah, we'll be fine and eventually we'll start winning again. So, we've lost a few pitches but we haven't lost any incumbent accounts.

But that doesn't mean people won't get fired. No, Bill won't panic. But he will calculate. He'll use it as an excuse to get rid of problems.

He's done it before. Three days after the Twin Towers did their Walls of Jericho impression, nine people lost their jobs. Nine out of 150. The reason given was the inevitable economic downturn. It was to protect profits for the year. Thing is, I knew the numbers. We had one quarter to go and we had already exceeded target for the full year. We paid out more in redundancies than we would have done for the last three months' salaries.

The promised economic downturn, the looming recession, well, it was this season's Emperor's New Clothes – never happened. But the dead wood had been stripped away. Problem people had been removed. Nice and neat and tidy. Since then nobody has given Bill an excuse.

Now though we're suddenly on a losing streak and London has been the victim of suicide bombers. Nobody has given Bill an excuse but one has come up anyway.

So this pitch I've been given by Amanda could save my job. So the question I need to ask myself is this: save my job or save my sanity?

Tough call.

I've locked myself away in a meeting room for some peace and quiet to get my work done. Out in the open plan the chance of peace and quiet is always below zero. There's more chance of finding an honest politician. A chaotic environment is essential for an ad agency. It proves that we're a wild and crazy bunch. Zany. Madcap. Nutty.

The door bursts open with a violence that you only see in movies when the police break in. Machine gun fire and barked commands should be the order of the day. Instead, I look up to see Rob's grinning head.

'What's your favourite word?' he asks.

'Eudemonic', I reply knee-jerk style. No thought, just spit the answer. I immediately regret it.

Rob's an account manager at the agency. He's one of the wild and crazy guys of the ad world. Just like everyone else. And he proves it constantly by playing these madcap games in the office.

'Fantastic!' enthuses Rob. 'Er, what does it mean?'

'It kind of means something along the lines of bringing about contentment,' I reply. 'Why? What's this for?' I ask.

'Oh it's just this game I'm putting together. I'm getting everyone's favourite word and I'll produce a list of people and the words and everyone has until Friday to match them,' Rob grins.

I groan.

So everyone will spend at least an hour each initially trying to match the name to the word. And they'll keep going back to it until Friday when they will hand in their answers. In the meantime they will work late all week and complain about it. It won't stop there either, because Rob will publish the results on Monday and everyone will talk about it all day.

'I'm almost done, actually' says Rob.

'Just got to get three more and they're all in a meeting at the mo.'

It's a great talent being able to speak and kiss my arse at the same time. Since Rob got promoted to account manager he has been spending every possible moment trying to impress me with his fun loving spirit and personality. Shame he doesn't do it with work.

'You should hear some of the answers!' he says and before I can stop him he's off.

'Onomatopoeia; antidisestablishmentarianism; alexipharmic; dystopia; euphemism; omnipotent; verisimilitude,' he lists.

I'm too busy for this. I shouldn't even be here. I just want to get my work done and leave.

'Rob,' I say, but he doesn't hear me because he's off again.

'It's brilliant. That was a selection of the pretentious offerings,' he says.

Great. Pretentious offerings. Well, at least I know which category my word has been put in, even if he didn't read it back to me.

'Then there's the obvious swear words – fuck, cunt, motherfucker, bollocks, cock, arse'.

'Rob, I…' I begin.

'Then there's the lewd and rude section: cunnilingus; ejaculation; fellatio; vagina; penis; orgasm…'

'Rob!' I shout. 'I've really got a lot to do, mate.'

'Oh,' he says. His grin collapses bringing his whole face with it.

'I'm sorry,' he says. 'I didn't realise,' he turns to go.

I'm working. He's wasting time. But I'm the bad guy. I'm the one who just neutered a puppy.

'Rob,' I say.

'Yeah?' he replies in his best hurt voice.

'Sorry mate,' I say. 'I didn't mean to snap. I'm just really busy,' I say.

'That's ok,' he says. 'I'll leave you to it,' he says and makes to leave.

'Rob,' I say.

'Yeah?'

'Can you do me a favour, please?'

'Of course,' he says. 'What do you need?'

'Can you change my word?' I ask.

'Of course I can,' he says. 'What do you want to change it to?'

'Anything at all,' I say. 'As long as it's not something pretentious.'

His grin is back.

'I can't just change it though,' he says. 'You've got to choose. Dem's da rools,' he says and clicks his fingers gangsta rapper style and finishes off with a Cobra. Clearly we're involved in something badass here so there's a certain way we need to behave.

My mind is blank and I can't think of a single word. I really don't have the time for this.

'Can't you just choose something for me, Rob?' I ask. Plead. Beg.

'Nopety, nopety, nope!' he says shaking his head.

My mind remains blank and I can't think of a single word.

'Bwaaa!' I hear myself say. Or something like that.

'What does 'bwaaa' mean?' asks Rob.

'It doesn't mean anything,' I reply. 'It was an exclamation of frustration! Because I don't know what else to say. Actually, strike that, it's a substitute word for when you don't know what else to say,' I say.

'Cool,' says Rob.

'And it sounds exactly like the noise made by a dying giraffe,' I say.

'Really?' asks Rob.

'Yes,' I say in my best earnest face.

Rob looks at me uncertainly but decides against pushing the issue.

'Great,' he says. 'Thanks! I'll leave you alone now,' he says and leaves.

I sigh to myself. So this is the career I've chosen for myself. A whole load of nothing that matters. This is the kind of company I've decided to work for. Society's cancer. The kind of people I've decided to work with. Satan's whores. In adworld, this is what passes for a creative environment.

'We need to think outside the box on this one people,' says the division's creative director. This is an initial concepts meeting on my new pitch. This was the meeting I was preparing for all morning.

'Absolutely,' says Rob, the word game guy. Filling space. Being heard. Eager. Enthusiastic. Sycophantic.

'What I want is for you to forget everything you've ever done before and treat this as a blank canvas,' says the division's creative director.

Around me heads nod pretend pensively.

'This, guys, is the wheel and we're about to invent it,' he's on a roll.

'This IS the greatest thing – forget sliced bread!' Beautiful.

'So, I've got just one question to ask you.'

He pauses for effect. He sits back. He glides into smug mode.

'If this were a car, what kind of car would it be?' he asks.

This is the most profound statement ever made. At least, that's what the expression on his face suggests.

Creative thinking for the creatively challenged. Same as it ever was.

For a moment I drift. I could be doing something else right now. Anything else. Anything at all would be more constructive. More beneficial.

I could be sticking pins in my eyes, for example. Or culling panda bears. Or ordering the tide to halt its advance, King Canute style.

Still, I suppose there are worse industries than advertising. Cosmetics, for example, and what they do to animals. Or there's fine jewellery where they charge millions for a lump of rock that's been mined by slaves earning less than the minimum wage. I could choose to be a number of things worse than an ad man. I could be a fascist and indulge in a little genocide. I could go and work for a tobacco company and spread cancer. Sure, there are plenty of industries worse than advertising. But it's a close call.

When I tune back in, Marsha is spouting on about some idea involving animals. Then again, Marsha is always spouting on about some idea involving animals. The Andrex puppy is her God. Not that she's alone. Everyone in Adland has their calling card.

Any minute now John will put forward the merits of a heritage and history campaign, Jack Daniels style. And everyone's mother, Ruth will want to use kids. Same as it ever was.

If advertising were a bodily function, it would be regurgitation.

I should be contributing. I should be steering the process here. I should be communicating my client's needs to my creative team who will then come up with a campaign that fits my client's requirements. If I feel it's moving off track I gently steer it back. That's my job.

Then again, I shouldn't even be here.

I should be sorting my head out. I should be focusing on my needs, not my client's. I should be getting my life back on track.

I should be doing a lot of things and work isn't one of them.

I don't normally do lunch. Too busy. And in my head I think I'd always prefer to leave an hour earlier than take an hour's break. The reality though is that I still leave late.

Sometimes, though, you just have to get out of the office. And today is one of those days. The morning brainstorm, well, boiled cabbage would have come up with better ideas. So right now I just need to be away from my colleagues. I need to be away from my boss. I need to be away from the agency.

If my agency were a disease, what kind of disease would it be?

So I'm sitting alone at a bench outside the King's Arms reading the Independent. Even though it's a lovely summer day there's a hint of a chill in the air and the breeze carries a familiar scent to my nostrils. Sunscreen and hash.

A shadow falls across my newspaper and I look up into the face of a silhouette outlined against the sun.

'Yo dude, wassup?' greets Clive.

'Hey mate, how you doing?' I ask.

'Same as ever, bro,' he says and sits down. 'How's the new plan coming along, man?' he drawls.

Oh yeah. My new plan. I'd almost forgotten about that. No, strike that, I had forgotten about it.

'Um, yeah,' I say. 'About that…'

'You haven't done anything, have you?' he asks.

'Nah,' I say shaking my head. 'Haven't had the time, mate.'

Clive shakes his head as he smiles a Big Brother smile at me.

'Still finding excuses not to live your life, eh dude?' he says. 'Just as well I'm here to look out for you,' he says and he reaches down to his rucksack and pulls out a stack of travel brochures.

My new plan, according to Clive, entails taking a break. Getting away for a while. Taking time out to assess my life. My needs and desires. My goals.

'This, dude, is the first day of the rest of your life,' he says mock serious. Clive shares my hatred of all things cliché. And because of this we use clichés all the time.

'Pick a start point and just allow the journey to take you,' he says.

It's that simple in Clive's head. No distractions. Do what you want to do. Live your life.

If only it were that simple.

'Thanks for the brochures, mate,' I say. 'I'll go through them this weekend. But I'm really busy at the moment and there are things I have to do.'

Clive sighs. Clive smiles.

'Have you got any meetings or deadlines this afternoon?' he asks.

'No,' I admit.

'Right then, we'll make a start now,' he says.

'But...' I begin.

'No buts,' he says. 'You just said you've got no meetings or deadlines this avo. Anything and everything can wait until later. We'll only be half an hour.'

'I'm really busy, mate,' I say getting up to leave.

'Half an hour, man!' he says. 'The other night you would have gladly given me half an hour. Thirty little minutes! Let's have a pint and flick through a few brochures to get a feel for it.'

He stops talking and looks at me. Really looks at me.

'You need this, bro,' he says. 'This will save your sanity,' he says tapping his temple with his index finger. 'This is your life, dude. You're the only one who can live it.'

'OK,' I sigh. 'Half an hour. But that's all I can spare.'

Some things suck you in. A TV spilling colour and images into a pub without sound, for example. Like a motor accident, you just can't help watching. Silent movies – the sequel. Chaplin would make a fortune. Again.

Travel brochures are the same. White beaches and ancient monuments. Different clothing. Strange trees. They suck you in.

The photos flash past in the brochures and Oxford Street becomes that much greyer. Turquoise water and golden shores render the appeal of the office as a destination a poor also ran behind Hell and Highbury. Waves rush in. I hear them fizz and bubble through the sand as they recede. I smell fresh coriander. Fresh lemon. Fresh coconut. I taste cool cocktails. I feel warm sun. Not London's oppressive wall of toxic smog, but a warm hug.

I open my eyes and it's all still there. Sure, I'm still sitting on the bench outside a London pub, but I can reach out and touch what I want.

Under half an hour and I'm hooked.

'OK,' I say. 'Sold! Helen wants the split to be permanent. I'm going to put the house on the market and I'm going travelling,' I say.

I never thought half an hour would become the rest of my life.

Selling up, moving on

'Things should move quite quickly,' I say. 'They are first-time buyers. There's no chain.'

I sip my skinny latte and look at Helen through my sunnies. It's not too bright but sunnies are essential when you've got a killer hangover raging through your skull.

'That's good,' says Helen. 'So that will be that.'

That will be that. The house is the last link between us. Selling it makes the break clean. How to dismantle a modern marriage, one easy lesson.

I put the house on the market the day after I went through travel brochures with Clive and immediately a queue formed to view it. I was going to do it the same afternoon but things got in the way. Not work. Beer mainly. I didn't make it back to the office and ended up getting pissed with Clive instead.

'Do you know what you're going to do with your share of the equity?' asks Helen.

'I fancy a complete change,' I say. 'I'm fed up with advertising but I don't know what I want to do. I've been thinking of using some of my equity to travel. Hopefully it will give me some ideas for the future.'

Not much choice anymore. Amanda went apoplectic. She was phoning me all afternoon. I ignored her calls. The next day I wandered in at elevenish, hungover and fit for nothing. Amanda sent me home.

I am so much cold product.

'How about you?' I ask.

'I don't know,' says Helen. 'I haven't put much thought into it. I've been too busy at work.'

Amanda has scheduled a meeting on Monday. It's not an official disciplinary meeting, more a chat about things in general. But I doubt I'm getting promoted.

'I'm working on a pitch,' says Helen. 'If we win it, it will be our biggest client. I'm enjoying the challenge though,' she says.

Helen's star is on the rise at work. Mine is passing her on its way down. If I were a colour I'd be green.

'Great,' I say.

Since we split she's been working longer hours, putting in the effort and focusing on her work. It's a distraction. It's a way of coping. It's better than spending too much time with her mother.

Helen's always had a spark of resentment towards her mother. And I can understand why. It seems more pronounced than ever though now that she's living back in the family home. Oh well, we always need an enemy.

'You won't believe it but my desk is clear for the first time I can ever remember,' says Helen.

She's the new golden girl of her agency. I'm the new leper of mine. Role reversal.

She's turned her back on her family and sold her soul to Satan. You can only ever juggle so many balls. Libra would call this "Westernised Foreign Policy". We entertain certain parties as long as they have something that we want and when it's gone we discard them quicker than yesterday's toxic waste.

But who Helen is becoming is her problem. Not mine. In my new philosophy on life this doesn't matter. I hate my job. I hate my industry. I hate my life. So why do I care enough about her success to be jealous? Maybe the normal state of things is to be terminally confused.

'Great,' I say.

Then silence.

'Any other news with you?' asks Helen.

I'm about to be fired. I'm over thirty and I haven't got a clue what to do with myself. My life is falling apart. I'm growing more bitter and twisted by the minute. I hate everything. I hate everyone.

'No, not really,' I say.

'OK,' she says finishing her coffee. 'Listen, I've got to go,' she says getting up. 'Busy, busy, busy! Let me know the developments on the house.'

'OK,' I say. 'Bye.'

I watch her leave. I finish my own coffee and head home.

Home. My home. The home I shared with Helen for six of our ten years together. Memories screaming at me from the walls. The oil painting we picked up in Paris. The papyrus of Abu Simbel. The photo of us on the Golden Gate Bridge.

More memories on the coffee table and bookcase shelves. The carved ebony family tree we bought in Zimbabwe, the didgeridoo, the bong.

Everywhere I look I'm reminded of Helen. The colours on the walls, the fun decorating the old place. The rugs we picked together. The curtains we picked together. The furniture we picked together. The house we shared together.

Flashback to the day we moved in.

At the third attempt we manage to get the shot. Not the money shot, but the memory shot. Thing is though, when the memory really counts you don't need a photo to remind you of the moment.

The first time round I had the camera set on night time vision and the photo was so blurry it looked like a Monet. Second time I slipped on the grass running back so it caught me on my knees half way to Helen who was at the door bent double from laughing at my fall. Third time round, we got it.

It was perfect. The shot of Helen and me turning the key for the first time in the door of our new home together. Our first home together. My right hand on hers, her hand on the key. Huge grins plastered across our faces looking back at the camera as it captured the moment forever.

Thing is it didn't capture my memory of the moment. I remember racing back to Helen to get in position and yeah I placed my right hand on hers for the shot. But it didn't show my left arm around her waist and the fingers of her left hand interlocking mine and our left hands holding each other so tight it felt like we would never let go. The photo didn't capture Helen whispering 'I love you so much' in my ear. The photo didn't capture me gently kissing the back of her neck or breathing in the gorgeous aroma of her hair.

But that's what I remember. Like I said, for the memory that really counts you don't need a photo.

After I checked the camera to make sure the shot was good I carried Helen over the threshold. We kissed. Then we laughed for no reason. We did that a lot back then.

The smell of lemon scented detergent still hung in the air from the rigorous cleaning conducted by the previous owners. Lemon scented detergent apparently made from real lemons. About as real as the Easter Bunny.

Helen giggled in my arms as I carried her down the hall past the sitting room door, past the bathroom door, to the foot of the spiral staircase leading up to the mezzanine floor. The mezzanine floor made forever bright and beautiful by the huge skylight overlooking it.

We kissed and gazed at each other. And we both giggled again. Our giggles multiplied rabbit style off the bare walls and bare floorboards and bare ceilings. Nothing to muffle the sound of our joy. Unrestrained joy bouncing tennis ball style back and forth colliding into previous echoes and fresh laughter.

Enveloping us.

Surrounding us.

Filling our home with song.

Joy.

Love.

Helen got down from my arms and took a deep, long breath.

'Woooohoooo!' she screamed at the top of her lungs and we stopped to hear the echoes carry through our empty shell of a home. Then she grinned at me. A smile wide as the Atlantic.

Then a fresh fit of giggles. Both of us again.

I ran up the stairs, my feet pounding out a beat on the wooden steps giving birth to a new cacophony. If a butterfly flapping its wings in Central Park can cause a typhoon in China, then what devastation were my pounding feet causing? At the top of the stairs I stopped and waited for the symphony to close.

For the music to end.

Silence to reign.

I waited for the perfect moment. For pure silence. That split nanosecond before the Big Bang. I raised my arms and closed my eyes King of the World style.

'Woooooohoooooo!' I screamed and Helen burst into yet another fit of giggles and raced up the stairs to join me. She leapt at me just as I was re-opening my eyes and I caught her, but I was too late and my legs gave way. We tumbled to the floor on the landing giggling like buffoons.

We were still wrapped around each other when we stopped laughing and we kissed. We snogged. We hugged.

And we snogged.

And we snogged.

'I love you so much, my princess,' I said.

'I love you too, my prince charming,' she replied.

Even on the dullest of dull days the huge skylight made it bright on that landing. On the day we moved in brilliant sunshine combined with virgin white walls to deliver the kind of blinding brilliance you expect from God's aura. Or a nuclear explosion. Even squinting hurt my eyes. It was beautiful.

Helen took my hand and led me to the office. At least, the room we had designated the office.

'You can have this room as your office,' Helen began all mock stern, 'as long as you keep it tidy.'

'Really?' I replied, 'so who made you the boss all of a sudden?'

'We held a vote when you weren't here,' she replied, 'and I was voted boss then.'

'Oh reheheheheally?' I said, 'and who is "we"?'

'Your imaginary friend and me,' she said. 'He knows what he's talking about, at least.'

'Does he now?' I asked.

90

'Yes. And he understands me. And we need to take care of you. So that's it. The matter is settled!'

'Well, I can't argue with that then, now can I?' I said and I kissed her again.

'Nope!' she said and she burst into a fresh fit of laughter.

We continued exploring the new house. Our new house. Our new home.

When the removals van arrived we got stuck into unpacking boxes. We had virtually no furniture as we had both been in fully furnished rented accommodation before then. But the boxes were never ending. Boxes and boxes of junk. Rubbish. Crap.

Kitchen gadgets that had never been used – a popcorn maker, a fresh pasta maker, a Soda Stream! Tonnes of shit that had died and not gone to whatever afterlife awaited them – two dead PCs, a dead laptop, a Playstation, two stereos, a printer, a video player, a TV, a tape recorder! Clothes we would never wear again (a few pairs of skinny jeans now three sizes too small but one day when Helen gets back in shape…the usual. And for me it was sporting gear for sports I would never again play – football, tennis – including six rackets – cycling). Clothes we had never worn once, some still sporting the labels. Half of the boxes were stuffed full of memories that would just sit in the attic and never again see the light of day. Well, not until we moved again.

The stuff we needed could have been moved in two cars easy. Instead we paid a removal company the guts of a grand to get shit we didn't need to our new home. Let the clutter commence!

But hey, that's what everyone does. The whole flock. Baa baa!

In any case, we didn't care. We were too excited to care. Our new home. Our new life. Our new start. Together forever.

It was only when dusk started settling that we realised we had no electricity. Until then we had not switched on a light or boiled a kettle or turned on a radio. We had been entertained by unpacking and our own giddiness. We hadn't even stopped for a cuppa. We were suddenly overcome with tiredness and hunger.

'Do you want to check into a hotel for the night?' I asked Helen.

'No!' she replied almost upset at the suggestion, 'I want to spend our moving in night in our new home!'

'Me too,' I grinned.

She beamed again and came over to me and kissed me.

'Let's get some candles,' I said, 'and a bottle of wine and a take away.'

When we got back from town I placed and lit candles all around the sitting room while Helen served up the food on disposable plates. We drank our wine from plastic cups and ate our dinner with plastic cutlery which bent and broke almost as often as it did what it was supposed to do. And we just laughed more and more. And yet a meal had never tasted better.

After we ate, we layered a few blankets on the floor as a base and placed our sleeping bags on top with a couple of jumpers for pillows. We held each other and watched the candles' dancing shadows on the walls and ceiling. And we chatted. We talked about our beautiful future and how perfect it was going to be. Our future travels. Our future successes. Our ambitions. We would grow old together. We would die together. We made love slowly, tenderly, the way Helen liked it. And then we held each other again. And chatted again. And watched the dancing shadows again. And made love slowly and tenderly again. Just the way Helen liked it again.

If I were a praying man I would have prayed for that perfect night to never end.

Selling the place is the best thing I could do.

Claire arriving is a welcome relief. I make a pot of tea and we sit in the kitchen.

'How have you been?' she asks.

'Oh, ok, you know,' I say. Saying something, saying nothing.

'Yeah,' says Claire, 'you sleeping?' she asks.

The answer depends on the specifics of the question. If, say, the question referred to natural sleep, then the answer would have to be 'no'. If the question allowed for alcohol and chemical assisted sleep then the answer would be 'yes'. If the question accepted passing out from alcohol, then the answer would have to be 'more often than not'.

'Sometimes,' I say.

Claire looks around the kitchen. My kitchen. The kitchen I've shared with Helen for six years.

'Must be weird living here without her,' says Claire.

I think this is what it must be like to lose a limb. Every day you walk around on two legs carrying two arms and then one day one of them is missing. Gone forever. Suddenly you can't take a normal step. You have to hop. You can never kick a ball again. Or wrap your legs around someone when playing in bed. And you only realize it's not there when you try to use it.

The first time I really noticed Helen was gone was that first night in bed. We had, of course, spent nights apart for one reason or another over the years. But this time was different. Suddenly being without her felt final. And I couldn't sleep.

'Yeah,' I say, 'it is weird.'

That first night though I realized something else too. I realized that being with Helen had never felt permanent. How can that happen? You love someone, you live with them, you get married. You plan the future together, you vow to be there always, but in the back of your mind you know it's a part-time gig. You know that one day it will come to an end and you will be able to move on. To get on with the rest of your life. The relief is tangible. You can touch it and it's hard as stone. When you break up you feel numb from the conflict of emotions. You're heartbroken yet relieved. I never really knew a double-edged sword until then. Distraught, devastated and disillusioned walk hand in hand with excited, elated, elevated.

'I see you've put the house on the market,' says Claire.

'I take it you're going to get something smaller on your own?' she asks

I'm shaking my head before she even finishes the sentence.

'Nah, I've got other plans,' I say.

'Oh, like what?' she asks.

'I'm going to use some of the equity to travel and think about what I want to do long term,' I say.

'Really? But you've already traveled,' she says.

Sometimes I wonder if we're even related let alone brother and sister. Maybe one of us was adopted. Fair enough, we look alike, but in attitude we couldn't be more different. Claire is someone whose idea of travel is a day trip to Calais.

'Yes,' I reply, 'and I want to do it again,' I say. 'Somewhere different this time. Not one of the usual backpacking routes, but somewhere I can get completely lost.'

'Like where?' she asks.

I pause. Sometimes you know exactly how it's going to go before it happens.

'The Middle-East,' I reply.

She crosses herself three times and says "Oh Jesus!" three times. Three times. Her own version of the Holy Trinity.

'Are you fucking mental?' she snaps. 'You'll get fucking killed! They're a bunch of lunatics over there who'll shoot you as soon as look at you! They're all brainwashed suicide bombers!' she screams.

I laugh. It just comes out. A big belly laugh right in her face.

'Don't be ridiculous,' I say. 'That kind of fundamentalism is a minority problem. I'll be fine.'

'They're completely barbaric!' she says. 'They behead murderers and cut hands off thieves!

'Then I'll be sure not to murder anyone or steal anything then,' I say.

'You know what I mean!' she snaps, 'there's no need to get sarky. They're different to us, that's all. That kind of behaviour is like savages! Cavemen,' she qualifies.

They're different to us alright. But what she means is they're not white. What she means is they're not Christian. I bet she probably wouldn't even mind so much if they were at least prods.

'So, sis,' I say. 'Do you still think we should bring back hanging and cut rapists' dicks off?' I ask.

'That's different,' she snaps. 'Rapists and paedophiles and murderers deserve it. But a thief is different. Robbing a loaf of bread to feed your kids is different.'

Great. Now every thief is Robin Hood. Or Aladdin.

'So what's the difference between beheading a murderer and hanging them?' I ask.

'Beheading is savage,' she snaps.

Now she's sulking.

I decide not to say anything.

We sit in silence for a moment.

She gets up and wanders over to the sink.

'And how they treat their women is disgusting,' she says and starts washing up.

She always starts cleaning when she wants to feel superior. It's like being able to keep a clean house is the ultimate in civilization. She may be chicken steps away from forming a lynch mob and causing a riot but at least she doesn't smell. As they say, cleanliness is next to Godliness. Then again, Hitler was always pristine.

'Granted,' I say nodding my head in agreement.

'I mean to say, making them wear those long, heavy, black dresses in that heat, forcing them to cover themselves head to toe is just cruel,' she says. 'And you know they only do that to hide the bruising from when their husbands beat them.'

Clearly abusive husbands don't exist in the west.

Our women just walk into doors.

A lot.

I remain silent.

'And they make the women do all the work,' she says.

I remain silent.

'And they can't vote,' she says.

I remain silent.

'And if a woman gets raped she gets stoned to death,' she says.

'Which country are you talking about?' I ask.

'All of those Arab countries!' she spits. 'They're all the same! 'Fucking Godless Muslims,' she says.

'Tell me, Claire,' I say, 'how many Arab countries have you visited?'

She takes a moment before answering. 'None,' she concedes eventually.

'Or Muslim countries?' I ask

'None,' she says.

'Or Middle-Eastern countries?' I ask.

'They're the same thing!' she barks, 'what's your point?'

'My point is they're not all the same,' I say. 'My point is that Dubai, for example, is quite liberal! My point is that not all women dress like that in the Middle-East! Fair enough, traditional Middle-Eastern women cover themselves head to toe. But so do the men. It's called modesty. And yeah, it isn't perfect and there are abuses but it doesn't make every Muslim man a wife beater!'

'All I know is it's the 21st Century and they're stuck in pre-history,' she says.

'You know, we're not so long out of the Dark Ages ourselves,' I say. 'It's only in the 60s that women were burning their bras. And if you think we live in an equal society, you're fooling yourself. You can see it everywhere from salary levels to household chore expectations.'

For a moment neither of us says anything, but the looks on our faces speak volumes. It's taking all of Claire's control not to slap me. And my face is probably saying something similar.

'You know what your problem is?' she says.

I remain silent.

'You're too bloody opinionated,' she says.

I remain silent.

I sigh. As I'm the one who is opinionated, clearly Claire's views can't be opinions.

Claire finishes washing up and leaves the dishes to drain. She sits down to drink her tea which must be gone cold at this stage.

'So, when are you thinking of going?' she asks.

'I'm not sure,' I reply. 'I've only just started looking into it. It depends on a few things, like selling the house, for example, but I would ideally like to go in October when it's starting to get cooler and I can take in some of Ramadan.'

'You seem to know a lot about it considering you've only just started looking into it,' she says.

I half chuckle.

'I've wanted to travel the Middle East for ages,' I say. 'I'm fascinated by the history, the culture, the people…everything.'

'Really?' she says. 'When you talked of travelling before with Helen it never came up.'

'It did in private,' I say. 'But Helen never wanted to go. She was afraid,' I say.

'Sensible girl,' says Claire. 'So how long are you planning on going for?' she asks.

'I don't know,' I say, 'three months, six maybe, a year, longer even. I think I'll just get a one-way ticket and see how it goes.'

'You can't stay away that long surely?' she says.

'Why not?' I ask

'Well, because you've got your life here,' she says.

'Oh yeah, my career. And my non-existent hobbies. And my ex-wife,' I say. 'What life?' I ask.

'Everything!' she snaps. 'Doesn't your family count?' she asks. 'And what about your friends?' she asks.

My family. Yeah, I'll miss the constant interfering. The constant squabbling. The constant bitching.

And what about my friends. My mates. When I was a kid I remember there was an outbreak of nits in the school. I lost closer friends in that shampooing session.

'Claire, I need to get away for a while, that's all,' I say. 'I'll come home at some point, I just don't know when right now.'

'Fine,' she says. 'If that's what your family mean to you, just go,' she says and gets up to leave.

She's fighting it but her tears will burst the dam as soon as she gets outside.

'Claire,' I say. I plead.

'Save it!' she snaps. 'I don't want to hear it,' she says and she storms out the door.

It seems I'm free to do what I want, as long as it fits in with everyone else.

Sleep when you're dead

At 11.30 on a Tuesday night there are a number of things that should be going through my head. Plans for the weekend, for example. Fun to have with family and friends. Things I need to do – personal things.

At least tomorrow is hump day and then it's downhill to the weekend. This is the kind of thing I should be thinking. But I'm not. Right now I'm too exhausted to look forward to anything.

I'm in a cab on the way home having just finished work. I'm famished and I know there's nothing to eat at home. I know this because I haven't been around long enough to buy any food. There might be some cornflakes in the cupboard but definitely no milk. Or at least, no drinkable milk.

No take away round my area will deliver at this time either. And I'm too tired to stop somewhere and pick something up. No, the options are dry cornflakes or hunger. I could do with losing a few pounds anyway. And let's face it, I'm not going to get to the gym any time soon.

The meeting first thing last Monday morning with Amanda, well, it didn't happen. Since then she has been saying that we'll sit down and go through things only for something else to pop up

98

and get in the way. She's putting it off because we're too busy. She's putting it off because right now she needs all the help she can get. Firing me would only give her a whole new set of problems right now.

God I'm tired.

Every night last week I worked late, went home with the intention of not drinking only to get pissed and pass out. I arrived at work every morning late and hungover. As each day passes I become more of an outcast at the agency. People who I used to consider friends, well, now they keep their distance. They don't want to be seen associating with me. I'm bad news. Oh well.

It's D-Day on Tuesday on that bloody pitch. As well as trying to keep all my existing clients happy I've been told in no uncertain terms that this pitch is the one we need. And we've somehow ended up resurrecting and re-jigging the frames campaign for it. It's not bad but it's no Carlsberg Probably.

God I'm tired.

My brain is at that stage when it simply can't think anymore. There's a heavy dull ache in my head – not a headache – but a brainache. Huge difference.

'Did you hear the result tonight?' asks the cabbie. It takes a second or two for the question to filter through the mulch that is my mind.

'No,' I reply, 'jus' finished work. Wasascore?' Christ, I'm so tired I'm slurring. It sounds like I've been on the piss all night.

'One nil to your boys. They were brilliant. A year ago if you had said to me that Spurs would go to Milan and beat them in their backyard I would've had you committed for a nutter! But this Spurs side has steel and no mistake!'

The cabbie works for the firm my company uses and he knows I'm a Spurs fan. The first season in the Champions League and I'm not even getting to see them play. How did that happen? My beloved Spurs. I don't do anything I want to do with my life. Instead I work. I don't even do anything I need to do to live. Instead I work. Christ, if I don't have time in my life for a love affair that began when I was five years old, how am I supposed to make time for anything else? Helen never had a chance.

There was a time when Spurs were my life. There was a time when I enjoyed life. There was a time when Helen was the biggest part of my life. Each time I've made a substitution I've brought on work. This isn't living. This is dying. Slowly.

Right, that's it, this weekend I am going to do something I want to do. Maybe I'll go to Spurs on Sunday. Or go to a gig. Or visit a museum. Or catch up with friends. Or I could do it all – out with the lads on Friday night, then to the British Museum on Saturday, visit Mum Sunday morning and then go to Spurs in the afternoon. It's a lot to cram in but it'll be fun. Besides, I can sleep when I'm dead.

I do have a problem though. My problem is I have to work all weekend. Sleep when I'm dead? I'm already dead.

The bar is dormouse quiet. No jukebox, no TV, no mind pureeing shrill squeaks from game machines. No banter. Just a few sad, lonely punters nursing their drinks and wondering what happened to their lives.

The peace and quiet of The Tombstone is exactly what I need after the week I've had. Right now I should still be at work but I'm not. If I have to work over the weekend then I'm not staying late on Friday night.

Jack tells me his back is giving him grief and that feels great. Not that I don't sympathise with him, but it's just nice to have a slice of normality. To know that the world is still spinning on its axis even though I'm too busy to witness it. I think the Germans have a word for that – schadenfreude.

Thing is, even though I've left the office and I'm sitting in a pub, I'm working. I'm tapping away at my laptop, building my presentation for the pitch on Tuesday. I eat a handful of cashews and take a slug of my beer. I shiver. The temperature is suddenly a touch cooler and I pick up a hint of sunscreen and hash. And my laptop screen is closed shut by someone's hand.

'Wassup dude?' says Clive. 'You can put that shit away right now and be a bit sociable with me, bruv.'

'How's it going, mate?' I say.

'Livin' the dream, fella' says Clive, 'livin' the dream. And you could be too. Booked anything yet?' he asks.

I sigh.

If I were a noun, I'd be procrastination.

'Mate, I've got so much to do. I'm so busy. I can't even think about booking anything now,' I say. 'But once I've got this pitch out of the way, then it's a different story.'

'Then there will be something else,' says Clive.

'No there won't,' I say. 'Seriously, mate, I've even put the house on the market.'

'Not being funny, bruv, but you had to,' says Clive. 'Now when are you going to book something?' he asks.

Clive never sees the full picture. He focuses on the goal and what needs to be done to achieve it. Everything else he thinks is a distraction. Maybe he's right.

'Mate, that stunt last week nearly got me fired,' I say changing the subject, 'and it still might,' I say.

'Good,' he says. 'If you won't change your life, then something needs to happen to change it for you.'

'It's not that simple,' I say. 'I'm going to quit my job. But it's got to be on my terms.'

Clive smiles at me. He leaves a big void of silence for me to fill.

'Look,' I say, 'I've got two months before I'll be heading off anyway. I've got a buyer for the house and it will probably take about two months for that too. So it will all tie in nicely. Besides, when I come back I may end up working in advertising again and I don't want to burn my bridges. I need to win this pitch and then leave on my own terms.'

Clive mulls this over for a moment.

'OK,' he says. 'Win the pitch then,' he says and he gets up.

'Where are you going?' I ask.

'You need space for a few days to win this thing, so I'll disappear for a while,' he says. 'Don't worry, I won't be far away,' he says and smiles before vanishing through the door.

fleeting moments

'He was such a good man', says a talking head. Other heads nod in agreement. Sombre. Sad. Other words beginning with s.

Sly.

Sycophantic.

Shite.

'Only the good die young,' says another talking head. Talking in clichés. More nodding. More pseudo sincerity.

They take a break to sip their drinks. The way yawning is contagious, well the same is true of drinking. One takes up a glass and the rest follow. Sheep bleating. Fish shoaling. I'm not a man, I'm a number. Robots.

'He was so fit and healthy,' another talking head says. More nodding. And I think if he were so fit and healthy, why did he die of a heart attack? If he were so fit and healthy, why was he so fat? You don't get his figure with salad and water.

Don't get me wrong, I didn't dislike the guy. Helen's Dad. Not bosom buddies by any stretch, but we could chat about anything. Unusual, considering we had nothing in common. I was always wary of him though. I knew him better than he thought I did.

'He was such a loving father,' says another talking head.

The herd nods.

The herd sips.

The herd gets ready for the next cliché.

I look at Helen. My wife cradling her vodka and coke into her chest above folded arms. A loving father. There are different kinds of loving. He might have thought of it as loving. She didn't.

I look at Helen's mother sipping her tea. Sooner or later someone's bound to say he was a loving husband too, even though they have been separated for eighteen years. Drifted apart was the party line. Irreconcilable differences. After everything he did though Helen's mother stayed in contact. They decided avoiding scandal was the best course of action. Instead of seeing justice done. Only a select few people know the truth. Loving father? Loving husband? I don't need to hear that crap so I get up and go over to Helen.

When I get to her I don't know what to do. Not so long ago it would have been obvious. I would have hugged her into me and told her everything would be all right. Stupid really. More clichés. How could everything possibly be all right?

'How are you doing today?' I hear myself ask.

'I'm ok,' she says.

I look at her and she starts crying. I take her drink off her and put it on the table. I hold her and she sobs into my chest.

'It's ok,' I say, 'let it out.' I hold her tight. I whisper shhhh gently. I cry. I stroke her hair and kiss her head.

People watch us without looking. Gossip. Scandal. They're back together – shock, horror! Fucking leeches.

Unfortunately it's not what it looks like.

After a few minutes she lifts her head and smiles at me.

'Thanks,' she says and I give her a tissue.

She blows her nose while I dab under her eyes with another tissue.

'Thanks for being here,' she says.

'Don't be silly,' I say and I hand her the drink.

'So how have you been?' I ask.

'Oh you know,' she says, 'surviving.'

Small talk is to language what the charts are to music. Helen takes up her glass and sips her drink. Then she gulps it down in one and shudders.

'Fuck! I needed that,' she says.

'Let me get you another one,' I say. She nods and smiles and walks with me to the bar.

'Is it bad that I'm not upset he's dead?' she asks me while we wait for the barman to bring the drinks.

'Well, you were crying five minutes ago so I think you are a bit upset,' I say. She shakes her head.

'I was crying because I'm upset for Mum and I feel guilty for not being upset that he's dead,' she explains.

'Right,' I say. 'Well, considering what he did to you, no I don't think it's bad,' I say.

'Then why do I feel so shit about it? I mean I've barely spoken to him for eighteen years. There were times I would have gladly killed him myself. And now he's gone I feel guilty about not feeling bad! How fucked up is that?'

Helen starts crying again. I hold her again and say shh. And tell her it'll be ok.

'Look Hels, I can't explain your feelings,' I say softly, 'and grief is a strange thing and there are no right or wrongs with this kind of thing. What I do know though is that you're a good person. You have never deliberately hurt anyone. The fact that you wanted to kill him but didn't just proves that you have a decent moral code built into your psyche. You can't help the way you feel but you can choose how to act. And you always choose to do the decent thing. Which is more than could be said for him,' I say.

I dab her face with a tissue and she takes another one to blow her nose. She nods agreement.

'Thank you,' she says.

'No problem,' I say. 'Hey, what else are ex-husbands for?' I say with a smile and she laughs.

'That's a bit better,' I say and I give her another hug. We take our drinks to a quiet table away from everyone.

'You know, I'm only here today for Mum,' she says when we sit down. 'I wouldn't have bothered otherwise. And now I'm here I'm annoyed that I'm here. I'm furious that she chose to stay in touch with him. That she wanted to avoid the scandal. I'm livid she let him off the hook. I mean were the maintenance payments really worth it? It's only money at the end of the day! And why has it taken me eighteen years to become angry with her over this? God I'm a mess!'

She stops to take a gulp of her drink and stays quiet.

'You know, you're bound to be confused,' I say softly. 'It's a lot to take in and a lot of emotions are going to surface. And in time you'll realise there's nothing wrong with the way you feel.'

Helen offers a half smile and looks away. We sit in a silence for a little while. All things being equal I didn't want to be here today either. And if Helen is only here for her Mum, I'm only here for Helen. What's wrong with us that we are both here to offer support to women who abandoned us? I keep half an eye on Helen, ready with tissues for the next attack of tears. Helen looks around the room scanning the faces of family, friends, acquaintances, people she doesn't know. Then, eventually, back to me. Her eyes are a little glazed. Not just from crying, but from alcohol. She's knocked back a few drinks in a very short time on an empty stomach. If I'm honest, so have I. You need to for days like this.

'You know, you're the only one I can talk to. The only one who truly understands me,' she says. I nod agreement. And I think, is this the drink talking? Or is this real honesty? And I have to ask myself, what is she telling me?

'I've realised since we split that my family, my girlfriends, everyone who I thought was close to me, well, they're not. We've drifted so far apart there's hardly any common ground anymore,' she says. 'And I'm scared.'

Silent tears fall from her eyes again and I carry out my tissue duty.

'Me too honey,' I say.

We look at each other. We say nothing. Well, we don't use words but our eyes are talking.

'Do you think…' we both begin together.

We stop together.

'Sorry…' we both say together.

We both let out a little half laugh.

'You go,' we both say together and we laugh a little more.

I decide to wait and let Helen speak. And she's about to. She leans forward and looks at me and barely lets loose half a syllable before…

'Hi you two,' says Geraldine, one of Helen's friends, as she leans in and gives Helen a big hug. We didn't see her arrive.

'I'm so sorry babes,' she says, 'you ok?'

'Yeah, I'm fine,' says Helen and she glances at me.

Two more of Helen's friends have just arrived right in behind Geraldine and have come straight over to offer their condolences. They take up seats with us as Geraldine goes to the bar to get the drinks. They ask all the questions people feel compelled to ask of someone suffering from bereavement. The conversation has shifted.

The moment is lost.

I haven't seen these girls since before we split up and they chat to me in turn and ask me how I'm doing. And every now and then Helen glances at me. And I glance at her.

But the moment is lost.

friend or foe?

It's easier to become an enemy than a friend. To be a friend you must constantly commit acts of selflessness over a significant period of time until your efforts have grown into responsibilities that have earned trust and become friendship. To be an enemy you only have to commit one selfish act. Betrayal, for example. Or adultery. Or simply not fulfilling obligations.

It's even easier to become an enemy when you're not friends in the first place. Like at school. Or in a team. Or at work. If you want to find out who hates you at work, all you have to do is miss a deadline.

At work, other factors help to make you an enemy too. Start coming in late and hungover. Take long lunch breaks in the pub.

It's a fine line. Stink of booze after lunch and you're sociable. Stink of booze in the morning and you're a party animal. Stink of booze all the time and you're an outcast.

This is why Amanda wants to see me. Strike that, other people want Amanda to see me. Amanda would prefer not to have this meeting. I sit opposite her and stare straight into her green eyes. I know this unnerves her, particularly as my face is Easter Island stone, bored rigid by years of nothing. She can't even see me staring because she's not looking. She's too busy shuffling paper and re-arranging her desk. But she can feel me looking in the same way the school kid who hasn't done his homework can feel the teacher looking at him and is going to ask him to read it out. All of her paper shuffling is a show. Trying to look busy. Avoiding the moment. But the moment won't be avoided. It won't go away. It never does, no matter how much we put it off.

After what seems like an eternity she stops, looks up and smiles at me. I smile back briefly before returning to granite. In a way I feel sorry for her. She's out of her depth. She's a marketeer who has done well for herself and risen up the ranks. She is now the MD of Plum, the retail division of the group. She may be MD, but like every other director outside group board level, it's just a title. Advertising agencies don't have departments, they have limited companies. An agency turning over £20m is probably made up of half a dozen separate limited companies. The entire advertising industry exists on massaged egos.

Amanda looks across the desk at me with those green eyes and she's wearing her best "earnest friend" face. It's a good look but genuine as a Downing Street dossier.

'Mate, is everything ok at home?' she asks.

Dear Lord! This is her opening line. She's been fretting about what to say to me for days and she opens with this? 'Is everything ok at home?' Ladies and gentlemen, we are proud to present management sensitivity at its finest.

You do the right thing by phoning and saying you need a few days off to get your head together. You get a call canceling your request so you can get a huge pitch out of the way first. You lose the pitch and are told that your job is on the line as a result. You get handed another pitch which you have to win to save your job. You work all hours to deliver the best pitch possible and juggle your existing clients' needs at the same time. You win the second pitch and you're still at work even though they promised you could have all the time you needed afterwards. And you get this: 'Is everything ok at home?'

They know what's going on at home. You told them on the phone. You've split up with your wife and your life will never be the same again. 'Is everything ok at home?'

'Fine,' I say.

'It's just that I've noticed you've been late a lot recently,' she says.

I've noticed, she says. I've noticed. She wouldn't have noticed if I had come in every day after lunch wearing only pink silk undies and suspenders.

I'm granite. She feels the need to fill the silence.

'And you seem to be drinking a lot,' she says.

'A lot?' I ask.

'Well, more than normal,' she says.

'For the ad industry?' I ask.

She makes a face like she's just been stung by a wasp and she sits back in her seat. She leans forward again with her "earnest friend" face restored.

'You're not making this any easier,' she says.

'Oh I'm sorry, Amanda,' I say. 'How could I make it easier for you?'

'Don't!' she warns and looks away.

I fold my arms and stare at the ceiling. Amanda gets up and walks over to her filing cabinet. She takes out a file, comes back and half sits on the edge of the desk.

'We've worked together here at Plum for four years,' she says. 'We've been friends for even longer. I don't want to lose you and I certainly don't want to be the one who has to make that decision.'

She flips open the file. My file. It contains details of every project I've ever worked on – not just here at Plum, but for every agency I've worked at over the years.

'This is impressive stuff,' she says. 'You have consistently produced quality work throughout your career. You're one of the best account directors in the business and we're proud to have you on board.'

With each sentence it sounds more like the company line. Trying to make me feel all warm and cuddly so I'll get back in my wheel and scurry for the company some more.

'Like I said, I don't want to lose you and I certainly don't want to be the one who has to make that decision. But the way things are going, you're not leaving me with much choice,' she says.

'Amanda,' I say, 'yes we go way back and yes we're friends. Or at least I thought we were and that's why I phoned you when I needed the time off. You know what's going on in my life at home and I can't believe you just asked me that question!'

She sighs and looks away.

'OK,' she says, 'fair enough, it was probably the wrong thing to say. And if it were up to me I would give you as much time off as you need. But the group board don't see it that way. They think you should not allow your personal problems to affect your work.'

I snort a half laugh.

'MD my arse,' I say, 'you're just a lap dog and you get brought in to do the shitty work they won't do.'

She snaps the file shut and gets up from the desk. She walks around to her seat and sits down. She opens her top drawer and takes out an envelope.

'Like I said, I don't want to lose you and I don't want to make that decision, especially after your frames campaign won through,' she says. 'But I don't have any choice,' she says handing me the envelope. 'That's a written warning. Get your act together or I will terminate your contract. You've got a fortnight to demonstrate an improvement and it had better be dramatic. Now get back to your desk and impress me.'

Amanda turns her attention to other matters and is already busily scribbling red ink notes through a printed presentation. I get up to leave.

'Oh and another thing,' she says as I reach her door. I turn to face her. 'Don't even dream of asking for any time off in the next fortnight,' she says.

When a guy's down, most people can't resist putting the boot in.

I am officially the enemy. I am out of the club. I am Saddam Hussein. We let him play with our toys and helped beat up his enemies. Then we kicked him out of the gang, took back our toys and beat him up instead.

Well, Saddam, I know how you feel fella. I am Saddam Hussein just in a different playground. The difference is I am in an axis of evil consisting of one.

We used to wait for God to fix our lives. Now we wait for reality TV. Same shit, different deity.

"Lord, please help me get the job," has become, "All I need is a break – my fifteen minutes of fame." Here, idol and idle are the same thing. Andy Warhol has so much to answer for.

We just want the best in life handed to us on a silver platter. Strike that. Make it a platinum platter.

As clichés go, the one that goes "nobody said life would be easy", is pretty good. On the flip side, nobody said it would be this fucking hard either.

Still it's a little easier than it was last week. Work has been a lot calmer since winning the frames campaign. This week I've even been able to leave at a reasonable hour most nights. Since my meeting with Amanda I've been getting in earlier too. Still hungover but hiding it better. Or at least, I hope I am.

And now at the weekend I don't know what to do with myself. I should start planning my trip, but I can't be arsed. I should start getting ready to move out, but I can't be arsed. There are a number of things I should do, but I can't be arsed.

I'm flicking through tv channels and drinking beer when my mobile phone rings. It's Helen. It's a very excited Helen. Excited because she's found a flat and she's had an offer accepted.

'It's a two bed in Chiswick,' she says. 'It's nice, but it needs some work. There's no chain so it's ideal for our situation.'

Our situation. We love putting nice friendly labels on everything. People losing their jobs is "rightsizing". People getting killed and tortured in Northern Ireland was the "Troubles". Collateral damage. Friendly fire. Rendition. Nice, inoffensive terms for extremely offensive content.

Our marriage falling apart is our "situation".

'That's nice,' I say.

'I got a bonus of five grand for winning the Zest account,' she says. 'I'm going to use the bonus to decorate and go on holiday with the girls.'

She has bought and is moving. She is decorating and going on holiday. She has left our relationship behind, sucked her thumb and moved on.

'Great,' I say.

'What are you up to then?' she asks.

I'm going to have the last beer in the fridge. I'm going to lace into that bottle of vodka. I'm going to watch shit on tv because I can't even decide on a dvd to watch. I'm going to sleep late.

'Not a lot,' I say.

If I were a Shakespearean character, I'd be Hamlet.

For a moment there's silence.

'Are you OK?' she asks. Concern is etched in her tone. Genuine concern. Maybe she's looking for me to open up. Maybe she's looking for me to ask her back. Maybe she has just hinted at a first move. After her Dad's funeral, it's a distinct possibility. But I don't want to be the one to say it. Besides, what if I'm wrong? One minute she's crying on my shoulder, the next she's moving into her new flat. I'm getting such a kaleidoscope of mixed signals I don't know what to think anymore.

'I'm fine,' I say. 'I've got to go. Busy, busy, busy,' I say.

I hang up.

My bottle is empty so I go to the fridge. Turns out I had already drunk that last beer. And I don't have any mixers for the vodka. So my choices are (a) Get dressed and go out to get beer and mixers (b) Neat vodka.

I'm mulling over my options – all two of them – when my phone rings again. This time it's Claire.

'Hi,' she says. 'Where are you?'

'At home. Why?' I reply.

'Because I'm in Ealing and was thinking of popping in if you were home. Is that cool?' she asks.

'Yeah, come on over,' I say.

'And pick me up a couple of six packs on your way and I'll give you the cash when you get here,' I say.

'Cool, see you in ten mins,' she says.

The doorbell rings and Claire breezes past me before I've managed to open it fully. I wait for the brood to waddle in after mother duck but the entire quintet is absent. I close the door and trace Claire's footsteps to my kitchen where she has discarded her coat over the back of a chair, turned on the kettle and is currently engaged in poking around in Old Mother Hubbard's fridge. Against all odds she still manages to find something to munch.

I pick up the beer from the table and open one. I hand it to Claire but she declines so I start drinking it and put the rest in the fridge.

'So how are the travel plans coming along?' she asks.

'I haven't really progressed them much,' I say. 'I haven't had the opportunity. I've been too busy.'

Claire says nothing. Just shoots me a look. Our mouths tend to spout incoherent babble, but our eyes always deliver the message.

Too busy? Last night I watched I'm a Celebrity, Get Me out of Here. Today, so far, I've indulged in further arse-scratching. It's 4pm and I'm still in my dressing gown. We always find excuses not to live our lives.

Procrastinate now! Tomorrow's motto today.

'What?' I ask, challenging her to articulate what she has already said in her look.

'Do I need to say it?' she asks.

'No,' I admit. 'I'm not ready. It feels like running away.'

She rolls her eyes Heavenwards and I can feel one of her legendary changes of tune coming on.

'It's not running away, it's getting away,' she says. 'Sometimes you have to do that for your own sanity. It will give you space to think. God, if I had the chance to travel the world for six months you wouldn't see me for dust!'

Great, the gospel according to Claire – my favourite! This from someone who struggles to decide between a week in Butlins or Mallorca. And she makes it sound like my travel plan was her idea in the first place.

Thing is, everything she said is right and I know it.

'How's the diet coming along?' I retaliate as she pushes the last forkful of cheesecake into her gob.

This time her look has teeth. Then she softens.

'Touche,' she concedes.

'Prick,' she adds with a smile.

I'm tempted to ask how her fitness regime is going too, but I don't want to push it. No, strike that, it's not that I don't want to push it, I'm just saving it as my ace.

But she is right and I should plan my trip. Or fix my problems.

I gaze at the pile of travel guides and brochures. They sneer at me. Mock me. Taunt me.

Fix my problems? I can't even run away from them.

'The album you *so* want to pick up now is by Third World Sweatshop,' says Jeff.

'Never heard of them,' I lie.

'They're as angry as Green Day, only good,' says Jeff.

This is supposed to be caustic humour. It's that superior British thing. The other two chuckle because they feel they should. If I know Jeff, and I do, it's not even his opinion. He probably read it in some up-its-own-arse magazine.

'I like Green Day,' I say.

Jeff sneers and does that cross between a laugh and a snort signifying that I'm being a Philistine.

'They are hugely *so* over-rated,' says Jeff looking away. The look is supposed to suggest boredom. He has to display boredom to a Philistine. It's in the rules.

Jeff is an account director at Plum, just like me. The difference is I'm older, more experienced and with a stronger client list. You could also read the difference as Jeff being younger, hungrier and with more drive and enthusiasm. Half full, half empty. Jeff is proving himself. He's proving himself by being cool and hip, if they're the right words to use these days, that is. He's proving himself by playing golf with directors at weekends. He's proving himself by kissing more arse than a politician kisses babies. He's proving himself by stabbing colleagues in the back.

The usual.

Hey, it's been happening since before Caesar, and it certainly hasn't stopped since.

Everyone does it.

The kind of thing Libra calls historically justified metaphorical murder.

God forbid you should have to prove yourself with the work you produce.

Trying to belittle me is just part of the ritual. Not that I care. I'm leaving all this shit behind anyway. I shrug and turn to the other two.

'You guys heard of this Third World Workhouse?' I ask them. I know I got the name wrong, I just want to see Jeff's reaction. He rolls his eyes to Heaven. Both the guys are shaking their heads. They've never heard of them.

'It's Third World *Sweatshop*!' spurts Jeff exasperated.

'Like, everyone is *so* talking about them!' says Jeff.

Clearly not, I think.

'Their debut single is *so* at number one,' says Jeff. Hardly a recommendation as every number one single for the last twenty years, with the odd exception, has been crap.

'They have, like, gained support solely through the internet,' says Jeff, 'They are the leading band in a new music scene called F.O.E.' And he enunciates each letter initial style even though those in the know refer to the music as Foe. As in opposite of friend.

I've already seen Third World Sweatshop live twice. They are a good band, no question. But genuine followers of Foe feel as though they've sold out by signing a recording contract. I bet this guy hasn't even heard the single.

'*Helloh-oh?!* Where have you guys been?' asks Jeff. 'I am *soh* not believing you're still into Green Day. They're, like, *so* last century,' says Jeff.

Where did this bloke learn English? He uses the words so and like as punctuation. More to the point, where did he gain his music education? If memory serves correct, and it does, when Jeff joined the company his favourite artist was Kylie and he harked back to the Stock, Aitken and Waterman 80s as the Golden Age of music.

This is the kind of conversation you have with colleagues at an ad agency when you're on the piss. We're on the piss because someone's leaving. Handy excuse. Not that we need one. It could just as easily be because we won a new account. Or someone got promoted. Or it's a Friday. Or the week has seven days.

But tonight it's a leaving do. So we're crammed into a trendy bar in Soho buying drinks at eight quid a pop.

I move on from Jeff and the other two non-entities. No scratch that, they move on from me. I'm bad news now and everyone knows it. Give me a bell and I'll announce my presence with 'Unclean! Unclean!'

I sidle up to Amanda and two other pseudo-directors. I've had enough drink to feel a little mischievous at this stage. The reception they extend to me is at best Arctic. Amanda has only just re-joined them. She has been to the ladies powdering her nose. And I mean that literally. I can see in her eyes, in her face, in her, that she's done a couple of lines. Just like those weekend rock stars the Arctic Monkeys sing about. It's the ultimate dilemma for a high flyer – pardon the pun – you must be able to party, but not let it affect your performance at work. And vodka Red Bull only gives you so many wings.

Seeing her like this reminds me of the time we nearly got it on. We were at a bash like this. Although I can't remember which one. If I'm honest they're all the same. Venues change, they're all the same. People change, they're all the same. Drinks of the moment change, they're all the same. Bands change, they're all the same.

But on that particular night Amanda was into me and I was into her, and everyone saw it. Smelled it. Felt it. Knew it. Stored it in their memory in case they ever needed it.

At one point we ended up in the ladies in a cubicle with enough Charlie to launch a small army of Whirling Dervishes. We snorted. We snogged. We nearly shagged. But the incessant banging on the cubicle door from women who needed the toilet put me off. Yeah, I could romanticise the moment and paint a prettier picture. But why would I do that? It was a near fuck in a shit-hole fuelled by alcohol and drugs. I can do romance and believe me, that's not it.

'Having fun?' I ask the three of them.

116

The response is aggressive nods with closed eyes. Amanda folds her arms across her chest and sips her wine. The two guys each hold their drink in one hand and fidget in a trouser pocket with the other.

Good.

On the defensive.

Women protect their tits and men play with their only true friends.

In their eyes I'm just a leper who shouldn't be there. If I were homeless they would walk past.

'Good turnout,' I say.

'Mmm,' is the general consensus.

'Fab response from the client on the Frames campaign,' I say.

I could have said 'good', or 'great' or 'nice' or anything else, but 'Fab' is so much more Ad, dahlink!

Global warming has thawed the Arctic. This takes a second. I have said the right thing and suddenly my leprosy is cured. The tits are once more free to breathe. The 'nads have been unclamped.

'Well, it's just so original the client had to love it,' says Nut Fiddler One.

'It's the best piece of work we've produced for a long time,' says Nut Fiddler Two.

'It's a shame some of our other teams can't learn from the experience,' NF1 again.

'Oh I think they are,' says Amanda. 'A couple of people have spoken to me about the strategy we employed and they've taken it on board. I'm pretty sure they're going to use it in the future.'

'Fab!' says NF1.

'Groovy!' says NF2.

'The creative team really pulled out all the stops on this one,' says Amanda.

Fuel to my fire.

'Absolutely,' says NF1.

'Award winning work,' says NF2.

'Fuck, yeah!' says NF1.

'It's just so fucking original,' says Amanda.

'Actually, it's not,' I say.

In a nanosecond their enthusiasm is quenched and the Arctic atmosphere has returned. Anything else I chose to say at the time would not have conjured the same reaction. Anything at all.

Like, "Myra Hindley for baby-sitter!"

Or "Mugabe for the Nobel Peace Prize!"

Or "The Queen for the guillotine!"

None of these would have got the same reaction as suggesting the work wasn't original.

'Haven't you ever seen National Geographic?' I ask. 'Their whole campaign is based around a frame. We have just re-produced what they have been doing for decades. Our campaign is good but it's not original.'

Tit protection and nut fiddling are suddenly the order of the day again. And silence. Yep, the three of them dole out huge chunks of silence for a few seconds.

'The big difference,' says NF1 eventually, 'is our use of 3D. That's what makes it original.'

'Absolutely,' says NF2.

'Definitely,' says Amanda.

'That's not original,' I say. 'OK, it's a little different, but it's still borrowing an existing concept,' I say.

'Whatever,' says NF1 and he looks away. I'm dismissed as a minor nuisance.

'Ooh, eloquent,' I say. 'Your grasp of the language is without equal! Your ability to produce good England is, like, so, whatever!'

Clamped tits and cupped nuts are accompanied by steely silence and stony gazes.

My career is, like, so fucked.

Oh well.

Whatever.

Time's up

'Killing people is not something we take lightly,' says the voice of Libra. That Stephen Hawking meets James Earl Jones voice. The voice of authority. The voice of knowledge. The trusted voice of a born leader.

'Violence was always a last resort,' he says. 'Like all freedom fighters before us we exhausted all diplomatic options before considering violence. The sad truth is that politicians only sit up and take notice when violence is used.'

I look around the bar and I see a sea of nodding heads.

'History is built on this truth alone. And yet again those in power have forced the hand of the weak to take up arms to further their struggle. And those in power condemn our acts as illegal even as they send our sons and daughters to their deaths in their own illegal wars. Not just illegal but unethical. Immoral.

At least our efforts are targeted at our enemies alone. Nobody innocent gets hurt in our attacks. I doubt the civilians of Iraq and Afghanistan and other nations too numerous to mention can say the same.

Our government is still refusing to heed our warnings and we have been left with no choice but to escalate our struggle.

Within the next twenty-four hours we will strike our next blow against the forces of evil.'

The image of the silhouette and scales is replaced by a newsreader. The spectacle is over. The sound gets turned down on the TV and the hubbub of a busy pub returns within a few seconds, everyone talking about the same thing. Libra. The Scales of Justice. Who they will target.

I finish my drink and go home to have an early night.

When I wake up the next morning I turn on the radio straight away. Then I turn on the TV. Then the computer. I want the news as soon as possible. I need to know if Libra has done it yet. Whatever it is.

Then I do nothing. Just sit and listen. Sit and watch. I never normally turn on anything that can make noise before I leave home. Unless you count the kettle boiling. That's all I can normally deal with first thing.

But today's not normal. Today we have been promised something. A surprise. A terrible surprise.

Someone is going to get hurt today. But it's ok because it won't be me. Libra said he won't allow innocent victims to suffer in his attacks. He will only hurt those he targets. Then again, in Libra's wider context, none of us is innocent. We all profit from government foreign policy. From the dead empire. From our shameful past, present and potential future.

I'm sure I'll be ok though. And everyone I love. Then again, I'm sure the victims of the July 7th Tube attacks thought they would be ok too.

On the radio Kurt Cobain sings "Take your time, hurry up, the choice is yours, don't be late," and I secretly urge the DJ to end this classic song prematurely so I can get the news.

I should be shaving.

But I'm not.

I'm waiting. In the same way it was impossible not to stare at the tsunami waves engulfing the Japanese coast and washing people, cars, trees, buildings away, it's impossible to get on with living my life until I know the details of the terrible attack.

On the TV Lorraine Kelly tells us that after the break they will talk to a woman who will show us how to make plant pots

120

out of every day household waste, plus there will be a competition to have a dinner date with Michael Bublé and there will also be the news. They break for ads and some Z list actor tries to convince us to switch to Tesco Mobile. If anything, right now, that advert bugs me more than anything else I've ever seen before.

My computer has eventually booted up. I really must tidy it up and clear some memory. Nowadays it would be quicker using carrier pigeon than trying to log onto my email with this thing.

On the radio Kurt swears that he doesn't have a gun over and over. I get the point, Kurt, now please shut up and switch to the news.

On the TV another Z lister urges us to switch to O2. OK, maybe the Tesco advert isn't the most annoying ever.

Why didn't I get Sky in? I could have any news specific channel on now instead of this mind rot.

BBC news won't load on the PC, so I type in Sky News. The wait is interminable. Ice ages don't last this long.

Kurt is eventually replaced by the DJ who introduces the news. Finally! But it cuts to ads instead and another no mark urges us to switch to Vodafone.

Sky news eventually loads on the PC and a super quick scan yields two potential headlines relating to the Libra story – Government Minister Attacked and MOD Targetted. I click on the first story and the little-green-thinking-strip lights up two mini bars and hangs.

On the TV some vapid tart is trying to convince me to spread inedible foul tasting shit on my toast because it actively reduces cholesterol. She doesn't tell us that it also actively reduces the will to live, but maybe that's just a side effect.

The radio is now endorsing a brand of lager publicly known as hooligan juice while encouraging us to drink alcohol sensibly. It's probably the worst advert in the world.

My PC's thinking strip has moved onto five bright green mini bars. Finally, the TV morning programme signature introduction shot emerges on the screen accompanied by its theme music. This happens while the radio jingle announcing the news blares out of my stereo and my PC's thinking strip escalates to ten bars and loads the story. It turns out the government minister attacked is no more than a verbal assault by the opposition leader about his fraudulent expenses. Apparently in the last three years the British taxpayer has forked out £250k for renovations on his villa in the south of France.

On the TV the newsreader leads with the story that the MOD's budget would be cut by a whopping 1% if the opposition took power.

The radio leads with the same story and then both move to the minister's south of France expenses. The next most important item for both media is the operation David Beckham needs to have to rectify an in-growing toenail problem.

Libra hasn't done anything. Yet.

At work everyone is focussed on the news. Well, focussed more so than usual. But it's different too. Everyone's anxious. Expectant. Nervous. Impatient.

We all want to know what Libra's planning. Who he's going to hit. How bad it's going to be.

The David Beckham story is just annoying everyone today. I mean genuinely annoying them. No matter how much people tell you these inane nothing news stories irritate them, it's not true. Secretly we yearn for them. Seek them out. Click on them incessantly. If we didn't and if the stories were genuinely unpopular, the media wouldn't focus so much attention on them. But today is different. Today everyone just wants the real news. The only story that counts. Libra.

Anyone can tell you that production rates vary day to day, hour to hour. But this morning nothing gets done. No question, more work would have been accomplished if we had all stayed home. We're all pre-occupied with the news. Well, lack of news.

By lunchtime the doubters are beginning to whisper. The told you so brigade are setting up their victory dance by calling Libra a fraud and dismissing his threat. They can't wait for six o'clock to come round so they can gloat. But if six o'clock arrives and nothing happens does it really mean the threat is over? After all, he has already carried out numerous acts of sabotage and killed a junior politician. Surely that means he's serious?

After lunch people start working properly again. If anything was going to happen it would have done so by now, they say.

They focus on their work. The work that should have been done this morning and the reason they are now going to work late this evening. It's quieter in the offices than I've ever heard it before. Nobody chats except for on the phone and the only other noises are serious industry. The clickety clack of typing on keyboards, the clicks and whirrs of printers churning out paper, the humming white noise of computers and other machinery.

For the entire afternoon it's heads down and focus on work. We should have thought of this kind of threat years ago.

From 5.30 a few people start to drift home but most of us are too busy. Most of us would have been working late anyway but now we're going to be later. The smugness of the told you so brigade is palpable. It almost has an identity of its own. I'm trying, like so many others, to disguise my disappointment. A lot of people think that Libra was the kick in the arse the government needed. The told you so brigade are now coming up with different theories. He lost his bottle. He was never going to do anything. He was thwarted by our security forces. Our intelligence. Not many people believe that last one.

In the five o'clock news Sky virtually dared him to do something by announcing that with an hour to go on the 24 hour deadline nothing had happened. They showed the PM smiling going into parliament and then leaving later in the day. They showed Buckingham Palace with the Royal Standard flying high. They showed other different important buildings and people enjoying a busy day. And the news report had a sneering quality to it. Like it was Murdoch's own private "fuck you" to Libra.

The six o'clock news came and all the stations joined Sky's gloating bandwagon. Nothing had happened. The security forces thwarted nothing because there was nothing to thwart. After the top story of Libra's impotence they all moved onto the more mundane stuff and one thing was very apparent – after this Libra would never again be taken seriously.

I was resigning myself to that fact along with the rest of the population when the newsflash broke. I can't even remember what story Sky were relating when it was interrupted with a confused and hurried report. The leaders of the British armed forces in both Iraq and Afghanistan were dead. Both assassinated.

Rock Bottom

Both leaders had been assassinated at 17.55 GMT. Both shot through the head at close range. At the same moment couriers were delivering tapes to the major TV and radio stations. Tapes from Libra notifying them of the assassinations. The armed forces in Iraq and Afghanistan only learned of the assassinations when alerted by the news stations. Both men were in their quarters at the time. In the confusion and chaos that reigned the assassins vanished and it had taken until ten past six for the reports to be confirmed. Sky was the first channel to play the tape:

'People of Britain and the world,' said the voice we had all come to know. Respect. Fear. Love. Loathe.

'As promised, today the Scales of Justice has taken another step towards balancing the scales of history. The most effective way to kill a serpent is to remove its head. Today we have removed the heads of both British serpents in Iraq and Afghanistan. They have paid the ultimate price for their wrongs as will anyone who tries to take their place.

The knee-jerk reaction of many people will be to claim that these men were merely doing their jobs. They were just obeying orders. They had no choice. This kind of thinking is tired and old. It was used by the Nazis and other monsters throughout history. These excuses will no longer be tolerated.

The only orders we must obey are our own ethics. Our jobs are now to follow our own moral paths.

Nobody believes we should have invaded Iraq and Afghanistan. Nobody believes we should still be in either country.

As the leaders of the British armed forces in Iraq and Afghanistan, these men were enforcing illegal and immoral campaigns. They have received their just desserts. And anyone who steps into their shoes will receive the same.

The British government now has three days to commence the withdrawal from Iraq and Afghanistan. If the government refuses, the men and women of the armed forces can also bring about the withdrawal. And if the government refuses, it will suffer severe consequences.'

My mobile phone rings and I see Helen's number flashing on the screen. Great. These days I only ever hear from her when she's got news. And it's normally good news. For her.

'I've been promoted,' says Helen in her bestest excited voice. 'I'm now an account director! And there are rumours that we're going to launch a new company to focus on the specialism. I'm being touted as possible MD!'

If I were a flavour I'd be sour.

In a strange sort of way our combined situation hasn't changed that much really. Between us there's not much difference in job satisfaction. Thing is though, if your head is in the oven and your feet are in the freezer, your average temperature is fine, but you're far from comfortable.

'That's great,' I say. 'I'm really pleased for you.

'Thanks,' she says. 'So, what's new with you?' she asks.

Well, on Monday I was issued with a final warning at work. I no longer care about anything. Nothing interests me and I don't know why I keep breathing.

'Not a lot,' I say.

'Have you decided where you're going to go on your travels?' she asks.

The brochures stare at me accusingly from the coffee table where they lie unopened. Where am I going to go? Heaven? Hell? Some sort of afterlife? Worm food?

'Not yet,' I say. 'I'm still looking at options. There's just so much to see and do.'

'I can imagine,' she says. 'God, you must be so excited about the possibilities!'

If I were an activity, I'd be watching paint dry.

'Yeah,' I say.

She waits for me to continue speaking. I wait for her. I have nothing to say but I don't want her to go.

'Listen, I'd better...' she begins, but I cut her off.

'So, what did you do at the weekend?' I ask.

'Erm, let me think,' she says. 'It seems so long ago I can hardly remember,' she says chuckling. 'Oh yeah, on Friday night I went to Mamma Mia. It was fantastic! At the end everyone was standing and singing along!'

If she were an emotion, she would be enthusiasm. She has wanted to see that show since it opened years ago. I was never keen.

'Who did you go with?' I ask.

'Oh, um, er, one of the, er, girls at work had a spare ticket because, um, her, er, boyfriend had to work late and couldn't make it,' she says.

She never was any good at lying and always stumbles over her words when she does.

I know everyone she works with.

'Who?' I ask

'Oh, she's, um, a new girl,' she says. 'She, um, only started last week. She's, er, she's new in town...'

The air hangs thick with silence.

If she were a broken commandment, she would be the ninth.

'I'm glad you enjoyed it,' I say.

If I were a temperature I'd be Kelvin.

'Thanks,' she says quietly. 'Listen, I have to go. My dinner's ready,' she says and hangs up.

OK, it is now official: I've hit rock bottom and started to dig.

Red plant in the corner. Played for and got. Two reds left in nice positions.

It must be months since I had a game of pool. Gary called me earlier out of the blue to see if I fancied a pint over a few frames. I haven't seen him – or any of the lads for that matter – since that Saturday night up town weeks ago.

I'm playing quite well considering it's been so long. I'm two frames up and in control of the third. Gary still has five yellows. My only problem is the black which is hugging the cushion.

I play my next shot – red to the corner pocket with a little left hand side to take the black off the cush. Perfect.

Gary taps his cue on the ground three times to acknowledge his appreciation of a good shot.

'How are all the lads?' I ask.

'Couldn't tell you, mate. I haven't seen them,' he says.

'So what have you been upto?' I ask.

'Not a lot really,' he says. 'Working mainly,' he says.

I line up my next shot. Easy red to the middle with a little screw back to leave me on the black. Beautiful. Couldn't have positioned it better with my hand.

'Fair enough,' I say. 'Did you do anything at the weekend?' I ask.

I line up the easy black to finish.

'Yeah! You're not going to believe this, but I went to see Mamma Mia,' he says laughing.

Miscue. I must have misheard. The black rattles the jaw and settles on the back cushion behind a yellow.

'What was that?' says Gary laughing in disbelief.

'Er, miscue,' I say. 'So how come you were at Mamma Mia?' I ask.

'It was a last minute thing,' he says taking his shot and potting a yellow. 'A girl at work had tickets for her and her best mate,' he says potting another. 'But her mate got held up at work. I know it's not really my thing but I wasn't doing anything else and I thought there might be a shag in it.'

He misses his next shot.

'Your shot,' he says.

I'm numb. I can hear the blood rushing through my head. I can feel it pumping faster and faster in my heart. I can't breathe. I take my shot. I foul. Badly.

'Jesus Christ! Where's your head at?' he asks laughing.

He pots one of his yellows.

'Did you get a shag out of it?' I ask quietly.

'Nah,' he says.

He pots the other yellow but misses the black. Old rules. Only one shot on the black. Easy shot to the corner. I aim.

'Well, not on Friday,' he says. 'I had to wait until Saturday.'

The black disappears in the corner pocket. The cue ball hits all four sides before going down the adjacent corner.

'Unlucky mate,' he says.

If he were a word it wouldn't be mate.

Doctor Clive

Thing is, eventually everyone fucks you over. Inevitable as sunrise. And sure, a lot of the time they won't mean it or even know they're doing it, but they will fuck you over nonetheless. Other times it's deliberate as eating and they know they're hurting you but in their minds that's ok because they want to hurt you. Other times they know what they're doing would hurt you if you ever found out and they pray and hope and beg that you never do. But eventually you will. And when you do find out it hurts so much you want to die.

What I don't get is the level of deceit that goes with it. Something tells me this wasn't a one off or even the first time. Something tells me they've been having an affair for a while.

How can she look me in the eye and tell me she loves me while she's fucking someone else?

After this, nothing will ever be the same. After this, you realise you're completely alone.

When you start thinking about the depth of the deceit you suddenly start doubting everything. The questions stack up gridlock style. Has she ever loved me? How long has this been going on? Is this the first one? The only one? How deep is the betrayal? Has he fucked my wife in my home? In my bed? In my car? On my boat?

You wonder if she's in love with him.

You wonder if he's in love with her.

Inevitably you wonder if he's better than you. But that's blokes for you.

You rack your brains to find out what drove her away from you. What was missing from the relationship? Were there any signs? And then you think: what fucking signs?

She looked you in the eye, she held you close and tight, she made love to you, and all the while she was fucking someone else. How are you supposed to read signs that don't exist?

And if that sounds hypocritical then you don't know me. I don't cheat. Sure I've had one night stands and secret flings, but I've always been single at the time. And I've never done anything with anyone in a relationship. Well, not knowingly in a relationship. Don't get me wrong – I'm not Mary Poppins, it's just one thing I believe in. If you love someone you don't do that to them. Simple.

She looked me in the eye and smiled at me. She told me she loved me. And all the while she was fucking someone else.

So you wonder why she was with you. Why you were still together for so long. Married after all that time. If she was that bored, if she had such a low opinion of you, if she hated you that much, then why did she stay for so long?

She gazed past my eyes, deep into my soul and told me she loved me. And all the while she was fucking someone else.

Did she stay out of habit? Was it easier to stay with me than end it? One thing is for certain, she didn't stay for the money. Or the glamour. Might sound obvious but I thought she was with me for me. Guess not.

Who am I kidding? Of course there were signs. They're just a little more subtle in real life than in the movies. Couples don't descend from happiness to misery in one dramatic fall. It takes chicken steps. Lots and lots of chicken steps. Everything does. Everything works on a series of natural progression. And we avoid the issues because they're so small. Miniscule. Not worth causing trouble. But they build up. Little issues. Tiny bug bears start to accumulate and become an obstacle which grows into an obstruction which becomes a barrier which turns into a barricade and before you know it there's a mountain of tinder dry problems ready to ignite into a massive bonfire. Then it's too late. Just a matter of time. When a bonfire is built it's impossible to dismantle. You have to burn it.

Sure there were signs. Little inconsequential signs that I didn't deal with. I should have addressed them but I didn't. I should have told her I didn't like her turning down my music when she arrived home. I should have told her I didn't want to watch the X Factor on Saturday night when we were at home together. I should have told her that I hated that she always valued her mother's opinion more than mine. Strike that, anyone's opinion more than mine. But I didn't. And she should have told me her issues with me but she didn't.

Still though, we ignored little issues. Then she held my heart in her hands and told me she loved me. And all the while she was fucking someone else.

And it makes you wonder if you've always been a joke to her. Was I just there to pick up the tab? Pay the mortgage and bills? Did she make fun of me with her lover? With her friends? Her family? My friends?

All the intimate little secrets we shared, did she share them with others as a joke?

One thing's for certain, she played me for a fool. And I'm sure everyone knows it. She looked me in the eye and told me she loved me. And all the while she was fucking someone else.

I'm looking at the policeman with my right eye that's barely open. I've just woken up. Even if I were fully awake I'd only be able to see the policeman with my right eye that's barely open.

My left eye is swollen shut. My right eye is not far off from being swollen shut. My nose is broken and my bottom lip is split. Two teeth are missing. A rib is cracked. My torso is bruised so much my skin is more purple than any other colour. I don't know this yet. At least, I don't know the full extent of the damage. But I can feel it.

I'm concussed in a hospital bed under observation. The medical staff are observing my condition. Monitoring my progress. The police are waiting until I'm lucid enough to understand the charges. D&D, GBH and causing an affray. There may be grounds for the first two, but I didn't cause the affray. Clive started it. Thanks Clive. He, of course, vanished before the swine turned up.

'And how are you feeling today?' asks the good doctor. I don't see him approach. He comes at me from my blind side. My left side.

'Sore,' I croak. This is at the third attempt. The first two attempts never got past my teeth because my mouth is so dry. I try to swallow and clear my mouth, but there's nothing there. I can't even make saliva.

'A bit dopey,' I say. The effort of talking opens the scab on my lip and it starts to bleed again. I taste the blood.

'Cold,' I say.

'Well, you're on strong painkillers,' says the good doctor, 'which is why you feel a bit dopey. But trust me, if you feel sore with them you would be in agony without them.'

I nod.

'As for feeling cold,' says the good doctor, 'I can offer no explanation.'

I was admitted last night after that stupid fight. The fight started by Clive. It was part of my therapy Clive assured me. I needed to let off steam. It was just stress relief. A tension blower. I needed to release some anger. Get it out of my system. This is what Clive told me.

But I couldn't start a fight. So Clive started one. I tried to stop him. I didn't want to fight so I tried to stop him. Although, if I'm honest, I didn't try very hard. If I'm honest, I did want to fight. Maybe it was the beer talking.

Or maybe I'm just different to who I thought I was.

Flashback to last night.

'I just feel so helpless,' I say. 'It's like five minutes ago I had everything I wanted. I was married to my beautiful wife. I owned my beautiful home. I was successful in my beautiful career. I had my beautiful life. And now I've got nothing.'

'Man, that's a bad break,' says Clive. 'You deserve better than that, dude.'

I nod. I cry. It's all I can do.

'I do need to ask you a question though,' says Clive.

'Yeah?' I say, 'what?'

'What are you going to do about it?' asks Clive.

I'm struck dumb. If my face were a state of being, it would be confused. Clive sees this and asks again:

'What are you going to do about it?'

Actually, it was more of a demand that time.

'I don't know what you mean,' I say. 'What can I do?' I ask.

Clive sighs and shakes his head. He sits back and looks away. His head snaps back straight at me and he leans in close. So close I can smell the smoked hash on his breath. So close I can see the mottled green and blue filaments of his irises. Same as mine. My mirror.

'Your ex-wife and one of your mates are having an affair,' says Clive. 'In all probability it started while you were still together. So, what are you going to do about it?' he demands again.

I'm the kid who started the fire in the barn. I've done nothing wrong, but this is how I feel.

I'm the best man who lost the rings.

I'm the one who left the window open for the burglars.

'I don't know,' I admit. 'It's not like they've committed a crime and I can report them. So I'm not sure if I can legally do anything.'

Clive rolls his eyes Heavenwards.

'Bruv, you've got to grow some balls,' he says. 'Some things aren't covered by law. Make no mistake about it, this is the worst kind of crime – betrayal.'

According to Clive I've got to break my conditioning. According to Clive I have to act more human and disobey the rules once in a while. According to Clive I need revenge.

For my new situation, Clive is my therapist. He's going to prescribe a series of treatments for me between now and when I go to the Middle-East. He tells me that before I head off I've got to realize that what I've got is a blank canvas of a future. I can do what I want. I can be anyone.

The first treatment was the fight. As cures go, I've had better.

The only thing that's fallen apart faster than my old life is the armed forces in Iraq & Afghanistan. The army hasn't seen this many deserters since the First World War. The government has refused to withdraw from either country, but the forces are so depleted with more soldiers disappearing each day that the situation is becoming untenable. The deputy commanding officers in both countries have been temporarily promoted to lead the forces, but it's clear neither of them wants the job. And nobody's jumping at the opportunity either.

The three days have lapsed and the world is waiting for Libra's next move.

At the end of my hospital bed the good doctor is reading my chart.

'I'm going to run a few tests,' says the good doctor. 'You may feel some discomfort but I need to check your progress.'

I nod and he leans into my face with his pen light and shines it into my half open eye. He forces my eye a little more open and pain shoots up through my forehead and directly into my brain. I thank the God I don't believe in that I'm on strong painkillers. He forces open my fully closed eye and shines his light saber into my head.

'What's your name?' he asks.

I look at him but I can't see him. All I see is a bright white spot where his face should be. After his torch I can only see round the edges. If I want to see him I have to look past him and even then I can't really see him. I know this will go eventually but right now it's the most irritating thing in my life.

The bright white spot in the centre of my vision is more annoying than my cracked rib that makes my breathing shallow and jabs pain into my core with each cough. The bright white spot in the centre of my vision concerns me more than my broken nose that drips blood down the back of my throat drop by drop by drop. The spot is a bigger burden to bear than the thought of the dental bill for my two missing teeth. The spot is like itchy blood that moves when you scratch it. It's the splinter that reminds you of its existence only when it is touched. It's the huge bogey up your nose or the itchy crotch or the fart that's waiting to explode, but you can't deal with it because you're in public.

And then suddenly I decide to not let it irritate me.

I look straight at my bright white spot in the centre of my vision where the good doctor's head should be and I tell him my name. I tell him where I live. I tell him my date of birth. I tell him my mother's maiden name. I tell him what I do for a living. I tell him that I am not confused and that I will speak to the police. He doesn't ask me for these things but I tell him anyway. All he asks is if I know my name, but I know where he's going with this and I'm ready. If I can deal with my bright white spot in the centre of my vision I can deal with anything.

The good doctor calls the police into the room. There are two of them but I could only ever see one through the window of the door. They read the charges and tell me when I have to appear at the Magistrate's Court. They tell me that the three blokes are not pressing private charges and are sorry that they gave me such a good kicking, but I just wouldn't stay down and kept coming back at them. It was self-defence they say. All the witnesses agree.

So it seems the sixty-four million dollar question is:

What is likely to happen to me in court?

I ask them.

The answer is that it all depends on a number of factors. They tell me my lack of a criminal record will help my case. They tell me my professional career will help. They tell me my background and education will help. They tell me my age and settled, married lifestyle will help. They tell me I'll probably be handed a small fine and a warning. About £100 probably.

I smile.

The benefits of a good reputation. A slap on the wrist and I'm off the hook. Well worth it.

You'd pay more than that for a paintball session. Or go-karting. Or white water rafting.

These bruises will heal. The bones will knit. All my physical injuries will be gone in a few weeks. And everything else that hurts too.

You'd pay more than that for a bungee jump. Or a sky dive. Or a million other adrenaline pumpers.

And none of them compare to being in a scrap. I had forgotten.

The release. The buzz. The fun. It was the ultimate tension blower

Who says crime doesn't pay?

I can't wait for my second treatment.

Therapy, Clive style.

New Me

There are times when I think I could get used to this impaired vision. Having the use of only one eye, albeit temporary, means I get to be a kid again. Now when I wake up I'm Steve Austin, the Six Million Dollar Man, coming to from being knocked unconscious by my enemy. Except this time, because of the painkilling drugs, the coming to bit is for real.

I take in my surroundings slowly, trying to remember where I am. Except I already know where I am, but it's ok to pretend. In some episodes, Steve Austin did wake up in a hospital. But he was always in a top security single room. Clearly he had BUPA.

Where Steve's blurred vision would slowly bring bright overhead lights and pristine white ceilings into view, I get to see the pastel green paintwork peeling back to reveal mildew patches the size of melons. Lower down, cast iron radiators deliver Arctic chill through blistered, flaking rust patches. Yet lower, linoleum tiles bear cavernous scars and amputated gaps from long forgotten battles with razor sharp metal furniture and the traffic of a million human souls.

137

Christ, even the hospital building looks sick. These tuberculoid walls. These leprous radiators. These cancerous floors.

How is anybody supposed to heal in here?

I blink and swallow, Steve Austin style.

'Wassup dude?' asks Clive from my left side. With my impaired vision I can't see him there. He must have turned up while I was sleeping.

'Hey mate, how you doing?' I ask.

'Cool fella,' says Clive. 'Man, you look shit.'

In spite of myself I chuckle. Which hurts.

'Come around to my right side', I say. 'So I can see you.'

'Nah, I'm good here,' he says. 'Nobody can see me here.'

I can't turn my head to see him but I can hear him flicking through a magazine.

'When do they reckon you'll be out?' asks Clive.

I swallow so I can speak. I have to do this every time to moisten my mouth. Think of a dewdrop to cover the entire Sahara and you're still way off the mark.

'Couple of days,' I say. 'Why?'

'So I can prepare your next therapy session of course,' says Clive.

He sighs.

'You need to learn to look after yourself properly again,' says Clive. 'Without counting on me or anyone else.'

I swallow.

'You mean like that time at school?' I ask.

'You got it, dude,' says Clive. 'Exactly like that time at school.'

'Oh,' I say.

Memories flood back tidal wave style.

I swallow.

But I don't say anything. I'm afraid to speak. I'm afraid to ask. But I need to know the answer.

I swallow again.

'Clive?' I ask.

Nothing.

I swallow.

'Clive?' I ask again.

Nothing.

I swallow.

'Clive?' I ask again.

Slowly, gently I push my elbows backwards on the bed until they're both under my sides and propping me up slightly. My broken rib sings at me and I'm sure other patients, even the deaf geriatrics, can hear my heart beat. Beads of sweat pop out of my now pulsing forehead. I ease my weight more onto my left elbow and turn my head. My eyes feel like they'll burst out of my head. I turn to see Clive. But I can't see him because he's not there.

Clive's gone.

Amanda doesn't take the news well. The news that I'm in hospital. She warned me not to take any time off and here I am concussed on a hospital bed. Holiday and sick are the same in her eyes.

She didn't like it that I handed in my notice in the same breath. I'd already handwritten the letter and told her I'd post it today. This is part of my therapy. Clive told me I had to change my work life. He told me I had to quit my job and work as a freelance until my trip. It makes perfect sense. I know lots of people in the industry and I can get work for a few weeks no hassle.

Amanda didn't like that at all. Oh well.

According to Clive, I have to change parts of my life that tie me to the past. That tie me to Helen. If I have a blank canvas of a future, if I can do what I want, if I can be anyone, then I have to stop being me. I have to change who I am.

The last link between Helen and me was the house, I thought. But Clive says that the strongest links are the ones nobody sees. The habits. The routines. The shared experiences. The shared friends.

It's impossible to remove all of those, but you have to change what you can.

Moving into a new environment at home will help. Moving into a new environment at work will help. A new company where nobody knows me. Scratch that, in the incestuous, nepotistic advertising industry that's impossible. But at least not everyone will know me. At least, it will be different enough.

When enough parts of me have changed I'll feel able to move on, Clive tells me. And already I feel it working. I haven't been in a scrap since I was about ten years old. OK, I was useless and took a huge kicking. But it felt good. I'm different already. Mao said that every journey starts with a single step. Well, I've taken mine.

The PM though has not taken his first step. He is clinging to the past. It's like he only has one plan and can't think of any other strategy.

He arranged for the deputy chiefs in Iraq & Afghanistan to be promoted permanently. And now they're dead permanently. Libra had them assassinated within a day of their promotions.

So, now it's the Prime Minister's move again. I doubt he'll take his first step.

But I have taken mine. So I'm officially unemployed. Three months ago the concept would have brought on an anxiety attack strong enough to make waves on a seismic reader. I would have been stressed about the mortgage. I would have been stressed about paying my car loan. My credit cards. My other loans. Loans that have grown cancer style and metamorphosed into living entities in their own right over the years. Living entities with add-ons. Transformer loans with extra millstone features and triple bonus interest points. A student loan became a holiday loan grew a home improvement loan became a laser eye surgery loan grew a boat loan.

So glad to see I focussed on the important things in life.

Now the reality is that I am unemployed. I'll find work again soon so I don't see what the fuss could be. But three months ago it would have been the end of me.

And, just for argument's sake, if I don't find work? Well, the millstone round my neck would be repossessed for a start. And the boat I haven't sailed for eight months would be taken away. And my colossal 4x4 carbon footprint. But I'm pretty sure I get to keep my eyes and they can't reverse the surgery. So I win really.

Unemployment isn't so bad. Why is it that the thought of confronting something is always a million times worse than the confrontation itself?

And why do we always focus on the wrong things when we worry? If I were suddenly unemployed three months ago I wouldn't have worried for a nanosecond about putting food on the table. Food just happens. You go to the supermarket and it's there. I can't remember the last time I looked at a price of a product in a shop. If it's there and I want it I buy it. Simple.

The price of bread or milk, I don't know. The price of anything I don't know. I couldn't even hazard a guess. Actually, that's a lie. I know how much property costs. And cars. And ad campaigns.

Christ, when did I become so shallow?

No, I don't really know the cost of anything that matters. The guy who knows that is the guy who walks ten miles a day just to fetch clean drinking water. More than knowing the cost, that guy knows the value.

I know neither the cost nor the value and it shows in everything I do. Everything I am.

But that's all about to change. I've already taken big steps to change my life. This afternoon I get discharged and I'm free to launch my plan. And it will liberate me just like that time at school.

My plan.

Our plan.

Clive's plan.

That time at school

The bar is dormouse quiet. Inside it's a good three degrees cooler than outside. Clive is sitting at my table with two fresh pints in front of him. He grins at me and gestures an offering palm to one of the pints.

I sit opposite him, lift my glass and we clink, cheers, drink.

'Wassup, dude?' asks Clive.

'Same old,' I cliché.

'The bruising looks better, bruv,' says Clive.

'Yeah, it is,' I say, 'thanks.'

I've been out of hospital for a week. A week of rest and recuperation. The best thing about rest and recuperation is it gives you time to think. A week of thinking time. A week of decision making. A week going crazy with boredom.

At this stage I have no doubt that daytime TV is a government plot to get the unemployed off their arses looking for work.

'Hardly any pain anymore,' I say. 'Even in my ribs.'

'That's good news, dude,' says Clive. 'You're healing inside and out.'

'Yeah, I guess so,' I say.

We both stop talking long enough to drink a decent draw on our pints marking the cessation of small talk.

Down to business.

'So how's your plan coming along, man?' asks Clive.

'All on schedule,' I say. 'I've left work and I'm going freelance until my travels. The house sale should be complete in about six weeks. And the ideal time to begin my travels from a weather perspective is about three months from now. So it's all good,' I say.

I lift my pint and drink.

Clive treats me to one of his looks. The look that says I need to say more. But I have nothing else to say.

Clive says nothing.

I fidget.

Clive insists on saying a whole pile of nothing.

I drink again.

Clive says yet more nothing and does even less. Just looks at me. That look.

I squirm.

'What?' I ask eventually.

'Don't "What?" me!' says Clive laughing. 'You know damn well what! What about the rest of the plan?' asks Clive.

I clear my throat. I look away.

'I, um,' I begin, 'I'm, er, I'm not very comfortable with it,' I say.

The worst thing about rest and recuperation is it gives you time to think. A week to doubt. A week to find flaws in plans. A week to become indecisive.

'So you would prefer to be a mug?' asks Clive.

'No, it's not like that,' I say. 'It's not that simple. Its'…well, it's…it's complicated.'

'Complicated?' says Clive. 'I don't think so. It couldn't be simpler, so let me spell it out for you: Your ex-wife and one of your so-called best mates are having an affair. And they must pay.'

Clive stares at me. A hard, cold stare.

I look away. When I look back he's still staring.

'Can I ask you a question?' I ask.

'Shoot,' he says.

I pause. This is more difficult than I thought it would be. The words are lined up on my tongue but my mouth is struggling to open. My brain forces the issue and over-rules my mouth.

'Have you done anything on my behalf?' I ask.

Clive smiles a knowing smile.

'I couldn't possibly comment,' says Clive and laughs.

'Mate,' I say, 'Gary spent two days in hospital,' I say. 'He's in a right state.'

Clive takes a swig of his beer but his eyes don't leave mine. He puts his glass back on the table and savours the flavour.

'Good,' says Clive, 'the bastard deserved it and more,' says Clive.

'Mate, I know you're just looking out for me,' I say. 'But please don't beat people up for me.'

'That's gratitude!' says Clive laughing.

He leans across the table to me.

'Bruv,' he whispers, 'if you don't want to hear the answer, don't ask the question,' he says. 'And yeah, I partly did it for you, but I partly did it for him too. Like I said, he deserved it.'

I shake my head and look away.

'Don't give me that!' says Clive laughing, 'I know you're not disgusted with me.'

I look back at him.

'I know you too well, bruv. We're twins, remember?' says Clive. 'Yeah, I know you're not disgusted with me. In fact, you're secretly delighted I gave him a kicking. In fact, there's a part of you that's gutted you didn't do it yourself,' says Clive.

In spite of myself I can't help grinning.

'You make good points, oh brother,' I say. 'But that doesn't make it right.'

He grins back at me and we clink glasses again. We drink and put our glasses back on the table.

'The thing is, bruv,' says Clive, 'I love your ideals because they're also my ideals. But there's a problem with us liberal lefties and that is we're too soft. The US reneges on Kyoto and we hit them with a protest march. Yeah, right on! That'll teach 'em! The PM lies about Iraq's military might, takes the country to war under false pretences and we organise a fucking leaflet campaign. That showed 'em, huh?!' says Clive.

'Effectively nothing happens. The bad guys stay in power, the good guys become more impotent and the world is a poorer place. These people are committing crimes and they must pay. It's the same with Gary and Helen. You can't afford to allow yourself to be an impotent leftie on this one. You're the only one who has been wronged in this situation,' says Clive.

He takes a swig of his drink.

I remain silent.

'Yeah, I may do the odd thing that isn't endorsed by law,' says Clive, 'but that doesn't make it wrong. Somebody has to take the right action for our side.' He takes another gulp of his drink before going on.

'I always ask myself the question: If I knew Hitler before he gained power and I had a chance to kill him knowing what I would prevent in doing so, would I take that chance? As long as my answer is always a resounding "Fuck yeah!" then I'm going to continue scoring points for our side,' says Clive.

His speech over, we both take a slug of our drinks.

'Go ahead,' says Clive, 'ask me the question.'

'What ques…' I begin, but then I stop playing dumb.

'OK,' I say, 'what did it feel like kicking the shit out of him?' I ask.

Clive grins again and I grin back.

'You know exactly what it felt like,' says Clive.

And he's right, I do.

I know exactly what it felt like.

I know because I've been there before.

'Just like that time at school?' I ask.

'Just like that time at school,' says Clive nodding.

Yeah, I know exactly what it felt like.

We must have been about nine years old. Clive and I, like most twins, were inseparable. We didn't need anyone else so it was always just the two of us. Nobody ever bothered us. Nobody ever came near us. Nobody ever talked to us.

And then something happened. I can't quite remember what it was but for some reason Clive wasn't around so much anymore. Maybe it was a girlfriend – nine year old puppy love coming between brothers. Or maybe Clive found a new temporary friend.

Or maybe we'd had a fight. I really can't remember, but whatever happened, suddenly I found myself alone. A lot.

As well as being twins, Clive and I were always best friends. But, like I said, we lost touch. It wasn't me – he moved away. It's understandable really. I mean, who is still best friends with their best friend from when they were nine? It happens all the time. People meet, hang out for a while and move on. It happens with adults let alone kids. And yeah, it even happens with twins.

It happens most when you meet a long term partner. You tell yourself that it won't happen, that you'll take things slowly, that you'll introduce your new partner to your mates and everything will be hunky. It hardly ever works out that way though. It's not long before you're not doing the things you always did. You don't go to football anymore. You don't play any sports. You don't go to the pub with the lads. You don't have a few games of pool. And you don't notice until you're with your mates and nobody knows what to say. It used to be that you would see these guys a few nights a week and you would be talking all night. But now you have nothing to say and even less in common. That's when you realize that your life now revolves around your partner. Things will never be the same again. It's funny, but you never realize what's important in your life until it's not there anymore.

Well, for a long time Clive wasn't there. And it was then that the bullying began. It started with names. Shithead, faggot, weirdo, spastic, queer, retard, bitch, wanker…the usual. I doubt if those kids even knew what half those names meant, they'd just heard them in the playground same as everyone else. It wasn't long before a name would be accompanied by a punch on the shoulder, almost like a joke exclamation mark. One of them would shout spastic and, wham, land a punch. And it always got the desired reaction of a laugh from whoever saw it. They soon got bored with that though so did things to spice it up. One would call me a name while another one kicked me. Or two of them would call me a name and land a punch each on a shoulder. That one they called the double bubble.

After that they got really creative. All three of them would sometimes call names and throw punches hard enough to knock me sideways into one of the others who would do the same. On the game would go with them taking turns at screaming insulting names and punching me into each other and me, their punchbag, bouncing around between them. This game they called pinball and would only end when the same name was called twice. I found out then just how many insulting names there are on the market.

They got creative with their weaponry too. Sure there were the obvious tools of torture like compasses, pencil tips and wet towels. But that wasn't enough for these guys. Let me tell you now a bulldog clip is extremely painful on the nose especially if you are powerless to remove it.

I thought this would never end. This was now my life and I just had to accept it. Clive had gone, I was on my own and these bullies were the closest people in my life. Strike that, they were the only people in my life.

Until, one day, Clive was back. He was still preoccupied with whatever fling he was enjoying so he wasn't around all the time. But he was there enough to be a presence in my life again.

Clive advised me to stand up for myself. He told me I had to fight back or I'd never stand up for myself. That I'd always be weak. I listened to him as I had always listened to him. He was always the 'big' brother. He always knew best. He was right and I knew it.

I was bricking it. But I did it. The next time an attack came I fought back. They kicked the shit out of me anyway. There were three of them and I had no friends. Except Clive.

So Clive came up with a plan. For three weeks I submitted to them. I gave them my lunch money and did their homework. In return they didn't hit me. The plan was to make them think they had kicked the fight out of me and I'd be their bitch forever. After a week was up the soreness from the kicking they dished out had gone and I was ready for revenge. But I bided my time for the full three weeks. They became my secret hobby. If I had gone on Mastermind my specialist subject would have been 'The Movements and Routines of Mike, John and Paul.'

We knew we wouldn't have to wait long for our opportunity. I remember it was on a Friday that Paul and Mike both got detention. I couldn't tell you what they did but it didn't matter anyway. We just wanted to get John on his own. When the bell

147

went at the end of the day we rushed to get ready and we raced out of the school gates, but we didn't go home. We hid in the alley we knew John walked through on his way home and waited for him.

Soon enough he passed the spot where we were hiding and we jumped out behind him. Clive struck first and it was perfect. Before the bicycle chain had whipped around his face fully, blood spurted from above his eye. When the chain took hold Clive yanked it with a vicious fury that spun John's head and ripped the skin across his cheeks, nose and forehead. He went down clutching at his damaged head, too shocked to scream with tears diluting his blood. Once he was down we whipped him a few times with the chains aiming mainly for his head. He was in the foetal position and had his head protected and cradled in his hands so we stopped with the chains and started kicking him all over his body. Clive was working his back while I aimed for his ribs and stomach. When he moved his hands to protect his midriff we changed attack to his head and balls. I kicked him more ferociously in the balls than anywhere else. It gave me great satisfaction. But not as much satisfaction as when we were finished. I leant down and grabbed his ear with one hand while Clive forced his eyes open so he could see his attackers. I leant into his ear so my mouth was touching it.

'I'm smarter than you,' I whispered. 'I'll always be smarter than you. I'll always be more ruthless. I'll always be tooled up. You tell a fucking soul and I'll cut you a cunt and feed you your balls. Understand?'

He nodded through the tears and Clive and I walked back towards the school laughing.

We waited for Paul and Mike to finish their detention and watched them go their separate ways.

Of the three Paul was by far the most stupid and the easiest to follow. We waited until he was only a few hundred yards from his house before we ran up behind the fat fucker and dragged him into some bushes. The chain did its work again and once I got bored with that I knelt on his back, took his pencils out of his bag and stabbed at his lardy frame until all the points were broken into his fat. He was blubbing like a baby and I could smell that he'd shat himself. I got off him, rolled him onto his

148

back and saw that the little baby had pissed himself too. And then Clive thought of the crowning glory. Lying on the grass a few feet away was a steaming dog turd. I caught the lard-ass by his school tie and pulled with both hands. To save himself from being choked he propelled himself backwards with his heels. It's just as well because I wouldn't have been able to move the mini-whale without his help. Of course, he didn't know where I was taking him but he was so gripped by fear that it didn't matter. Once I got to the dog shit I rammed his head into it and rolled it back and forth. The smell nearly made me vomit. But what was more sick was the way he was crying like a toddler. Seriously I had never before and never since seen a nine-year-old cry like that. It was pathetic. I think the little shit thought we were going to kill him. Clive just stood over us. He didn't need to open his eyes this time because this pile of rectal matter had already seen his attackers. I whispered my speech in his fat little piggy red ear and we walked away laughing.

Mike was the ringleader and he was going to have to wait until Saturday morning when he went to the shop to get his comics. It was almost too easy. He left the shop exactly the same way I had seen him leave before. He was reading the Beano and had the others tucked under his right arm. As he walked through the deserted playground we struck. Clive caught him flush with the cricket bat at the back of his head and his blond hair was already turning red before he hit the ground. Clive threw the bat away and we just got stuck in kicking him until he was crying and begging us to stop. Pathetic. Clive again came up with the cherry on top. He rolled up the Beano as tight as he could while I pulled down Mike's pants. The pathetic little shit didn't even resist. So I got to deliver my little speech to my tormentor while tears ran down his cheeks, blood flowed from his head and his comic stuck out of his arsehole. He'd never think of the Beano in the same way again.

They never touched another kid again. Still though, when I was alone I was still scared of them. I thought they would try to get revenge. But they never did. Even when I was alone all I had to do was stare at them and smile. In return they would look at the ground and shuffle slowly away.

Eventually, I wasn't scared of them anymore.

Control of destiny

According to Clive, I have to change parts of my life that tie me to the past. That tie me to Helen. If I have a blank canvas of a future, if I can do what I want, if I can be anyone, then I have to stop being me. I have to change who I am.

I'm selling the house and going into rented accommodation. I'm going to get away from London for a while and travel the middle-east. I've quit my job and I'm going freelance until I leave the country.

And then I get a call out of the blue from an old mate, Phil, who needs a freelance AD and has heard I'm on the market. It's three weeks since the fight and I'm all but healed. I still get reminders of the damage if I move too suddenly or bash the wrong part of my body against something, but to all intents and purposes I'm fine.

I haven't worked at all in the last three weeks and I'm ready for a project. I go to see Phil in his office on Wardour Street.

'Hey mate, good to see you, how's it going?' asks Phil as we shake hands.

'All good mate,' I say, 'you?'

'Couldn't be better,' says Phil wearing a big grin. A grin so big, wound so tight, the elastic is in danger of snapping. The easy and fun attitude he projects is betrayed by his eyes. His exhausted eyes on the verge of hysteria. His shattered eyes kept open and awake by coke. Lines and lines of the stuff. His hostage eyes screaming for help.

Phil's a busy guy and hasn't got time to chat right now so he just takes me through the project and promises he'll make time for lunch in the next week or so.

I'm in complete control. By the look of things, Phil lost control a long time ago.

The campaign is for a new client. And the campaign was won by Phil through his expertise and experience in the relevant field. Problem is, Phil and his agency can't conduct the project because it would cause conflict with one of their incumbent clients. Because of this they have farmed it out to a sister company. A sister company whose resources are already stretched to cracking. They need an outsider to come in and do it.

I have ultimate power. I'm in complete control of my destiny.

I tell Phil that it's all cool. I don't care where I work or with whom. I'm freelance and my own boss. I am the master.

Phil emailed a contract to me yesterday and I read through it last night. It's all good – tied in for three months. Perfick! I sign it now.

The way I feel now, the power, the control, Gods must be envious.

I am surprised though and I say this to Phil. I didn't think Hex had a sister agency. I thought Hex was independent. One of the last true cavaliers.

It was, Phil tells me, until two weeks ago.

Then it was bought by the AdCom Group.

The AdCom Group is to advertising what Microsoft is to computing, absorbing all competition until no competition exists anymore. Subsuming anything different, anything original, anything new. Forcing its will. Forcing conformity. Imposing its own religion.

My old agency, Plum, were bought by the AdCom Group about 18 months ago. That's when it all started going downhill.

The AdCom Group is to creative thinking what boybands are to music.

Phil tells me that the takeover sealed the deal on the contract with the new client. Until then it was a toss-up between Hex and another agency. AdCom swung it.

If the AdCom Group were a car it would be a Volvo.

The good news is that the new client loved Phil and the Hex team but they were just worried that the agency was too small to cope. Not anymore.

If the AdCom Group were a professional it would be an accountant.

Now that Hex is part of a larger group, one with muscle, the new client feels more at ease.

If the AdCom Group were an extreme sport it would be tiddlywinks.

Suddenly, much like Han Solo, I have a very bad feeling about this. My stomach starts to turn. AdCom is the mother ship.

If I were a historical figure I'd be Nostradamus. I see exactly where this is going. My throat is suddenly very dry. AdCom owns Hex.

You take two and two. You add them together. And sometimes you don't get four. Sometimes you get the $64,000 answer. I start to sweat. AdCom owns my old agency, Plum.

I know what Phil is going to say before he does.

'In many ways,' says Phil, 'it'll be like going home for you. The agency conducting the project is Plum.'

At home there's a message on the answerphone and I only realize then that I've had my mobile turned off since I went into the meeting with Phil. The message is from Helen. Great. I'm still in my old home. I'm going back to my old work. And my ex-wife is phoning me up for a chat. Clive would not be happy with my progress – or lack thereof – today.

I phone her back on her mobile and hear the hubbub of a pub in the background. She asks me to hang on so she can go outside to hear clearer.

'Hiya! Sorry about that but I'm out with work tonight,' says Helen as she makes it outside the pub.

'How are you? How have you been? It's been so long since we talked,' this all spurts out without a breath. No answers required to her questions. She's just filling space. There's a giddy energy to her. Upbeat but nervous.

'I just got back from Greece where I went with the girls for a week,' she says. 'It was great! Although, I can't say I'm refreshed. It was more of a party place than we anticipated. I need a holiday to recover,' she says laughing.

The originality of ad people.

'We were pissed every night,' she says. 'I know that doesn't sound like my kind of holiday, but I had a great time.'

Not her kind of holiday. Three months ago the very thought of it would have horrified her. Getting pissed every night is not her style. She'd rather be at work than in Ibiza. If she were a state of mind she would be denial.

'So how are you?' she says. 'Come on, you haven't said anything yet,' and she laughs. 'Only kidding, I know I haven't really let you get a word in edgeways, have I?' and she bursts into a fit of faux giggles.

I tell her I'm fine and we share small talk. We say nothing and we continue to say it for a number of minutes. Eventually though the small talk starts to peter out.

'So, you called me earlier,' I say. 'You said you needed to chat. Is everything ok?'

'Well, there's something I need to tell you actually,' she says. Something's wrong. Her voice is suddenly very quiet. Giddy upbeat to somber downcast in the beat of a hummingbird's wings. She's gone from Mayfair to the Old Kent Road and didn't stop at Go.

'I did something I would never dream of doing while I was on holiday,' she says. 'I've been very foolish and I wouldn't blame you for hating me. I slept with a complete stranger.'

It's like jumping into cold water, or getting an electric shock. It's the kind of jolt that makes you realize you're still alive. This is not the girl I married. This is the anti-Helen.

'Why are you telling me this?' I hear myself asking. 'Are you deliberately trying to torture me?'

'Of course not,' she snaps. 'I wouldn't have told you because it's none of your business anymore. But I wanted you to hear it from me rather than anyone else. The thing is, Evelyn was on holiday with us.'

Now I understand.

If Evelyn knows then Tom knows. If Tom knows then he will delight in ensuring I know. She's right. It was better to hear it from her. Yep, eventually everyone fucks you over.

'Besides, eventually we were both going to end up with other people,' she says. 'One of us had to be first. I know it's not ideal and I'm not very proud of myself. But it's happened and that's that.'

I think of Gary. For some reason I think this is betraying him more than it is me and this makes me smile.

'You're right,' I sigh. 'I suppose it's just another step in the process of moving on.' This is the kind of thing mature, normal, modern people say. It's just moving on. No emotion attached. Being grown up about it.

In my head I hear Clive telling me to grow some balls.

'So, was it a one off or are you seeing him now?' I ask.

Why I ask this I don't know, but I ask it anyway. Maybe deep down I enjoy emotional kickings.

'Definitely a one off,' says Helen. 'I was drunk and foolish. I'm not ready for another relationship but I'm definitely not going to start sleeping around.'

'Me neither,' I say.

For a few seconds neither of us says anything.

There is no silence more awkward than the silence on a phone line.

'Have you, er…?' begins Helen, 'have you, er, have you been with anyone since we split?' she eventually asks.

'Not so much as a peck on the cheek,' I say.

Silence again.

'Maybe you should,' says Helen, 'it might do you some good.' I never thought I'd witness the day my wife would encourage me to go on the pull. The world's a pretty fucked up place.

'I'm not ready,' I say. 'Going on the pull is way down the line. Besides, I wouldn't know where to begin nowadays. It's been so long since I chatted anyone up I wouldn't know where to start.'

Helen bursts into laughter.

'What's so funny?' I ask.

'You? Not knowing how to chat anyone up? says Helen, 'that's like a fish that can't swim!' she says.

'Darling, I haven't the slightest idea what you're talking about!' I say all mock modest and we both laugh a little at our own private joke.

For a few moments neither of us says anything. We both sigh.

This just isn't right. This is my wife. The love of my life. We made vows together. We were meant to spend the rest of our lives together. We were supposed to die together.

'We used to have fun, didn't we Hel?' I say.

'Yeah we did,' says Helen. 'There were a lot of good times.'

'So what happened then?' I ask.

'Don't do this,' says Helen.

'Why not?' I demand. 'I have a right to know. I'm so fucking confused I can't think straight. I don't know what I've done and I don't know what to do! At least if I knew what I'd done…where I went wrong…I mean did I ever hurt you? No! Did I ever abuse you? No! Did I ever mistreat you in any way at all? Fucking no! So what the fuck did I do?' I'm screaming down the phone by the time I finish.

Helen's crying. I'm fuming. It takes a moment for her to gather herself.

'You know I can't fault how you treated me,' says Helen, 'you were always brilliant. But you've changed. You know that! I kept trying to tell you.'

In my head I think sickness and health. In my head I think better or worse.

'What do you mean "changed"?!' I demand, 'Everyone changes for fuck's sake!'

'I know,' she says. 'But you've become so angry. So bitter. So moody. One minute you're the life and soul of the party, the next you're verging on suicide. I couldn't cope anymore…especially when you refused to get help,' says Helen.

'A shrink?!' Is that your answer for everything?' I ask.

'Of course not!' she snaps. 'But you could have at least tried it,' and she bursts into fresh tears.

Hearing Helen crying I melt. Well, at least I haven't changed in that respect. I soften.

'I'm sorry,' I say. 'I didn't mean to shout. I didn't mean to make you cry.'

Helen gathers herself again.

'I know,' she says. 'It's ok.'

But it's not. It's far from ok. She knows it. I know it. And something needs to change.

'Are you ok?' I ask.

'Yeah, I'm fine,' she says. 'How about you?' she asks.

'Yeah,' I say. 'Well, no, not really.'

'Yeah,' says Helen, 'me neither. Leaving you was the hardest thing I've ever done and it's not getting any easier,' she says.

What does that mean? Does she want to give it another go? Or is she just saying what she's feeling? And how am I supposed to react to that? Right now I would do anything to get her back. Win her back. Even therapy. I want to tell her to come home. I want to tell her I want her back.

'You mean I don't own the monopoly on emotional turmoil then?' I hear myself say.

She sniffles a giggle.

'No,' she says, 'I'm afraid not. I've got a stake in that pie too.'

What's going on in my head? I want to tell her I'll get help. Just come home.

'Yeah, I think between the two of us though we own majority shares,' I hear myself say.

Why can't I tell her how I feel? What the fuck am I doing here?

'Yeah,' says Helen. 'It will get better though.'

Now. Now's the chance. Just say it.

'Yeah,' I say.

Coward. Emotional retard. Gutless swine.

'Listen, it's started to rain and I'm outside so I'm going to go back in,' says Helen. 'I'll call you soon. Maybe we can catch up over a coffee?'

'Yeah, let's do that,' I say.

Tattoo a yellow stripe a mile wide down my spine. Oh look, it's already there.

'Helen?' I hear myself say.

'Yeah?' she asks.

'Erm...'

'What?'

'Well, er...' I say.

'Hate to rush but it's really starting to rain now,' says Helen.

'Nah, it was nothing,' I say. 'You head off. Talk soon.'

'Ok, see you later,' says Helen and hangs up.

Earthworms have more spine.

I'm not the only one having trouble escaping my past. After the deputy commanders were assassinated the PM appointed new chiefs of staff who were flown in from Britain immediately. Suicide mission. That's what everyone thought.

Well, everyone except Libra. He had other ideas.

'We warned the government that it would face severe consequences if it refused to withdraw the troops from Afghanistan & Iraq,' said Libra on the latest tape. 'Tomorrow those consequences will be realised.'

For 24 hours the world once more held its collective breath. What would he do this time? Everyone expected the assassination of the new chiefs as a minimum, even though they were now under round the clock armed guard protection. Some anticipated an attack on parliament. Others thought it might be an assassination attempt on the PM and Minister of Defence. Whatever he had planned, the world waited and watched the way children everywhere wait and watch for Santa Claus on Christmas Eve.

The next day nothing happened. But it was the most disruptive nothing in history. The armed forces went on strike. In Iraq & Afghanistan not a single troop attended their post. Not a single soldier stood to attention. Not a single patrol was conducted. The orders were given as normal. But this time they just weren't obeyed.

And it wasn't just in Iraq & Afghanistan either. Across the world British troops refused to do their duty. Even in Britain some of the forces stood down for the day. And the world watched in wonder.

The message was clear. They were still armed forces and they were still serving their country. But they would no longer act without question. They did not agree with these illegal wars and they would no longer fight them.

Sure they were still British soldiers. But now they belonged to Libra.

Clo/e Shave

It doesn't seem to matter how much I say it, or what way I say it, it still doesn't help. It's different this time. I'm freelance. I'm in control. I'm my own boss. But I'm still going back to Plum. I try to calm myself that going back to Plum isn't going to be so bad. It's different this time. I'm freelance. I'm in control. I'm my own boss.

No, it's not working. So I arrange to meet Clive to chat about it over a drink. Clive will know how to deal with it.

I go to the quiet pub we arranged to meet at and sit at the bar nursing a pint. I'm waiting for Clive and thinking about the meeting. I'm trying to move away from my past but every turn I take brings me back into the bosom of memory. Right now I could rip off someone's head. Right now I could happily break bones. Right now I could do damage.

'Bleedin' thugs,' says the bloke sitting at the bar just up from me. He's wearing a tweed flat cap and looks old enough to remember when England was Catholic and Henry VIII was the Great Defender of the Faith. The last thing I want is some walking corpse cosying up for a chat but I just happen to be sitting there when he starts talking. He's not even talking to me,

159

but really he is. He's pretending to be talking to his copy of the red-top tabloid he's reading, but he's really talking to me.

'In my day a bobby would've clipped 'em round the ear and sent 'em home,' he says.

Sweet Jesus, do people really talk like this? I just thought it was a poor stereotypical joke.

I remain silent. But I could scream.

'Still, at least it was a queer they killed,' he says and starts to chuckle. He looks up from his rag and I can see from the corner of my eye that he's focusing on me.

'That's one less poof on the planet, eh?' he says to me.

Clive's philosophy of scoring for our side certainly has appeal and I don't think I would ever tire of punching this guy.

'Mmm,' I murmur by way of reply.

'You're not queer yourself, are ya?' he asks laughing.

I pause and glare at him.

'No, I'm not gay,' I say evenly, 'but I do have some gay friends.'

His face looks as though he's just bitten through a lemon.

'Still,' he says, 'I don't condone what those thugs done. Bloody animals want hangin'. No discipline, that's what it is. They should bring back National Service.'

He's referring to the killing of a gay teacher who was beaten to death by a gang of pupils at this school when they found out he was gay.

'I dunno what the world's comin' to,' he says. 'It wouldn't 'ave happened in my day. This current generation has ruined the world. There's no respect no more. This was a great country once. Now it's over-run with poofs, thugs, wogs and pakis,' he says shaking his head.

He moves away from the bar and goes to the toilet just as Clive walks in. I get up and gesture for Clive to follow me and we head to the toilet.

Clive closes the toilet door and I grab the old codger, spin him around and pin him to the wall.

'Wouldn't have happened in your day?' I ask.

'There was respect, was there?' I ask.

'Ever heard of the Kray twins? Jack the Ripper? John Christie? All those priests who are only being found out now?' I ask.

His wide-open eyes stare straight into mine, frightened rabbit style. His mouth opens and closes but no sound issues from it.

Now I'm in control.

Now I'm the master of my destiny.

Now I'm the boss.

Instilling fear like this into another human being is the ultimate power trip.

'That was your generation and before, you cunt,' says Clive jabbing a finger into the old guy's chest.

'Don't dare hand us a broken world and blame us for the breakage,' says Clive and slams the prick's head into the wall. The tiles instantly splatter with blood and his flat cap falls into the urinal. No loss. It already stank of piss.

'National Service?' I ask.

'So we can produce more bitter and twisted bigots like you?' I ask and I knee him between the legs. He drops to the floor crying.

I look at Clive and Clive looks at me. We grin at each other before kicking the shit out of him. He's unconscious when we leave the toilet. Clive stops at the door for a last glance at him. Then he says: 'If old people hate the world they helped to create so much, why don't they just fuck off and die?' he asks.

Not thinking is what we do best. The less effort the better. It's probably why we're so in love with routines. As Libra says, practice makes permanent.

Practice becomes habit becomes routine becomes tradition.

But even traditions change. Evolve. Move on. After all, we used to make human sacrifices to appease the Gods. Now we just give up chocolate for Lent.

Then again some people do things for Lent instead of giving up something. Like helping out at a homeless shelter. Or a charity shop. But for most of us that's just too much effort. Too much thought. It's thinking outside the box. No, give us a routine, an easy way out and nine times we'll take it. I know I do.

I look in the mirror ready to do it again. I'm getting ready for my first day back at work. My first day back at Plum. The clippers have been charging for half an hour plugged into an extension lead plugged into the socket in the hall. The number three setting is already in place muzzling the metal teeth. Number three – no shorter, no longer. Just the way Helen likes it. Same old, same old. Nothing changes, the rest remains the same. Routine is as routine does.

The thing is, people tell you you're lucky when you've lost your hair because you don't have a choice. There's only really one way to wear it – gone! But that's simply not true. In fact, of all the disastrous hairstyles out there, the most disastrous belong to men who have gone bald. The Bobby Charlton sweeping comb over. The Trappist monk. The fuzzy mohair. The half mullet. Even if he clearly thinks it's a full mullet. Lady killers every one. Or maybe not.

I do mine once a week. Number three – no shorter, no longer. Just the way Helen likes it. Thing is, if you let it get too long, you're in danger of going down the disastrous hairstyle route. Too short and you're a thug. It's a fucking minefield.

So I look in the mirror ready to do it again. Ready to do the number three. No shorter, no longer. Just the way Helen likes it.

I deploy automatic pilot, flick the switch on and glide the clippers slowly up my temple. Its pleasant zhoom vibrates in my head and my hair sprinkles in the basin. I zhoom row by row of my head and my hair floats down to the basin forming a carpet.

I flick the switch off and brush the hair off the number three guard. I remove the guard and brush the hair off the silver teeth restoring their nakedness. I replace the guard and flick the switch on ready to zhoom the next patch of hair. I stop. I turn off the clippers and look at them. I look at myself in the mirror. Really look. I've looked the same for years. Since my hair started receding.

If I were a TV programme I'd be a re-run.

If I were part of a song I'd be the chorus.

If I were a festival I'd be Groundhog Day.

I remove the guard and the teeth glint in the bathroom spotlights. The teeth grin up at me, free from the oppressive muzzle now nestling in my left hand. I look at the muzzle before

162

dropping it into the bin. Turning on the clippers again, the teeth seem happier. Smiling. Grinning. The clippers zhoom the same patch of my head without the oppressive muzzle. And the naked teeth zhoom onward and my hair sprinkles past my eyes raining salt and pepper and carpeting the basin further. The clippers eat lines of hair and I imagine this is the way the turf at a football stadium must feel – carpet short. Neat lines. Regimented. And then it's done. But it's not done. It's not good enough. Not short enough. If I were a film I'd be Rebel Without a Cause.

Muzzle numbers one, two, four and five follow muzzle number three into the bin, along with everything else in the clipper's aluminium case. There were implements I never bothered to find out the use of and now I never will. And now they enter the scrapheap as virgins. Never used. Never wanted. More old maids than virgins.

And maybe that's just the way Helen likes it too.

But I keep the brush for brushing the clippers. And I brush them now and more hair joins the carpet in the basin.

But it's still not done.

I rinse the basin, then fill it with hot water and wet my head. I massage shaving oil onto my head slowly, deliberately, calculatingly. I put a fresh blade in my Mach 3 and with robot smooth motions I glide my razor across my scalp, clean shaving my head stroke by stroke.

Not the way Helen likes it.

If I were a movement I'd be revolution.

And then I rinse my head. I run my hand over the smooth surface of my scalp only to find pockets of resistance.

I fill the basin again.

I wet my head again.

I oil up again.

I shave again.

I get my scalp smoother.

But not perfect.

Not the way I want it.

Definitely not the way Helen likes it.

And I wet my head again and oil up again and shave again. And I focus on the rough patches. I come at them from different angles this time. And I shave harder this time. Over and over. Harder and harder. Over and over. Harder and harder.

Until I slice my scalp. The intensity of the sting brings tears. And I feel the blood trickle down the left side of my head. And I see it flow in the mirror. And the blood river runs south to my ear, then east to my face, then south again down my cheek past my ear lobe and follows the line of my jaw to my chin where it drips, drips, drips.

And it's cool.

All change, no change

My first day back at Plum. Already it feels different. The weight of responsibility does not bear down on my shoulders. Today and forever more I will not be Atlas carrying the world.

Delegation is key.

Organisation is key.

Not putting up with unreasonable demands from above is key.

It all looks good. I'm the Senior Account Director on the new client account. I've got an Account Manager and two Account Executives as well as support from the team PA. I also have a cracking creative team to call upon.

It's all good. Just as it should be.

First thing there's a meeting to discuss the project. I've got my strategy outlined and I'm in control. I will refuse to take on more responsibility than this project. This client.

It's foolproof. Safe. Piece of piss.

I walk to the meeting room with Gemma, my Account Manager, and already in there are Kate and Tom, my Account Executives. They're all ready. Eager. Enthusiastic. Prepared.

We just need my mate, Phil and Hannah, the Divisional Director, and Thunderbirds are go!

Phil arrives looking, if anything, more wound up than he did on Friday.

'Hey mate,' he says grinning the big, forced grin again, 'how's it going?'

'All good, mate,' I say, 'couldn't be better.'

'Great!' he says with an almost maniacal stare, 'like the new look by the way. Very Yul Brynner!'

'Cheers mate, did it myself!' I say and I give him a fashion twirl so he can see the whole thing.

'Fuck man, that's some shaving nick! Jesus Christ, were you trying to give yourself a lobotomy?'

I rub the scab on my scalp. It must be two inches long.

'Mate, do yourself a favour and next time go to the barber!'

Before I can say anything Hannah walks through the door followed by Bill, the FD.

'See you couldn't keep away then!' he says laughing as though it's the funniest and most original joke ever.

Smug prick.

'How's it going?' I ask shaking his proffered hand. I remind myself that he no longer has any power over me. I grin.

He sits down.

'Shall we get started?' he says.

'You're sitting in on the meeting?' I ask.

'Yep,' he says grinning. 'Standard procedure now. We need to get the numbers right from the start. So I sit in on the first meeting for each new client,' he says.

The grin he's wearing, well it's normally only seen on a crocodile. Or a shark. Hyena. Snake. Death.

Hannah looks at me and smiles an apology.

I now fully understand the look of utter despair on Phil's face. But that's ok. I am in complete control. I will not put up with any shit.

'Fine,' I say and turn to my notes.

I am an irresistible force.

'We've got a perfect team set-up,' I say, 'with Kate, Tom, Gemma and myself on the account management side, as well as the creative hub at our disposal...'

'Let me just stop you there,' says Bill cutting in.

'Why do you need two AEs?' he asks.

166

I pause, unsure of the nature of the question. I look at Phil and Hannah in turn, but their faces are blank. Taut. Stretched to breaking point.

'Erm,' I begin, 'because of the volume of work,' I say.

'You don't need both of them,' says Bill. 'Tom, you can go back to your desk. We'll get you involved on another account that needs you.'

'With all due respect, Bill, you don't know what's involved in the project,' I say. 'Tom, please sit down,' I say to the young lad who suddenly doesn't know what to do or where to be. I'm certain that all he is certain of is that he would rather be anywhere else right now.

I will not be bullied by Bill's position.

'OK,' says Bill sitting back crossing his arms and wearing his Death mask again 'Educate me.'

He is an immovable object.

The numbers of troops striking increases every second day and includes more senior officers as the stalemate continues.

Yet he refuses to withdraw the forces.

Other public workers have started their own strikes in support of the soldiers.

Yet he refuses to withdraw the forces.

MPs have started resigning in support of the troops.

Yet he refuses to withdraw the forces.

He's running out of options. He's running out of time. He's tightening the noose around his own neck.

There is only one thing more ominous than Libra speaking, and that is Libra not speaking.

And Libra hasn't said a word for days.

I outline the work involved in the project, which is heavily front end loaded. I explain how important it is to get it right from the start to avoid having to amend things down the line. I tell him that if we invest the time and effort at the beginning it works out more cost effective in the long run. I deliver a winning argument that cannot fail.

I am the irresistible force and the immovable object.

'And you're telling me it will take two AEs as well as you and Gemma to do that?' he says. 'The fact is we prepared a pitch and won the account on a tight budget. And I intend to see us stay well within that budget. Tom, you can go and this time don't sit down again no matter what he says,' says Bill throwing a nod in my direction.

Tom gets up and leaves.

'Now, where else do we need to trim the budget?' asks Death.

When the meeting is over I have been granted half a day with a junior creative team and my production budget has been slashed to 70% of the original. As well as that I've been drafted onto another account for two days to help out as the team is running seriously behind schedule. Big shocks.

When an immovable object is met by an irresistible force you find out very quickly that one of them doesn't exist.

Compromise

Sometimes you know exactly how it's going to end before it begins. Helen leans against the door frame of my new kitchen, arms folded, her right leg crossed in front of her left. Two piece black suit – jacket and skirt. White blouse. Plain black shoes. Professional. Business. Work, work, work. Busy, busy, busy.

We chat while waiting for the kettle to boil. More chart rubbish destroying real music.

I've already done the grand tour. Somebody once used that expression years ago – The Grand Tour. On that occasion, it was funny. The tongue in cheek irony poking fun at a poky pad with a grand price. Since then everyone uses it but nobody thinks it's funny anymore. Maybe that's because it's not. But it's become part of our language like so many outdated, useless proverbs and we won't give it up. Even though it's as dead as a dodo. Haha.

After Helen told me she found a flat I got my arse in gear and found one myself. We had a buyer lined up for the house so I didn't have much choice anyway. Then after her holiday story, well, I couldn't get out of the old house quick enough. So I picked one to rent quickly to speed up the move. And now she's in my new place to haunt me all over again.

I've ended up in a one bed flat above a parade of shops. It's nice and clean and a funky shape, but it wasn't what I was really looking for. I wanted an open plan apartment in an old warehouse – the kind you see in American movies all the time. But they were way too expensive, so I compromised.

That's something we are doing more and more. Compromising. My warehouse apartment became a one bed flat in the same way the astronaut settles for being a train driver. The Porsche becomes a Skoda. The knight in shining armour turns into the night guard in uniform. The promotion and twenty percent pay rise becomes more responsibility for the same money. Nobody gets what they want and everyone settles for less.

So anyway, we've already done the grand tour and now it's time for a cuppa. Helen wanted to come around and see the new place. My "bachelor pad" as she insisted on calling it. The way she says it though is mock serious. Nervous. In one little phrase she's underlining the fact that I'm free to do what I want, but warning me against doing what I want. She doesn't want me but nobody else is allowed to have me either.

I make the tea and we move to the sitting room. It's nice. Pleasant. We can do this. Mature adults. We've already talked about what we've been doing. The weekend. Family. Friends. That kind of thing. Things since the funeral. Coping. The usual family dramas. The mundane nothing. Yeah, coping. We really can do this. I'm sitting next to my ex-wife on my sofa in my flat at a respectable distance and there is no tension at all, sexual or otherwise. We really can do this. I was a little jumpy – nervous, before she came round. But everything's fine now she's here. We can do this. Mature adults.

'So how are things at work?' I ask as I put my tea down on the coffee table. I'm so relaxed and comfortable now I don't even mind what's coming next. The inevitable onslaught of unqualified successes as she flies up the ziggurat, while I grasp hopelessly at my greasy-poled career. Fair play to her. She deserves her success – she's worked hard enough for it.

But Helen's quiet. She hasn't answered me. And when I turn to look at her tears are streaming down her face.

'What's the matter?' I ask and I take her tea from her trembling hands. I grab a handful of tissues from the box for her.

'That fucking bastard,' she says. She doesn't have to tell me – I know she's talking about her company chairman.

'He's talking about pulling the plug on Concept,' she explains between sobs. I put my arms around her and stroke her head just like I did at the funeral.

'He says he can't afford for the new enterprise to run at a loss,' she says. I provide her with tissues just like I did at the funeral.

'Even though the budget we put in place and he authorised has us making a loss in the first year,' she says. I rock her gently and say "shhh" just like I did at the funeral.

She sobs and sobs and I rock her gently.

'So if he approved the budget why is he now changing his mind?' I ask.

'Because suddenly other parts of his empire are struggling,' she says, 'and he must "re-focus on the core business",' she says. 'So my start-up takes the hit for other peoples' failures even though we're on target. And if Concept goes I go because there's no position for me anywhere else in the group,' she says and she bursts into uncontrollable sobbing.

'Oh God, what am I going to do?' she wails between sobs.

And I hold her tighter. And I give her more tissues. And I stroke her head. And I rock her gently. And I shhh her and tell her everything will be ok. Just like I did at the funeral. Just like I always used to.

And then it hits me.

She needs me. She is the one who has kept contact open. She is the one who doesn't want me but nobody else is allowed to have me either.

She needed me at her Dad's funeral. She needs me now.

As soon as real problems come up she comes to me. Not to her Mum. Or her sister. Or girlfriends. She comes to me. I'm her crutch.

I understand her and she knows this.

'What am I going to do?' she asks.

I look at her and I dab at her tears. I kiss her forehead and say shhh.

This is my opportunity. My chance. Make a decision one way or another and move away from this impotent limbo. I can choose to end it properly now and break all ties. I can tell her I'm not a crutch that can be used when needed. I'm either a full part of her life or I'm not. She can't have both.

Or I can choose to try again. Get back together. Offer her the comfort of safety. If it all goes pear-shaped at work she can fall back on me until something else comes up.

And without needing to think through these two options I know which one I want.

'Why don't you amend your budget and cut some costs so that you can realise profit by the end of the year?' I say. 'Show him that you're adaptable and can move with the business needs. Show him you're hungry to succeed and can think and move on your feet,' I say.

I don't know why that came out of my mouth. It's not what I meant to say at all. I meant to say that we should give our marriage another go. Try again. That if she lost her job I would be there for her. If she lost her home, if her life fell apart, no matter what happened I would be there to pick up the pieces.

But I didn't say that. Instead I engaged auto-pilot and moved into work speak. I'm such an automaton. Such a sheep. Worse, such a coward.

I can still save this. I can still say what I want to say. But I don't.

Helen has stopped crying and she's clearly thinking about what I just said.

'It's such a tight budget already though,' she says.

'There's always room to cut,' I reply automatically.

'Do you think it will work?' she asks.

'You've got nothing to lose,' I say. Coward.

'You know, you're right. I'll give it a go,' she says and she gets up. She smiles at me.

'Thanks hun. I'll just clean my face and head off.'

She heads to the bathroom.

Fan-fucking-tastic! I choose neither of my two options and end up hitting middle ground. Again. Shot to pieces in no-man's land. Mice are more assertive.

How to compromise your own future – one easy lesson.

Back out there

The only person I can trust is Clive. It's been like that since before way back when. Clive always tells me the truth. Sometimes it's more pain than I can bear but at least I know it's the truth.

So when he tells me I need to get out there, I need to go on the pull, I need to get laid, well, I believe him. If Clive says it, I must be ready.

But already this feels like a mistake. A gentle way back in, Clive said. Right now self-circumcision with a rusty blade would be more gentle.

'If you could have any plastic surgery,' she asks, 'what would you have done?'

This is her question.

Not, "Do you go to counselling for your problem?" or "Do you think everyone secretly wants to be gay because it's cool? Like, gay is the new black?" or "Have you ever been with a prostitute?"

Nothing interesting like that.

Not even the obvious faux thinkers' "Why are we here?" or tongue in cheek funny, "Do you come here often?" or even honest and up front, "So, why are you speed dating?"

No, she goes for, "If you could have any plastic surgery, what would you have done?"

It's like Blind Date only without the intelligence. Clearly she's as vapid and vacant as she is ugly and grotesque. Don't get me wrong, she's attractive physically, but it's superficial.

Synthetic.

Fake.

Plastic.

She might as well be a Barbie Doll.

Then again, here I am at a speed dating night. Who am I to label anyone superficial? Synthetic? Plastic? Vapid? Vain?

Maybe she's just like me and is here under duress. Clive thought it would be a laugh. A gentle way back in. After incessant badgering I agreed to go.

'So you think I need plastic surgery?' I hear myself asking. Her forehead crumples into a confused frown. Clearly this isn't how she's expecting it to go.

'No, it's not that,' she says, 'it's just that I want to get surgery done and I'm interested to know what you would have done.' She smiles a perfect smile, teeth straight as US State borders. She's interested to know what I'd get done in the same way that world leaders are interested in eradicating poverty in Africa. What really interests her is talking about the plastic surgery she would like to have done and she's hoping her question will open up the same question to her from me. I'm not going to indulge her little ego trip though.

'I wouldn't have anything done,' I say.

'Oh,' she says. There's that confused frown again. It seems like she's worked out one answer only to her question and if she doesn't hear it she gets thrown completely. I'm guessing the same will be true of her other two questions. Time to have some fun.

I wait for her to speak again and just before she does I get there first.

'I don't need any,' I say. The confused frown returns. It's like she's never considered the notion that someone might exist who doesn't require surgery.

'You, on the other hand,' I continue, 'need shed loads. Let's start with your eyes.'

'My eyes?' she asks horrified, 'What's wrong with my eyes?'

'Honey,' I reply, suddenly camp as a row of tents, 'those crows' feet could be river valleys,' I say pointing at the area around her eyes silky smooth without so much as a laughter line for miles.

'And as for those lips, well I've seen thicker printing paper,' I say. Her face begins to collapse around the outraged 'o' shape made by her mouth.

'Also, clearly your parents thought it cruel to tape your ears to your head in order to pin them back. Well, I wonder if they think it's cruel now when they see you walking around with those satellite dishes sticking out the side of your head. Tell me, can you pick up Sky Sports?' I say.

The tears begin cascading down her cheeks as she gets up from her seat and starts to run.

'By the way,' I say, 'have you ever heard of Clearasil?'

When I say the word Clearasil she's already through the door and out on the pavement. Her two friends follow her throwing evil scowls my way.

'Dude,' says Clive, 'what happened?'

I just look at him and shake my head.

'Dude, what did you do to the nice lady?' he asks laughing.

I tell him what happened and he laughs some more.

'Man, you can be a heartless bastard,' he says, 'but hey, no sweats, she'll get over it.'

'Mate,' I begin, 'why are we here?'

'Do you mean in this establishment tonight or is it a deeper, more philosophical question?' asks Clive.

'The former,' I say.

'I thought you knew the answer to that one, man,' says Clive, 'we're here to get you back in the game. We're here to get you laid. And dude, this isn't marriage you're after tonight. Just a shag. Plain uncomplicated sex,' says Clive.

'Like such a thing exists,' I say.

'Dude, you have got to lighten up,' says Clive, 'you don't have to like these girls. They're not looking for Mr. Right at a speed dating night either. They're just out for some fun. You know a shag probably won't happen tonight but it's just a gentle way back in. And you never know, one of these girls must just be looking for Mr. Right Now. So relax and have some fun. Just go with it. OK?'

Gentle way back in. Me bulge. But I concede defeat with a sigh.

'OK,' I say.

After that I just go with it. I answer the questions in the way the girls want them answered and I ask questions that mean nothing in return. At the end of the night nobody has ticked me as someone they would like to see again and that's fine by me. I didn't tick any of their boxes either.

That night though, for the first time since we split, I go to sleep not thinking of Helen.

Shoaling

I look to my left along the platform and then to my right. At 7.30am it's the proverbial sardine tin. There are so many open umbrellas above the crowd it reminds me of the first week of Wimbledon. Every year.

It's not even raining. Well, not really. It's that embarrassing misty drizzle cousin of real rain. If it were really raining my fellow commuters wouldn't be sheltering under brollies on the exposed section of platform, but huddled together even tighter, packed under the excuse of a roof that runs to the halfway point of the platform.

My fellow commuters. So many different faces all looking the same. That haunted, vacant expression brought on by years of whoring for Satan. Years of career dis-satisfaction. Years of worry about jobs and money. About mortgages and loans. About family. Partners. Kids. Parents.

A screech of feedback introduces the tannoy.

'Ladies and gentlemen, we are experiencing minor delays this morning as a result of the adverse weather conditions. London Underground wishes to apologise for any inconvenience caused.'

177

All around me the predictable chorus of moans and groans erupts along the platform. And less than ten seconds later it subsides and my fellow commuters go back to reading their newspapers and books. Listening to their iphones and mp3s. Grooming and picking as though nothing had happened. We've become so good at launching into inaction that we deserve the lack of service we get.

From leaves on the track to the wrong type of snow, London Underground's excuses for delays are legendary. But this beats all. If light drizzle constitutes adverse weather in Britain then cockroaches are an endangered species.

In Northfields, the next station along, a train has been sitting on the platform for at least seven minutes. Coming from Heathrow it will already be packed with tourists and their luggage as well as commuters trying to get to work. There's no way I'll get on that train. No point even trying. Why am I even standing in the open waiting? I move away from the yellow line, the barrier that protects us from train and tracks.

Behind the crowds I manage to find some space and room to breathe. I wonder what an intelligent species would make of us. This daily flocking and herding. This institutionalised harassment and torture that we accept. No strike that. That we welcome. We used to be a nation of fighters. We fought for equal rights. We fought for the vote. We fought for freedom. Now we just fight each other for elbow room in a sardine tin.

I decide to wait for the mess to clear. For a train with space. It might take ten minutes. It might take an hour. I don't care.

I go to the waiting room where only three other people sit and wait and I take a seat and read. I read the first paragraph three times but I don't take it in. I can't take it in. I'm too distracted. I keep looking out the window at the crowd. I look at them craning their necks to see the train that still sits at Northfields. I look at them looking at their watches and then looking at the train information boards then looking at the station clock then looking at their watches again. I look at the crowd looking up the tracks in the other direction, not really sure what they're looking for but they're looking all the same. I look at the crowd doing nothing. This shoal of sardines flitting this way then that. Aimlessly but altogether, just waiting to get into the comfort of their tin where they can moan and groan at some new harassment.

I look at my watch. I'm waiting for a train with space. It may take ten minutes. It may take an hour. I don't care.

At least I tell myself I don't care. The trouble is I do. I get up and wander out to the platform where I re-join my shoal. I look at my watch. I look at the train information boards. I look at the station clock and then at my watch again.

Inside I fume. Right now I hate my work. I hate my commute. I hate my life. I hate myself.

But I continue to wait this interminable wait for a train anyway.

I stand my ground waiting for my train and the rain starts getting heavier. It's still not quite the real deal but it's no longer the embarrassing relative. This stuff can actually get you wet.

After a few more minutes of shoaling, the overcrowded train pulls in and a handful of relieved souls disembark only to be replaced by three times as many victims. I don't make it onto this tin and the doors close.

Inside, my fellow commuters manoeuvre their bodies into contorted shapes to fit sloping windows and doors, luggage and feet, armpits and elbows, coughing, sneezing and spluttering heads. The windows fog with the condensation of my fellow commuters' breath infected with thousands of different bacteria and viruses. And then the germ factory pulls away leaving me behind on the platform.

But at least I'm back at the front of the yellow line for the next one. And I'm right at the spot where the doors open. Pretty damned fine manouvering to secure such a prime location against the odds. Almost like securing a one bedroom studio apartment in Notting Hill for the bargain price of £500k.

It seems things are moving again now as I see the next train pulling into Northfields. Sure, this will be overcrowded too but I've got a fighting chance of making it on this time.

The train leaves Northfields and grinds and squeals its way towards us along the glistening tracks. It's suddenly real rain now and the sky has turned a heavy grey rendering everything dull and lifeless. A hundred metres away from the platform the train stops and sits. The fin-jerk reaction of the shoal is to look at watches, then the train information boards, then the station clock and then back to watches before staring at the motionless hulking locomotive.

The rain falls harder running off brollies onto other commuters so that even those under umbrellas still get their share of the soaking. The train moves towards us again. This time Wonder Woman style. Slow motion. Torturing us yet further. The face of the train smirks at us with its window eyes and grinning grill mouth.

And as it approaches, as it looms into view, as it grinds onward, I think how easy it would be to end it all now. Just jump. And all the worry goes. No more mortgage. No more loans. No more family and friends. No more germ factory commutes. No more anything. Peace at last.

But I don't and the smirking face passes me by and I'm sure it whispers to me from its grill mouth. One word.

Coward.

The hits keep on coming

It's not as bad as before, I keep telling myself this. This is the thing about going back to Plum. It's not as bad as before.

I walked through the door and before I had control of my client account it was wrested from my grasp. But it's not as bad as before.

The early mornings and late nights began again instantly, but it's not as bad as before. I keep telling myself this.

I have no support whatsoever, but it's not as bad as before. I keep telling myself this.

And the hits just keep on coming.

At least though, as a contractor, I gct paid a higher rate than if I were on a salary. I've started telling myself this.

You can probably see where this is going.

I go down to the accounts department to enquire about my cheque. The accounts department is in the basement. It seems to be an unwritten rule that accounts departments get put in the most dismal part of any building. As I walk through the door the six pasty, miserable faces look up and grunt greetings at me. No natural light for the bloodsuckers. It must be a vampire thing.

I go to Geraldine who looks after suppliers. She tells me she has done her payment run. The cheques have been signed and sent out she tells me. There wasn't one for me.

Apparently there's a problem with my invoice. I billed at the wrong rate. AdCom has a policy that no contract Senior AD gets paid more than £250 per day. I had agreed a rate of £300 with Phil. At £250 per day I'd be making the same as a salaried SAD so what's the point in taking the risk of being a contractor? In fact as a package it works out a lot less without pension, private health, paid holidays and other benefits.

This is all mildly annoying but I'm not too upset. I've got my contract. I'm protected. I say this to Geraldine but, to be fair, I'd get more of a reaction from a corpse. She barely even shrugs. Nothing she can do. Out of her hands. Not up to her.

I sent the invoice to Phil who signed it off. But Geraldine knew the rate would present a problem so she brought it to the attention of Bill. He has the invoice now. He's had it for a week and nobody thought to let me know there was a problem.

I begin to mention this but I see in Geraldine's face that there's no point. She doesn't care and wouldn't be able to do anything about it even if she did care. She and proactivity have never met. Neither knows the other exists.

I go to Bill's office.

Bill greets me with his shark smirk. That's ok, I'm ready to play hardball. Besides, I have my contract. My signed contract. Bill will have to pay the invoice.

'Bill,' I begin, 'there seems to be a problem with my cheque.'

'No,' says Bill, 'there's a problem with your invoice.'

'The rate,' I say.

'The rate,' agrees Bill.

'Well, I hate to disappoint you, Bill, but it's the rate agreed in my contract,' I say taking a seat and smiling.

Bill reaches into a drawer, pulls out a stapled document and tosses it across the desk at me.

'You mean this contract?' he asks. That was handy – the contract being in his top drawer ready to be retrieved at a moment's notice. He's been waiting for me to come down to his office and ask about my cheque. He's had the invoice for a week

182

and he has been ready for me for a week, but he was always going to wait for me to make an appearance. Cunt.

'That looks like it,' I say.

'Flick to the back page,' says Bill grinning his Death grin.

I look at the smug prick wondering what he's playing at. I pick up the contract and flick to the back page.

'Is that your signature?' asks Bill.

'Yes it is,' I say.

'Now show me where the rate is agreed,' says Bill.

I flick through the contract but don't see a rate. I flick again, slower this time. Still nothing. I scan every page carefully, every line looking for the figure. A figure. Any figure.

There isn't a single mention of money at all. But I remember seeing it.

'This is impossible,' I say.

'The contract I signed specified a fee of £300 per day,' I say.

'Clearly not,' says Bill. 'None of our contracts specify fees. At least, not to contractors.'

I know I've seen it. I think. I think some more. And then it hits me.

'It must have been in the email! That's it! I must have read it in the email,' I say.

'I doubt it,' says Bill. 'We never mention figures in emails either. Company policy.'

'I've seen it written somewhere,' I say and get up to leave.

'When you realise you don't have a figure in writing I'll pay your re-issued invoice at £250 per day,' says Bill grinning.

'Even if I don't have it in writing I have a verbal agreement with Phil,' I say.

'Not worth the paper it's not written on,' says Bill.

'Phil is not authorised to make that call. And I won't pay it. Save yourself a lot of bother and just raise an invoice for £250 per day,' says Bill. 'You know it makes sense,' says Bill and he grins at me again.

That crocodile smile.

That shark smirk.

That Death grin.

The prick delights in other peoples' pain. I bet he smiled that smile when he made those six people redundant. I bet he grins that grin each time he cheats on his wife with another PA.

I want to smash his face until his own mother wouldn't recognise him. I want to punch him until it hurts me. I want to scream and rant and lash out. I want to do damage.

But I don't. I remain calm. I get up and walk out without a word. As I pass through his doorway he snorts and sniggers.

He'll get his.

Cunt.

He had to do it. He was left with no choice. No alternative. His hand was forced and he took the only option available. Inevitable as death. As Prime Minister he had to do something.

After the strike he called on his chiefs of staff to dole out punishments including court martial proceedings. Instead nothing happened. The numbers were just too vast and they were all guilty of the same "crime". To take action would have meant suspending all of them until court martials could be heard and that would have obliterated the armed forces. This stalemate continued for weeks as the world looked on. The Prime Minister's position grew more precarious each day and his impotence was being mocked from all corners of the globe. So he took the only option he could and he's gone after Libra.

And when I say he's gone after Libra I don't mean like before with the inept police raids on Foe gigs. Lame publicity stunts to make the public think the situation was under control. This time he's pulling out all the stops. Every tape and scrap of evidence is being analysed, hunting for clues.

Rewards have been offered for any information which helps the case. So far all the leads have ended up as dead ends. But the heat is very much on. If the rumours are true, he's even put a price on Libra's head. Bounty hunters are being lured by a figure of £500k. Allegedly.

The couriers delivering tapes to TV stations have been interrogated too. Another dead end. Libra, it turns out, uses a different company each time. He sends them to a different location where the biker finds the tapes in addressed envelopes

184

and enough cash to pay for the deliveries twice over. The couriers know nothing. They're just messengers.

The Prime Minister is trying to turn the tables. He has even used Libra's words against him.

"This terrorist has told us that to kill a serpent you must remove its head," said the PM. "Well, we're going to remove the head of the Scales of Justice. We are going to hunt down this terrorist and bring him to justice for the terrible crimes he has committed!"

Every day people are being brought in for questioning. Every day there are raids up and down the country. Special teams have been assembled in MI5, MI6 and the SAS. But so far they have got nothing. Zero. Well, nothing that's been made known to the public anyway. Rumours abound about progress that has been kept top secret. Some say they are very close to capturing Libra. Some say they already have a number of his closest deputies. Others say the trap to catch him is about to be sprung.

One thing is for sure, they certainly don't have him yet. The tapes keep on coming. The army still goes on strike. And the PM grows more frustrated by the day, which is understandable.

His situation is becoming untenable. Pressure is mounting on him to resign. He believes that catching Libra will save him.

To kill a serpent you must remove its head. Now, it seems, it's just a race to see which head gets removed first.

Our country

Getting back out there is tough. Nothing seems to fit. There's always something wrong. Something about her will annoy me. She might be too chatty. Or boring. A soaps fan. Too old. Too young.

Hark at me! Like I'm the perfect catch!

But believe me, it's tough out there. Last week I was on a date with a girl I met at a leaving party at work. She's a friend of one of our graduates and just came along to the bar. We got chatting and I got her number. We seemed to click so I called her and asked her out. Let me say now, stapling my eyelids shut would have been more fun.

Flashback to the date.

We sit across from each other in the restaurant. Silence. Not just silence, but awkward silence. Her name is Sarah, she's 22, a graduate in micro-biology from Oxford and, well, that's it. She hasn't started her career, she barely has a past and there isn't much in the way of conversation. Sure, she's pretty and pleasant, but there's no connection here whatsoever.

That might sound like I'm laying the blame at her door but I'm not. If anyone is at fault here it's me. I should know better.

Or at least I'm old enough to know better. And yet here I am chasing women a dozen years my junior, sometimes even more. What the hell am I playing at?

And what's wrong with me? I was on a date with a gorgeous woman in a nice restaurant and all I could do was think of other things I'd have preferred to be doing at the time. I could have been at home reading a book, for example. Or at the theatre. Cinema, even. I could have been out for a few drinks with Clive. I could have been conducting self-circumcision without anaesthetic. I tell you, it would have been less painful. But no, there I was being an idiot and wasting time.

Yeah, it's tough being back out there. There's always something wrong. Something about her will annoy me. Too vacant. Too self-absorbed. Too shallow. Too something.

At the risk of sounding like a complete hypocrite though, the silence with Sarah was Heaven compared to a date a few weeks back. And this time I really should have known better. My sister Claire set me up with a girl she knows. Not even a friend, just someone she knows. I'd met her twice before and for some reason decided it was a good idea. As good ideas go it's right up there with the Charge of the Light Brigade. Like I said I really should have known better.

Flashback to the date.

It's been seven minutes and thirty-two seconds since I've said anything. I've made appropriate ooh and aah noises where necessary and thrown in the occasional chuckle to show I'm paying attention but to all intents and purposes we're sitting together but completely alone.

In that time she's been telling me about the latest developments in the Big Brother house. No scratch that, she hasn't been telling me but chatting at me as though I know what and who she is talking about.

On the jukebox, Kurt Cobain sings: 'I wish I was like you, easily amused,' and I catch myself nodding. Thankfully my date doesn't notice. Good old Kurt providing synergy.

Yeah it's tough being back out there. But don't get me wrong, I'm not a serial datist or anything. I'm just trying to break a decade of conditioning. It's just part of my therapy.

Thing is I don't ever remember being this choosy before. Like everyone else I've got my share of cringe and shudder memories. Those chew your arm off at the elbow horror stories. Yeah I was never really that fussy before Helen. But now? Now if my date has a pet then forget it. I'm not interested. Definite no-no if she has a kid. I don't want to know if she lives too far away. Likewise if she lives too close. If she works unsociable hours there's no point. And I'm never going to snog a smoker. And if I find out she reads celebrity gossip magazines then it's over before it begins. If she shares a flat or lives with family or just doesn't live alone then I'm not sticking around. Boy band fan? You must be joking!

There is a problem with being this choosy though. According to Clive I've reduced my options to minus. According to Clive I'm looking for a woman who doesn't exist. Not the perfect woman. Something far worse. According to Clive I'm after a woman with no history. That woman, if she existed, would be bad news. More damaged than damaged goods.

If Clive's assessment is right I'm in big trouble. I can't spend the rest of my life chasing rainbows. That way lies insanity.

Thankfully Clive, as ever, has the answer. The solution.

According to Clive I need familiar surroundings. I need my posse with me. I need to find my zone. I find my zone, everything else falls into place.

So tonight we're going to step back in time. Tonight we're going to an 80s club.

We hit the club at around 11.30 after a few looseners in the pub. We're greeted by Rick Astley on giant TV screens dancing his dance and reassuring us he's never gonna give us up. Tubed fluorescent lighting blinks on and off in sequence against the Death black ceiling. UV light picks out every speck of white in the crowd. Not a night to wear a dark top if you suffer with dandruff. Some of the guys have even dug out their white Michael Jackson style socks for the occasion. Scary. Or maybe they just never put them away in the first place. Scarier.

We get drinks and find somewhere to stand and look cool. If looking cool is possible at an 80s disco that is. Above us on the giant TV screens, Rick Astley morphs into George Michael urging us to wake him up before we go go. It seems 80s DJs still haven't learned how to mix. I look at pretty boy George with his perfect bleached teeth and perfect bleached hair and perfect bronzed tan dancing and prancing in his three-quarter length trousers and plimsolls banging his tambourine and I ask myself: How did we never spot that he was gay?

All around us blokes stand in groups each with one hand in a trouser pocket while the other cradles a drink, their eyes prowling the crowd predator style. As well as white socks, some guys have dug out their New Romantic suits. I even spot a keyboard tie.

Girls in groups dance and laugh and sing. Most of the crowd are old enough to remember the decade with only a few young intruders. The 80s. Our own country. Disastrous hair. Disastrous clothes. Disastrous music. But ours. And we're willing to defend it with our lives.

Clive asks me if I'm hungry and points to the other side of the club. A hole in the wall offers a view to the kitchen beyond where people race through clouds of steam preparing deep fried delights.

We wander over to the magical portal and see burgers grilling and chips frying. Paper plates and plastic cups. Ketchup and mayonnaise bottles oozing diseased gunk. We hear cheap meats sizzling and the fat bully manager barking orders at spotty, disinterested teens moping behind the counter. We smell frying onions and garlic mushrooms and, yes, oh God yes, curry sauce. Ah the 80s! Home!

Now it's complete. Now I'm back. Now I'm in the Zone. And suddenly I catch myself moving to the music. Not dancing, but swaying with attitude. And it's good.

I grin at Clive and see him grinning back at me. He's bopping too and it's like I'm looking in a mirror we're so on the same wavelength. We order food and while we're waiting the music improves. A Town Called Malice leads into Blue Monday leads into Panic leads into Road to Nowhere leads into Rock the Casbah. OK the DJ still can't mix for shit but at least they're cracking tunes and I'm itching to get onto the already thronging floor and dance like a teenager again. I just need my food so I can wolf it and go. Now I realise food was a mistake but I've ordered and paid and I'm still famished anyway.

And then it's there. Clive and I grab our grub and munch like we've been fasting for years. And still while we stand and eat we sway with attitude. Both of us aching to get on the floor.

Atomic leads into The Whole of the Moon leads into When Doves Cry leads into Oliver's Army while we wolf as quickly as we can so we can get out on the floor. And wouldn't you know it, as the last strains of Oliver's Army play out, as we cram the last mouthful of food in on top of the previous two mouthfuls, as we try to wash it down with beer, as Elvis Costello fades out singing 'I would rather be anywhere else...' the DJ plays Come on Eileen.

I look at Clive and Clive looks at me. We each look at our near empty glasses. We look at each other again and say one word in unison: 'Bar?'

Wavelength, baby, wavelength!

At the bar we stand waiting for the music to improve again. But it just gets worse. You wouldn't think there's far to fall after Come on Eileen, but the DJ pulls out all the stops to bring us the ultimate dross of the era. It seems he plays the entire Stock Aitken and Waterman back catalogue interspersed with every novelty tune released through the decade. Shuddup a your face and the Birdie Song are wedged in between Sonia and Sinita. Bros and New Kids on the Block follow Star Trekkin' and Agadoo. And then, just when we thought the barrel had been well and truly scraped, Shakin' Stevens gets an airing. Yep, we're even so lucky, lucky, lucky to be treated to a trio of Jason and Kylie numbers. The DJ knows no shame.

And nor do the crowd on the floor. None of the 80s generation is out dancing, just the young 21st Century gang.

At 1am Clive and I decide to leave. We clearly missed the best half hour while we were stuffing our faces and there can't be much time left. We drain our glasses and turn to go. We weave our way through the crowd toward the exit. The heat of the club gives way to that fresh night time air as we reach the door. Disappointed. Despondent. Dejected.

But it turns out there's time for one more touch of magic. One more flirtatious fling with the past as Teenage Kicks swamps the air around us. I look at Clive and he at me. We grin and turn back and head straight for the floor. We jump and dance, strut and slide. And we're not alone. On the floor we're surrounded by 80s kids. All the young pretenders are now standing at the edges. On the periphery where they belong.

Teenage Kicks becomes Mirror in the Bathroom becomes Going Underground becomes Turning Japanese becomes Heart of Glass becomes I Fought the Law. I sing at the top of my lungs surprised I still know most of the lyrics. And then surprised when I realise I've forgotten the chorus. My face aches from grinning and I want this to last forever. I'm sure I'm not alone but I didn't realise how great my teens were until they weren't there anymore.

The thing about 80s discos is there are rules. You go to a night club in the 80s and there's a strict format to be followed. Sure, you're free to do anything and anything can happen. But it can only happen within the structured formula. We've had the disastrous DJ, the disastrous music and disastrous clothing. We've had the greasy food lacking in nutrition. We've had the beer and dancing. We've had the boys standing around trying to look cool and the girls standing around singing and dancing, trying to look alluring. And then, right on cue, with a quarter of an hour to go, the DJ redeems himself. The slow set. The window of opportunity. Those three or four songs where you can approach the girl you've been eyeing up all night and ask her to dance. If she says no then you have a dilemma. You can stay and chat and try to convince her to dance as the clock runs down or just chat and see where that leads. Or you can move on to someone else and lick your wounded ego later.

The slow set. The place where it's acceptable to have Whitney Houston saving all her love for you. But the DJ does way better than that. He gives Eric Stewart of 10cc the opportunity to convince us that he's not in love. I turn to Clive but Clive's gone. Randy bastard. No doubt he's already on the floor with his tongue down someone's throat while feeling up her arse. I'm not sure I can be bothered. The bar's closed and I don't have a drink. Clive's gone and I'm unlikely to see him again tonight. I've spotted a couple of girls through the evening...well, one in particular, but I don't see her now. Time to call it a night. I turn to leave and I've gone a few steps when I get tapped on the shoulder. I turn quickly not sure what to expect and find her standing there, the girl I had been eyeing up, her hands behind her back and her feet crossed where she stands.

'Leaving already?' she asks coyly, 'I thought you were going to ask me to dance.'

'In the 21st Century?' I say all mock shock, 'surely it's the lady's prerogative to ask the gentleman to dance,' I say.

'True,' she concedes, 'but tonight it's not the 21st Century. Tonight we've gone back in time. Tonight it's the 80s,' she says grinning, peering out from under her blonde fringe and swaying gently.

'Mon dieu!' I say smacking my forehead with the heel of my hand, 'you're so right! How can you ever forgive me?' I ask holding out my hand which she takes.

'My lady,' I say, 'would you care to dance?' I say kissing the back of her hand gently.

'I thought you'd never ask,' she says and we head for the floor.

The DJ does his job perfectly. I'm not in Love gives way to Purple Rain gives way to Fast Car. Three songs. Perfect.

On the floor we ask each other's names. We ask who we're each here with. Where we live. What brought us to 80s night. All the usual small talk.

Filling space.

Saying nothing.

All the necessary unnecessary questions have been asked halfway through Purple Rain. All the right boxes have been ticked. We lapse into silence. She looks away and so do I. But it's brief. In the next heartbeat we turn to each other and kiss. We kiss until the end of the slow set. For the rest of Purple Rain and all through Fast Car we say nothing, just kiss.

Fast Car ends and we still kiss. The music stops completely and we still kiss. The DJ announces that the night is at an end and we still kiss. The lights come up and we stop.

We stand for a moment holding each other blinking in the glaring lights that have chased away the magic.

And I really am a teenager again. A teenager in my mid-thirties. The thing about 80s discos is there are rules. I think to myself, will she let me walk her home. I think to myself, will she give me her number. I think to myself, will I see her again. A teenager again. Awkward. Lacking confidence. Unsure of what I want and how to behave. And just when I'm about to ask if I can walk her home to Camden from Central London, just when I'm about to demonstrate my lacking confidence, just when I'm about to prove I'm a teenager trapped in a 30+ body, she saves me.

'You're nice,' she says, 'but I'm not going home with you tonight and you're not coming back to my flat either. I'd like to see you again and I'll give you my number,' she says.

'OK,' I say and I realise I'm relieved.

I watch her wander over to her mates and get her bag. She comes back over to me and gives me her card. And I give her mine. We both look at each other's. It turns out she's a lawyer. A grown up career. I imagine her fighting for the rights of the weak. Railing against oppression. Making the world a better place.

We look at each other and smile.

'I'm going to go and get a cab with my friends,' she says. 'How are you getting home?'

'Oh I'll probably get a cab. Clive has already gone I think. But that's ok – I'm a big boy,' I say and lean in to kiss her.

We kiss briefly, say our goodbyes and she goes over to her girls.

I turn and stroll to the door, hands in pockets and feeling warm. I realise I'm grinning.

A perfect night.

Perfect Christmas

Mum phones me while I'm at work. It's 8.15pm and I should be long gone by now. But I'm not. Mum didn't even phone my mobile, but my direct work line instead. She knew I'd be here.

Even though she has phoned my direct line, she asks me if I'm still at work. She asks if I'll be much longer. I tell her I'm just catching up on emails that came in while I was in meetings all afternoon. I came out of the last meeting, organised my work schedule and resources, actioned a few urgent items and began checking my emails. As I say this another email comes in. I know this because I downloaded a soundbite to alert me when a new email arrives, so now when another one lands in my inbox Yoda tells me I have a message from the Dark Side.

I have a quick look and see that it's from my new divisional director scheduling a meeting with the whole team for 8 o'clock in the morning. Great. In less than twelve hours I need to be back in here. My mobile beeps alerting me to a new text message. It's from my new divisional director telling me about the meeting tomorrow morning. He must have sent a web text to the entire team. When I get home I have no doubt there will be a message on my answerphone too. Out of curiosity I go to my Facebook page, and yep, sure enough there's a mail from my new DD inviting me to attend a team meeting tomorrow morning at 8am.

I'm beginning to understand how Libra feels. The Prime Minister has upped the ante by bringing in emergency anti-terrorist legislation which means that the government can access any CCTV footage at any time without a warrant. Teams have been set-up to trawl through the back catalogue showing the locations where tapes were left by Libra. Thing is, all the locations are blind spots – no CCTV on any of them. So they've gone after tapes of Foe gigs. Protests. Demonstrations. Anything and everything to try and find something. Teams are even set-up to monitor Google Earth and other satellite packages to spot anything out of the ordinary. Big Brother? Orwell didn't know the half of it.

Mum tells me I'm working too hard. Glad she's cleared up that mystery for me. She tells me the stress and pressure of a career like mine aren't worth the salary they pay me. She tells me that my health will suffer, that my marriage has already suffered, that it will send me to an early grave and other cheery thoughts.

Then she moves onto Christmas. She and Claire have been talking about the holidays. About the arrangements. I haven't even thought about it yet, but it's not that far away. Only a few weeks.

Mum wants to know what I'm doing this year. Helen and I used to alternate between her family and mine and this year was due to be with Helen's crowd. I take a brief opportunity to curse myself again for not having sorted out my travel plans. I should already be gone. Sipping coffee in a souk somewhere in the middle-east, listening to a mullah call the public to prayer. At this stage the brochures and guides are likely to die virgins.

I guess I'll be at Mum's for Christmas then.

This news turns Mum into a six year old in a sweet shop. She gets so excited she's in danger of exploding. It'll be the first time in about eight years that we'll all be together for Christmas – my parents and their kids and grandkids. Unless I've found my early grave of course. She doesn't say that but I think it.

In her head she's playing out an American TV programme. Little House on the Prairie fused with the Brady Bunch. Something like that anyway.

It's going to be huge grins and heartfelt sighs all round. We'll gush at each other and lose count of the times we say 'I love you'. Compliments will scatter confetti style over everyone and we'll all have nice glowing feeling in our tummies. At least, that's the Christmas Mum plays out in her head.

She doesn't seem to have considered that nobody likes my brother's wife, my sister is capable of starting an argument with inanimate objects and their kids practice being spiteful to each other at every given opportunity and in extremely creative ways. She hasn't considered that Dad will try to hide in the shed pretending to be doing some essential gardening and that I'm hardly life and soul at the moment. It hasn't dawned on her that we won't be able to agree on a TV choice or a board game, that the kids will keep playing with their new toys at top volume and that she will get herself wound up cooking dinner. We'll all offer a hand but she will insist on doing it all herself and then complain bitterly about the lack of help and that she hasn't been allowed to enjoy 'her' Christmas.

'Her' Christmas. The perfect family Christmas. The perfect 2.4 happy, but quiet children. The perfect family unit with perfect marriages and perfect lives. Tiny Tim getting exactly what he wanted from Santa followed by the tastiest meal ever followed by the Sound of Music. Perfect.

Problem is it's not everyone's idea of a perfect Christmas. And that's where it begins to unravel.

Maybe perfect families do have perfect Christmases. What I know though is that dysfunctional families have dysfunctional Christmases. And we're not the perfect family.

I don't say this of course. I let her have her dream and finish chatting at me.

As I hang up from Mary Poppins, Amanda walks into my office. We haven't uttered two words to each other in the few weeks since I've been back at Plum.

'How you getting on?' she asks.

'Oh you know,' I say. 'Same old. Nothing changes, the rest remains the same.'

'That bad eh?' she says with a smile. She's being my mate and my defences automatically upgrade to red alert.

I lean back in my chair and fold my arms.

'What do you want, Amanda?' I ask.

'Nothing!' she says. 'Jesus, can't I even have a chat with an old mate anymore without it having an agenda?' she asks

'No you can't,' I say, 'with you there's always an agenda.'

She starts to cry. Real tears. Arms folded, head bowed. A sniffle and heave of the shoulders. And now she's sobbing with her right hand covering her eyes.

I try to remain stony.

Cold.

Hard.

But this is real. She's not that good an actress to carry this off. I get out of my seat and go to her. Put my arms around her. Give her a hug.

Now she really lets go. Tears and snot. Almost wailing. Unable to catch her breath in huge gulping sobs.

'Hey, mate, shhh,' I say. 'It'll be ok. What's the matter?'

'Fucking Bill, that's what's the matter,' she says. 'That cunt. I fucking hate him.'

'Everyone hates him!' I say, 'But what's he done this time?

She tries to gather herself so she can speak.

'He's...'she begins but her eyes well up again, 'He's...' and a new burst of tears and snot and drool and wails and sobs cascade out of her waterfall style. Broken river bank style. Destroyed dam style.

I hug her tighter and manoeuvre her to a seat. She sits and sobs. She cries and gulps.

I reach for the box of tissues on the desk and she takes one, two, three and blows her nose. She takes another two and wipes under her eyes expertly removing the eye liner that's run without smearing what's left.

'Take your time,' I say. 'Settle down and tell me when you're ready.'

She nods agreement and attempts to compose herself. She looks up and away to the left and fans her face with her hands open finger style and takes in big breaths, letting them go slowly.

Then she's ready.

'The prick told me this afternoon that he has to cut my personnel budget,' she says. 'He said that my client accounts weren't generating enough income this year. We're down ten percent on last year.'

'Jesus,' I say, 'he can't do that surely?'

'He can and he has,' she says. 'I have to reduce the cost by twenty percent.'

'Twenty? Why twenty when the revenue is only down ten?' I ask.

'Because apparently the trend is leaning towards it getting worse and we need to "budget for the future, not the past",' she says. The last part I'm guessing was a direct quote from Bill the Bull himself. She used the universal sign language of finger inverted commas to signify this.

Amanda tells me that Bill suggested she gets rid of the team PA and an account executive. And everyone else takes a five percent pay cut. She tells me that in true Bill style it might have been dressed as a suggestion but underneath the clothing it was an order.

And it gets worse. Amanda wasn't the only divisional director to have a meeting like this today. Two others were called in too, including, you've guessed it, my new DD. I think about my Facebook page. I think about my mobile. I think about my email and the team meeting scheduled for the morning. I think about Yoda and his message from the Dark Side.

Got that right pal.

Professional help

I didn't expect to be given a menu, but that's the first thing that happens. Well, the first thing after the initial chat and welcome and invitation to sit. As soon as my backside lands I'm handed a menu as though I'm in a nice restaurant and the maitre d' is catering to my every desire. But this is no restaurant and this maitre d' lacks for a tuxedo and wine list. And unlike a maitre d', she stands there hovering while I flick through the offerings.

Words jump off the page at me. Words like anal and fantasy and double. Words like bondage, dominatrix, slave. Words like nurse, schoolgirl, nun.

This might sound odd, but this is part of my therapy. That lawyer I met at the 80s night. Well, I tried calling her half a dozen times. I even rang the number twice. And on one of those occasions I heard her speak. 'Hello?' is all she said before I hung up, but at least I heard her speak.

Thing is, phoning her felt wrong. Like I was cheating on my wife. If only I could come round to the idea that she's my ex-wife and the ex part is permanent. But I can't.

I told all this to Clive. I needed to know what to do and I couldn't figure it out on my own. I don't want to live the rest of my life feeling guilty for being human.

Clive reckons I need uncomplicated sex to break the programming. He recommended I seek the help of a professional. And he knew just where to go to get it.

The cheapest meal on the menu is a hand job at £40. After that blow jobs and straight sex come in at £60 each. Anal sex is on offer for £120 while two girls could be mine for £200. Side portions are also available. Kissing costs £40. Touching £20. So I can come in a complete stranger's mouth for £60 but if I want to touch her tits it will cost me an extra £20. That's well fucked up, no pun intended.

And if all that's on the menu, you've got to ask the question: what's not on the menu?

Pretty damn sure the maitre d' knows this is my first time. Well, not my first time, of course, just my first time in a place like this. Yeah she knows. She's laughing in an "Oh bless, a virgin!" kind of way as I flick through the pages. I'm guessing my face has become a wide-eyed balloon around an 'O' shaped mouth.

I grow a little flustered because of the laughing and I just scan the rest of the menu quickly looking desperately for anything that might appeal. Something out of the ordinary. Something I haven't tried before.

And there it is. Twins. In a shower cubicle. Perfect.

These girls are gorgeous. One looks a little like Jennifer Aniston and as they're twins, so does the other one. They walk *that* walk toward me. You know the walk. The one that suggests sex. Screams sex. Is sex. Legs crossing over each other with each slow, sensual step. Pelvis grinding, ass gyrating as though chewing a toffee.

They both smile at me slightly open mouthed with a hint of tongue. When they reach me they each take one of my hands and lead me to the room. Our room.

The shower is already running with the bathroom steaming gently. They sit me on the edge of the red, silk bed and push me back slowly, gently, tenderly until my head rests on plush velvet cushions.

They snog and start to undress each other slowly, provocatively. As each inch of flesh is uncovered by clothing it's re-covered with a kiss. They work each other down to their lingerie before coming back to the bed where they start stripping me.

'Darling,' says Jennifer 1.

'Babes,' says Jennifer 2.

'Oi sweetheart!' barks a raspy voice that startles my eyes open. I didn't realise I had closed them. My fantasy is at an end and there standing in front of me is a pair of sisters. Twins in fact. But they're not Jennifer Aniston. Neither of them. Although one of them might weigh the same as two Jennifer Anistons. This had better be a big shower.

'Follow us darlin',' says one of them as the other one blows a bubble with her gum which invariably bursts on her face.

I follow my twin fantasy down a dim, musty corridor. We pass paper walls and cardboard doors behind which we hear moans and groans, grunts and screams, bouncing beds and banging headboards.

As I watch the twins waddle ahead of me I can't stop thoughts entering my head. Thoughts like: these girls have cornered the market in cellulite. And thoughts like: tattoos of football club crests don't even look good on blokes.

I'm led into a room that just about accommodates a double bed and chest of drawers. I'm guessing the en-suite is behind the door in the far corner of the room. The door that may open a third of the way before crashing against the bed. The bed that makes me itch just looking at it.

The striped blue and yellow wallpaper is peeling in several places revealing black damp patches on the naked, diseased walls. Botched attempts to stick it back down with sellotape or drawing pins were clearly the order of the day at some point until it was decided that there was more chance of finding an honest politician. The main carpet it seems was once a brown, swirly patterned nylon affair from the 70s, but is now a patchwork quilt with pieces of different carpet sewn in where bad things have previously happened.

The girls, the room, the bed, the whole place smacks of desperation. Then again, I'm the one visiting a brothel so maybe in this glasshouse I should keep my stones in my pockets.

'Awright darlin', says the talker handing me a towel, 'git yer kit off. The shower's busy at the moment, so we'll be here for a few minutes 'til it's free.'

'Oh,' I say, 'is that not an en-suite?' I say.

The girls glance at each other and burst into a false laugh. A fake laugh. Straight out of the Barbara Windsor Carry On Laughing school.

'Yeah, course it is darlin'. Welcome to the Ritz!' she says and bursts into another fit of giggles.

'Nah, it's just down the hall. They'll give us a knock when they're done.'

She turns to her sister and they start chatting. Well, she starts chatting while her sister chews her gum and blows bubbles. I don't even exist.

I undress and wrap the towel around my waist. I fold my clothes and put them on the chest of drawers. I sit on the bed. I look at the girls. I've disappeared.

A few minutes pass before a knock on the door starts the girls into action.

'Come on darlin',' says little miss chatty.

They leave the room and I follow. We walk further down the dark, musty corridor. To my right I hear a whip crack and the sound of a man crying. Ahead of us in the corridor a fat man in his 50s stands outside a room wearing nothing but a towel wrapped around him so that the head of his erection pokes out over the top. I look dead ahead at the back of the gum chewer's head and don't allow my eyes to veer down to his waist.

'Put it away, Fred!' says the talker before bursting into another round of Babs Windsor.

Just beyond fat boy the girls turn into the steaming bathroom. There isn't a bath in sight so I suppose it's really a shower room.

Still chatting to each other without acknowledging my existence the girls begin to undress and put their underwear in a cupboard. I just stand there, the ultimate spare prick.

Little miss chatty turns on the shower and both girls get into the cubicle.

'Well, what are you waitin' for darlin', a written invitation?' says little miss chatty. The gum chewer pops her gum at me. I take off my towel and put it in the cupboard noticing as I do that there isn't even a hint of an erection.

'Deary me,' says chatty, 'we'll 'ave to do somefink abaht that', and she grabs my dick and pulls me into the shower. Gummy starts lathering gel into me while chatty fondles and strokes my penis into something vaguely usable. Once it's fully erect she expertly rolls a condom on it, leans back into the wall, spreads her legs and pulls me in. Foreplay, it seems, is something that happens to other people.

I go to kiss her and she moves her mouth away and slaps my hands down from touching her.

'That'll cost you extra, sweetheart,' she says and then turns to her sister. 'And don't you let him touch you without paying neither.'

Gummy pops her gum in reply, which I think translates as 'I won't'.

Chatty tells gummy to work the soap on my back then my arse and then to slide her fingers up my bum. Instinctively I clench.

'Sorry darlin', don't you like that? You just struck me as the kind of bloke who would like a good finger up the arsehole,' she says.

'Or fist,' she says. 'But we won't do anyfink you don't want us to do.'

All this time I've been sliding in and out of her while she's been giving instructions to Gummy.

She shakes her head and Gummy's hand, which I hadn't realised was poised to enter, retracts from my arse. Instead of sticking fingers up my anus, Gummy starts soaping up my legs as she kneels beside me.

And still I slide in and out of Chatty who seems to be growing a frown. She reaches down to her sister's hair and pulls it away from her shoulder.

'How long have you had that?' she asks.

Gummy tries to look at the back of her own shoulder to where her sister's pointing at an orange mole but fails. She shrugs an answer which I take as 'I don't know.'

'You need to get that checked out,' says Chatty, 'I'll take you to the doctor tomorrow.'

And I slide in and out.

Chatty looks up from her sister into my face, seeming to acknowledge my presence. And suddenly she starts moaning and groaning. All the directions have been delivered and now she's moaning and groaning.

Her Babs Windsor laugh has nothing on these moans and groans for falseness.

If there is an opposite of an aphrodisiac, this is it. I feel nothing and my erection evaporates like a drop in the desert.

'What's wrong babes?' she says.

'I don't know,' I say, 'I just feel nothing,' I say.

'Do you want to try my sister?' she says looking at Gummy who shrugs and gets off her knees. They swap around and Gummy leans her back into the wall and spreads her legs. Chatty takes the condom off my dick and starts massaging gel into me working up an erection again. When I'm ready she puts a fresh condom on me and Gummy pulls me over to her. I start sliding in and out of her while she chews and pops her gum.

I slide in and out.

She chews and pops.

In and out.

Chews and pops.

In and out.

Chews and pops.

I only realise that Chatty has left us when I hear the toilet flush. I look around at the sound of the flush only to see Gummy's hand picking at her nails. She's been doing this all the while.

I've been sliding in and out. She's been chewing and popping. And cleaning her nails. Multi-tasking.

These girls do a great line in contraception and my penis is once again only good for pissing.

I push away just as Chatty comes back into view.

'You lost it again?' she says before doing her best Babs.

'That's not helping,' I say and she stops laughing.

'Well I'm sorry but if you can't maintain wood it's not my problem,' she says.

'So what happens now?' I say.

'Well, we've got another client in a few minutes so I'd say we're done. Dry yourself off and get dressed babes,' she says.

'But I haven't finished,' I protest.

'You look finished to me,' she says and flicks a nod at my penis. 'Besides, you've had both of us so that's that.'

'But I didn't "finish" finish,' I say, 'you know what I mean, I didn't come.'

'No orgasm during sex?' she says all mock shock, 'welcome to the life of your average woman love!' she says.

'Anyhow, like I said, not my problem,' she says and walks out of the room followed by Gummy.

I've never felt so used.

The end

I'm dying. Plain as the nose on my face. It's a certainty. That's what she tells me. Well, in a roundabout way. I hear it in her voice.

Sombre.

Serious.

Sad.

And yet I can hear her trying to hold back the laughter. She knows it would be inappropriate but that just makes it more of a struggle. She's very professional and even though she doesn't say it I know what she's saying. Or not saying as the case may be.

Cancer.

That can be the only explanation.

Or meningitis.

An incurable strain of TB.

What else could it be?

I play the message on the answerphone again. Looking for clues. My doctor's secretary's message. The one telling me that my doctor would like to see me. That I need to call her back to make an appointment. That he needs to discuss the results of a routine blood test conducted after an anomaly was discovered during my blood test after the fight.

I'm dying.

Leukemia.

Ebola.

Typhoid.

It can't be HIV. The "professionals" were the first since Helen and long after the blood test. Chance would be a fine thing.

On the answerphone my doctor's secretary assures me there's nothing to worry about.

Yeah right!

Why would she emphasise that point if the opposite weren't true?

I'm dying.

A brain tumour.

Bowel cancer.

Heart disease.

I'm dying.

I had so much to do. So many plans. So many places to visit. So many experiences to, well, experience. So much life to live.

And now it's over. I'll never get to travel the Middle-East. Or see Uluru. The Taj Mahal. Machu Picchu. The Grand Canyon.

I'll never skydive. Or bungee jump. Or fly a plane.

I'm dying.

It's so unfair.

Nothing to worry about, she says. As if!

She's not very good at disguising her fears for me. It's going to be painful. Excruciating. Agony.

It's going to be nasty. Undignified. Degrading.

I'm dying.

And I haven't lived. I've worked instead.

It's over. I may as well get a gun and blow my brains out. Run a warm bath and let the blade do the rest.

Cyanide.

Prescription drugs.

Throw myself off a bridge. In front of a train. A tall building.

Or take the 21st Century way out and strap myself full of explosives and take as many enemies with me as I can.

Clive wouldn't be this defeatist. Clive is a winner. Clive lives life and if he were told he had a finite amount of time left he would make the most of that time.

Clive is an eagle soaring. I'm a hamster in a wheel.

But I don't have to be.

So I'm dying. So what?

Why can't I skydive? Worst case scenario is the chute doesn't open and the pain just ends quicker. Or why not go during my travels in the Middle-East instead of in a damp squib at home in bed?

I reach for the phone and dial my doctor's office number but the surgery is closed so I'll have to call back in the morning.

And it hits me. If I'm already dying then I'm free to do anything.

I reach for the brochures that have stared at me for months. I get my pen and pad. I get my Lonely Planets.

I make plans.

'Still he sits on his throne and leads the country from one catastrophe to another,' says the distorted voice of Libra. 'The people have spoken, but he ignores them. The army has spoken, but he refuses to listen. His own ministers are resigning on a daily basis and speaking out against his actions, and still he sits on his throne and leads the country from one catastrophe to another.'

The Prime Minister's efforts at hunting down Libra have failed. He has called off the dogs and switched his focus. It almost seems as though his latest tactic is to ignore Libra and hope he goes away. But he won't.

'People of Britain and the world, this is the true face of so called democracy,' says Libra. 'We are told that we have a voice. We are told that violence is unacceptable and that goals must be achieved through diplomatic means. Yet when we venture down the diplomatic road we go backwards. Our voice is weaker. Our strength is lost. The sad truth is that violence works. Sometimes it is the only thing that works. And with a tyrant like him, it is the only thing that will work.'

Of course some people are saying that it is a ploy by the Prime Minister to lure Libra into making a mistake. Into showing his hand and making himself known. I can't see it happening though. Not now after all this time.

'I said before that violence was always a last resort for the Scales of Justice,' says Libra. 'We played by his rules, but that didn't work. And now we have reached our last resort. To kill a serpent you must remove its head.'

I'm dying. Oh God I'm dying.

It's one of those hangovers that starts at the back of the neck and pulses up the left side of the head and stabs through the left eye causing it to water uncontrollably. Thank the God I don't believe in that I'm still pissed or it would be even worse and I'm not sure I could handle that today. With each breath I taste vodka and everything seems to be swimming around me. I don't know how much I drank. I don't know how I got home. I don't know what time I finished. No doubt it was a great night but huge chunks of it are missing and I keep getting flashbacks. Oh God, did I really air guitar on the pool table of the Fox? I'm barred now and no mistake.

Every so often a shuddering yawn reverberates through my shattered body making me want to curl up under my desk forever. But I can't.

Apart from the fact that I'm super stupid busy there's something else happening today. Something unexpected. Something important. They found Bill the Bull.

Bill didn't turn up to work yesterday and he didn't phone in sick. And that's very odd. Bill is Mr Reliable. If Bill were an ad campaign he would be Sure For Men – He won't let you down.

He had important meetings lined up all day that he didn't attend. Nobody could get him on his mobile. He wasn't at home.

Then his wife phoned. She had been trying to reach Bill. She hadn't heard from him all day. Mr Reliable would have phoned by now or answered his mobile when she called him.

That's when the police were notified he was missing.

Since then everyone has been worried sick. Strike that, everyone has been giving the appearance of being worried sick.

Sycophants.

Everywhere I looked yesterday people were gathered in pockets talking about one subject.

209

Speaking in sombre tones. Coming to terms with the possible tragedy. Gaining perspective.

This many crocodile tears could flood the Sahara.

In the 21st Century everyone writes headlines. Everyone coins soundbites. Bill was firm but fair. Bill was a true company man. Bill was more loyal than a Tommy in the trenches.

Blah, blah and more blah. Filling space. Talking in clichés.

Epitaphs for the presumed dead.

Suddenly Bill is royalty. Everyone's favourite FD. The nation's penny-pinching prince.

Thing is, alive or dead the guy's still a prick. Have these people lost their memories? Being dead or missing doesn't change anything. Or is Saddam Hussein suddenly a saint because he's popped it?

Or is it wrong that I don't care about what happened to Bill?

Even if I did care I wouldn't have time to devote to it right now. I've got a client coming in for a presentation at noon and my meeting room has been taken by the police, so as well as everything else I need to source a new venue. Terrific.

Apparently the board room is going to be a police interview room for the whole day while they conduct their enquiries here.

All sorts of rumours are doing the rounds about Bill. Initially we heard he was dead, but that's not the case. Critical but stable is the latest. Another hour and he would have died so the story goes. Critical but stable. It's an odd combination of words. On one hand it suggests it's the worst it could possibly get. On the other hand it suggests he'll get better. On the mend. Can be repaired.

He probably doesn't feel that way though.

I've decided to ignore all the rumours. I don't need to hear them. Besides, rumours are dangerous. On the morning of 9/11 there were seven aircraft missing at one point and the White House had been hit and at least 10,000 people had died in the twin towers. We love drama. We love bad news. We love delivering bad news.

Flashback: I'm on my knees in the club last night at a table full of girls, all in their mid 20s. Clive is there with me and we're singing "You've Lost That Loving Feeling", at the top of our voices. A couple of the girls egg us on. A couple bury their faces in their hands for shame. A couple are laughing out loud.

And still we sing. That's the problem with getting laid, it boosts your confidence. Sure, I paid for it, but I still got laid. Sure, it was an awful experience, but I still got laid. And now I'm so buoyed on confidence that I'm stupid enough to get down on my knees and sing to a group of girls in a night club.

One of them gets up. The one. My target. I'd been chatting her up at the bar for ten minutes and when she went back to her girlies I followed her with Clive and made him sing with me. And now she's standing in front of me looking down into my face looking up into hers. She's grinning widely trying her best to suppress her laughter. I'm such a tool sometimes.

I shudder the flashback away.

The police are conducting an investigation into what happened to Bill. Nobody seems to know the details but this is bad booze. It smells and tastes like it's going to hurt bad.

'Do we have a room for the meeting?' barks my new DD as he walks through the doorway. No greeting. No good morning. No kiss my arse. Nothing, just straight down to business.

'Being sorted as we speak,' I say.

'AV facilities?' he asks.

'Yep,' I say.

'Refreshments?'

'Ordered yesterday.'

He glares for a second then walks away. If his face were a state of being it would be disappointment. He wanted an excuse to give someone a kicking.

I stare at him as he walks back to his office until Yoda stirs me with a message from the Dark Side. An email. From Liz, the team PA. The room is ready for the client meeting. What would I do without her?

The client seems pleased with progress and the meeting is wrapped up by 2pm. Better than that, my hangover is gone and I'm ready to deal with the rest of the day.

On my way back to my desk I get intercepted by Liz who tells me the police want to see me now.

The two detectives sit on one side of the board room table while I sit on the other. The older, heavy guy asks all the questions while the younger, skinny guy operates the tape recorder. In the digital 21st Century of CSI and forensic analysis, Scotland Yard uses a tape recorder. He even needs to press the record and play buttons together. He probably still brings it home at weekends, sets it up next to the radio and prays for the DJ to shut up so he can record the latest songs. And maybe I'm being unfair. Maybe their hi-tech equipment is back at the station and this is just what they use off-site.

The interview is so much like something you would see on TV that I have to suppress the laughter. I'm in an episode of The Bill. Or Morse. Or that one with David Jason. Any moment now I'll blurt out my lines. The lines. The immortal lines.

'You got me bang to rights guv!' I should say.

'It's a fair cop,' I should say.

'I woulda gotten away with it if it waren't for them pesky kids!' I should say.

But I don't say any of these things. And I don't laugh. I don't say much.

This is serious.

And I'm nervous. I don't have any reason to be, but I am. Right now I don't know how anyone could pass a lie detector test. These detectives have a way of making you feel uncomfortable.

At fault.

Guilty.

It's like they know I've done something wrong even if it isn't the crime they're investigating.

Bill has been the subject of a vicious assault. They can't tell me any details but the older, heavy guy says it's one of the worst assaults he's ever witnessed and he's been in the force for 25 years.

None of us at work are suspects. Yet.

They are just building up a profile of Bill from those who knew him best. That includes people at work.

And his golf club.

And his drama society.

And his local pub.

And ex-employees.

They are trying to ascertain if Bill had any enemies. If he had fallen out with anyone. If he was in debt.

They ask me lots of questions. Generic shit that they will ask everyone. When did I last see Bill? Did I ever socialise with him outside of work? Did I know of anyone who bore a grudge against Bill? That kind of thing.

I think of the six people he made redundant. I think of the secretaries he has had affairs with before firing. I think of everyone who knows the wanker.

Still, you put two and two together and get six million. The generic questions. The net spread so wide you could get a blue whale through it. They haven't a clue who did this.

Apparently Bill was found in a lock-up garage. The younger, skinny detective tells me this when the older, heavy guy takes a call on his mobile. The call was urgent and confidential so he left the room and went into the office next door which is also being used by the police.

The young detective had to get it off his chest. On the verge of tears he tells me they found Bill strapped to a chair in the lock-up. Just an ordinary lock-up. Shelves piled high with rubbish that no man can throw away. Half full tins of paint. If they were half empty you'd probably throw them out. Scrappy bits of wood. Dust sheets. Boxes of junk. Old work clothes. Ropes. Cables. Rusted lengths of pipe. Myriad tools that have long since been replaced. Their replacements that have also long since been replaced.

The usual.

Including the solitary strip light across the ceiling.

At first glance the only thing that looked out of place was Bill on the chair. But the first thing to hit you was the smell. The stench of rotten meat.

Bill was unconscious strapped to a chair. Barely alive. And now he's critical but stable. They think he'll survive but he'll never be the same again. He's been maimed. Horribly.

But hey, nothing's impossible. Medical science has advanced enough in recent years to perform all sorts of miracles. Nowadays we're curing cancers. Repairing damaged organs.

Conducting transplants. Treating infectious diseases. Re-attaching limbs.

TV has taught us that it's imperative to have a bucket of ice handy in case you sever a limb. You put the limb in the ice and get to the nearest hospital quick as a blink. Of course, if the limb is a leg, driving may be difficult. And losing an arm brings about another set of problems. I suppose the hope is that if you sever a limb there will be somebody there to help you. The ice serves to freeze the damaged limb in suspended animation and it can be regenerated later. This can be done with all sorts of appendages. Fingers, toes, noses, penises…you name it, if it can be severed it can be re-attached.

The second thing they noticed that looked out of place, the younger skinny detective tells me, was the bucket of water on the floor next to Bill.

In the 21st Century we have learned so much and moved onto another level of existence. We're sophisticated beings who can think our way out of problems. Out of crises. We're so sophisticated we have turned our back on our natural instincts. We no longer need to hunt. We no longer need to fight or defend. We no longer need to find a cave or tree for shelter. Nor do we need to strike flint to spark dead vegetation into fire for heat.

We've given up our instincts the way we've evolved out of our fins. They're lost and gone forever. We've evolved.

Moved on.

Built that bridge and got over it.

But then, as the proverb suggests, old habits die hard.

And so pregnant women nest. And men congregate around the Barbie. And even non-swimmers crave the ocean.

And there are some things that make a woman a woman. And some things that make a man a man.

The third and final thing that looked out of place was the blender.

At first glance Bill just looked unconscious in the chair. But when they got closer they realised he was wearing grey trousers. They just looked black because of all the blood. They couldn't see the blood on the black floor but around Bill a huge puddle of the sticky goo had formed.

214

He was about an hour away from bleeding to death. I bet he wishes he had.

But he didn't. And now he's critical but stable. Earlier in the day, the younger skinny detective tells me, Bill did regain consciousness briefly. Just long enough to give some details of his ordeal. Vague, sketchy details. The searing, excruciating pain. The fear. The horror. Watching it sitting in the bucket of ice. Then being removed from the ice and put into the blender. Watching his genitals being turned into a smoothie and then being force-fed that smoothie. Then vomiting that smoothie.

There are some things, no matter how tough you are, that break you. There are some things from which you never recover.

Some things make a woman a woman. And some things make a man a man.

And some things once broken can never be repaired. No matter how far medical science has advanced.

Bill didn't see who attacked him.

Of course he didn't. We were wearing balaclavas.

Apple Sours

Katie buys me a drink. It's called an Apple Sour. Just like Ronseal, it does exactly what it says on the tin. I think in advertising terms. Some people say you are what you eat. That's rubbish. You are your work. And what I mean about an Apple Sour doing exactly what it says on the tin is that it tastes of apple and it's sour. My face when I down it is the kind of face you pull when you bite into a lemon. Or a grapefruit. Katie laughs at this. It's not a pleasant drink Katie admits. I wonder why she bought it then. She also had one. Why would she drink it if she doesn't like it? Because it's got a secret she tells me.

'Apple sours freshen the breath,' she says.

'They're great for refreshing your mouth and making your breath smell nice,' she says. It's true. My mouth does feel refreshed.

'This is important,' Katie says, 'when you're about to snog someone for the first time.'

Katie snogs me.

Katie and I met earlier in the evening. I'd gone out for a few drinks with Clive. Katie was in the pub. Clive went to the toilet and Katie came over to say hi. I didn't see Clive again all night.

216

By the time Katie planted that snog on me, we were in a club. She had said that she wanted to go dancing. But when we got there I bought a couple of drinks and we stood at the bar. Before we had even touched the other drinks Katie bought the Apple Sours. Then Katie snogged me.

'Apple Sours rock,' says Katie and smiles. 'You have lovely soft lips. Let's go.'

'But we just got here,' I say. 'We haven't even touched our other drinks. Besides, I thought you wanted to dance.'

'Oh we're going to dance,' says Katie. 'We're going to dance at my place,' says Katie winking at me as she grabs my hand and leads me through the crowd.

Christ, have I really been out of the game so long that I no longer know how it's played?

Katie is snoring gently beside me. It's so gentle there should be another word for it. When you think of snoring you think of a rumbling, aggressive thunder. The kind of thing that could cause an avalanche. Katie's snore isn't like that. It's more like a zephyr rustling leaves. A faint whisper. Birdsong at such a distance it's on the edge of hearing. I'm staring at Katie snoring and I'm trying to understand what just happened. She's sleeping, snoring without a care. I can't sleep. It's been months since I had sex. Well, sex like that. Sex that I didn't pay for. Years since I had sex three times in one night. Christ, Helen and I didn't even do that on holiday in recent years. What's wrong with me? Most blokes would be grinning like Cheshire cats if they were me. Me? I just feel like a traitor. My marriage is over. I'm in bed with a beautiful woman. The sun's up and the birds are singing. And I've never felt so much like a sack of shit. My marriage is over. My marriage is over. My marriage is over. It doesn't matter how often I repeat the mantra, it still feels like betrayal.

Katie opens her eyes and yawns. She blinks a few times and rubs them. She stretches. She yawns again.

'Hi,' she says. 'Looks like a beautiful morning. Do you have any plans today?' she asks.

I've got a busy day sitting on my arse in front of shit TV. I've got a fridge full of beer to drink. I've got nothing to do and all day to do it.

'I have to leave,' I say.

I get out of bed and start getting dressed.

'Is something wrong?' Katie asks 'Have I upset you? Why are you leaving?'

Yes, there's something wrong. No, she hasn't upset me. I'm leaving because I have to.

'It's not you,' I say, 'it's me.' Cop out of all cop outs.

Katie pulls the duvet up to her chin and holds it tight. She's fighting back tears. She looks embarrassed. Humiliated. Vulnerable.

This is my fault. This is not Clive's doing. Helen hasn't landed this on me. This is not a failing of society or any politician. I can't pin the blame on anyone or anything else. I'm the perpetrator here. It's my fault. It's me.

'Look,' I say, 'I'm really sorry. But I'm in a really bad place right now.' Why can't I stop speaking in clichés? 'This is not your fault. You're a lovely girl,' I say.

Katie looks scared. On the bed-side table there's a pen and a set of post-it notes. I write my name and number on it. My real name and number.

'I'd like to see you again,' I say. 'But there's no pressure. Give me a call in a few days if you feel like it,' I say.

I leave.

Christmas

It's the first time for eight years that we're all together at Christmas. Except for Helen of course. We used to alternate Christmas holidays between her family and mine and there were a couple of occasions when either Jim or Claire were away with their families and I was home. So it's the first time in eight years. Hungover is the only way to greet that kind of dawning realisation.

Mum's been fizzing around in an excited blur for weeks. It's like somebody filled her full of blue Smarties and Coke and shook her really hard.

But I must say it's been nice. Pleasant. Calm. Even with Mum buzzing about like the Duracell Bunny.

I even went to mass with her last night. Voluntarily.

And then I went and worshipped at my own church with my brother and his wife. We worshipped until about 3am. And I'm feeling it now.

At least my sister's gaggle of kids hasn't arrived yet.

And without kids around it's way too early for this shit. There's something perverse about five adults being up at 7am when we don't have to go to work. Unless we've not actually made it to bed yet. But that's not the case.

We've done the present thing and the happy family thing and now I think everyone just wants to be back in bed.

'Right,' I say, 'I'm going to make breakfast.'

Something of a tradition started about ten years ago and we have enjoyed the same breakfast Christmas morning ever since – eggs Benedict and Champagne. I always play chef when I'm around and this year is no different.

Mum's got the turkey in the oven and is preparing veg. Frank Sinatra's insisting we have ourselves a merry little Christmas. My brother and sister-in-law are tidying up a bit before everyone else arrives and my Dad is lighting the fire. It's pleasant. It's nice. It's the kind of scene you get in cheesy American movies.

I even go over to Mum, peck her on the cheek, give her a big hug and wish her a merry Christmas. I tell her I love her and she tells me she loves me too. Then she tells me it will all work out fine in the end and I tell her I know.

Sometimes you know how it's going to end before it begins and I know I'm going to have a blazing row with someone before the day is through. I push the thought from my mind and tell myself I'm just being silly.

Dad sings along with Frank. Mum joins in. The rest of us abstain for no other reason than sometimes you can have a bit too much cheese on corn. Although I do catch my brother smiling and I am too.

We've got maybe a couple of hours before Claire arrives with the kids. A couple of hours of peace. A couple of hours of calm. Claire's kids are great and I'm looking forward to spending the day with them but they manufacture noise on a never-ending production line.

Even the prospect of noisy kids doesn't dampen my enthusiasm for the day and I'm determined to just go with whatever everyone wants and enjoy it. Well, whatever Mum wants anyway.

Over breakfast the fun mood continues. Even my brother's God-awful wife is playing happy families. So much so that we're all still sitting at the table chatting long after breakfast is finished when Claire swarms in with her gaggle.

If I had to pick a point when the day started to go wrong, Claire's arrival would be it. You can only have so much of a good thing, so the saying goes. On the flip side of that, we tend to endure an awful lot of a bad thing.

Claire's completely stressed out and ready to kill her kids. She's laying down the law with two of them who have been fighting all morning as she walks through the kitchen door. One of them is crying, the other sulking. The other three don't even make it into the kitchen but head straight to the sitting room to set up the Playstation. Bang goes TV for the day.

Claire's mood seems contagious and around the table the rest of us are suddenly the picture of misery. Except Mum who has decided to be Polyanna.

'Claire, darling…' she begins but that's as far as she gets.

'Don't start Mum!' warns Claire and Mum lapses into silence. Claire stops for a moment and takes in her surroundings properly and seems to come to a decision. The rest of us watch her to see what will happen next. She walks over to a cupboard and gets a wine glass. She comes over to the table, grabs the bottle of bubbly and fills her glass. As quickly as she filled it she empties it down her throat. She sits down and sighs.

'Fucking needed that,' she says.

The tone is set.

After that the day deteriorates whirlpool style beginning with leisurely loops around the top, gaining speed and depth slowly at first but quicker with each revolution until it's spiralling uncontrollably downwards into oblivion.

The kids seem to take it in turns to cry. It's almost passed from one to the next like that bopping electricity dance from the 80s. The circus just seems to gain momentum with each new phase. Noise and presents, sweets and video games, bickering and bitching, tears and mess.

Dinner arrives too soon after breakfast, so Mum gets a face on because nobody has an appetite. Mid-afternoon most of us are pretty well on the way to getting sloshed.

By the time we flop out in the sitting room, snidy comments have already been shot across boughs. The TV has been re-comandeered by the adults and the kids are bored without their video games. And of the adults, the only one really watching is Mum. Shitty Shitty Bang Bang. Dad's asleep. Jim and his wife are in the kitchen having a "chat". The raised whispers make the kitchen a No Go Zone for everyone else.

Almost out of boredom Claire starts speaking.

'It's amazing,' she says, 'but every year we spend a small fortune on Christmas presents and the kids end up playing with the boxes and wrapping paper.'

Before I realise what I'm doing my eyes have rolled Heavenwards and I let out a tired sigh.

'I'm sorry,' she says with irritation, 'wrong again, am I?'

'No,' I say quickly, 'it's just that everyone says that, don't they? It's become such a cliché.'

'I suppose so,' she says after a pause. 'I hadn't really thought about it. God, it's such a predictable thing to say,' she says with real self-horror in her voice.

'It's not just kids who do it, though,' I hear myself say.

'What? So, are you saying that adults play with the wrapping paper rather than the presents?' she asks and laughs.

'All the time,' I say. 'We work jobs we hate instead of focusing on the things we want to do. We offer up small talk instead of trying to resolve relationship problems. The music we listen to, the TV programmes we watch, the magazines we read – they're all becoming more and more wrapping paper with no content. We are actively trying to delude ourselves into thinking our lives are better than they really are,' I say.

'We have been given the greatest gifts ever and we're afraid to play with them. So we mess around with the wrapping paper instead. We're so afraid of failure that we don't risk anything anymore.'

'My God you can be depressing,' she says.

I sigh.

'If you've got such an insight into everybody's failings then what's the answer?' she says.

'I don't know,' I admit, 'I don't claim to have any solutions and I'm as bad as everyone else. But as far as I can see we live until we die and everything else in between is pretty much a failure.'

And as Claire is about to respond, as I get ready to retaliate to her retaliation, as we get ready to move to Def Con 3, my mobile rings.

Saved by the bell.

Helen.

And I think frying pan to fire.

'Merry Christmas,' she says when I answer.

Claire sits scowling with her arms folded.

'Merry Christmas,' I reply, 'how are you?'

'Yeah fine, thanks,' says Helen, 'you?'

Small talk. Filling space. Murdering language.

We insist on saying lots more nothing for a few minutes – any news? Where are you spending Christmas? How's work? That kind of thing. The usual.

She's just phoning to wish me a happy Christmas and see how I am. And then something I don't expect.

'Are you seeing anyone?' she asks.

'Er, no, no…you?' I say.

'No,' she replies. 'Been on any dates or had any flings?' she asks.

I think of the lawyer at 80s night. I think of my visit to the "professionals". I think of me singing on my knees. I think of Katie.

'No,' I say, 'you?'

'Not really,' she says.

What does that mean? Not really! Does it mean yes? Does it mean no? Does it mean I might be?

'Yeah right!' I hear myself say.

'What do you mean by that?' demands Helen.

I pause, kicking myself for letting my guard slip. And then it hits me. I'm not the one in the wrong here.

'You know what it means,' I say.

'No,' she says, 'I don't think I do.' If words were solid, if words were tangible, hers would be huge blocks of ice. Big enough to sink Titanic.

'Come on, Helen,' I say, 'Stop playing games. I know you've been seeing someone else.'

Everything in the room stops and suddenly everyone is looking at me. Including Dad who had obviously been pretending to be asleep in order to stay out of trouble. I leave the sitting room and close the door behind me.

'Oh really?' says Helen. 'Well that's news to me. Would you care to tell me who I've been seeing and how it's any of your bloody business?' she says.

I don't know how it's happened but mercury quick I've lost the high ground.

Before I say the name I realise how stupid it sounds. Helen always hated Gary. She always thought he was a slime. I say his name anyway.

'Gary!?' she shouts. 'Fucking Gary!? That prick?! That's who you think I've been seeing?'

Any other name wouldn't have been as daft. My Dad. My Mum. The Easter Bunny. Anyone.

'You're not then?' I whisper.

'No of course I'm fucking not, you moron!' she screams. 'Jesus Christ! If he were the last man alive and I were the last woman…' she says. Even at our angriest it seems we can't avoid descending to cliché.

'Is that really what you think of me after all these years? And to think I was having second thoughts about my decision to end it,' she says.

It's like jumping into cold water. Suddenly I'm alive. Animated.

'Helen,' I begin. 'I'm sorry. It was stupid of me,' I say.

'Yes it was!' she snaps. 'But worse than that, it was typical of you,' she says. 'At least typical of you over the last couple of years. Do me a favour and go fuck yourself,' she says and hangs up.

I stare at my phone and wonder how I could have been so thick. Foolish. Stupid. Helen called me a moron. Well if the cap fits…

Merry.

Fucking.

Christmas.

Sanitised genocide

The bar is dormouse quiet and cold enough to see my breath in the air. It may be winter outside but it's definitely colder in here. Jack the barman looks miserable as ever though so at least there's some consistency. He sees me walk through the doorway and he reaches for a couple of pint glasses and starts to pour.

'Jesus, Jack, is the air con stuck on Arctic or something?' I ask rubbing my hands together for warmth.

'The punters prefer it that way,' says Jack, 'they like the cold. Besides, they start to smell if it gets too warm,' he says.

I pay for the drinks and wander over to our table where Clive is sitting with his head back and eyes closed.

'Wassup dude?' says Clive as I sit.

He opens his eyes and picks up his glass. We clink and drink. He knocks back half his pint and lets go a huge belch.

'Nice!' I say.

'Natural,' he says wiping his mouth with the back of his hand.

'We waste too much time and energy suppressing natural instincts, bruv,' he says.

'If you need to burp, you should burp. If you need to fart, you should fart. If you need to kick the shit out of someone...' he says and leaves it hanging in the air.

I don't think we need to be twins in order for me to finish his train of thought. But I don't say anything. I just look at him. He grins at me.

'The leap from farting to fighting isn't so great,' he says. 'Come on, bruv,' he says, 'it's not such a big deal.'

'They weren't even seeing each other,' I say. 'She hates Gary,' I say. 'There's no way in the world she would have gone with him,' I say.

'That's not what you thought at the time,' says Clive and he stares at me. I stare right back and for a few moments neither of us says anything.

'Look,' I say eventually, 'I know it was my fault and that's why I don't want to make the same mistake again. I don't want someone getting hurt because of me for no reason,' I say.

'Bruv, you can't let one mistake change your plans,' says Clive. 'You know you're taking the right action and that it's not always going to work out perfectly along the way. But more often than not the ones we target will deserve what they get.'

'But it was a huge mistake!' I protest.

'No it wasn't,' says Clive evenly. 'The first World War was a huge mistake. The Atomic Bomb was a huge mistake. Electing Maggie Thatcher was a huge mistake. In the company of those events, kicking the shit out of Gary wasn't even an error of judgement. He's such a cock he deserved it anyway. Besides, at least you're big enough to admit when you've messed up. These days you can't find a single soul who voted for Maggie.'

'Yeah,' I say, 'it's amazing how often the shared accountability of democracy becomes mass denial.'

'Democracy isn't all it's cracked up to be,' says Clive. 'Granted, it's the best we've come up with, but that says more about our limitations and defects than it does about the brilliance of the system.'

'The great thing about democracy is that everyone has the vote. But the awful thing about democracy is that everyone has the vote. In a world populated by responsible beings it would be wonderful. But we live in a world populated by morons. Worse than that, they're lazy morons. Strike that, we're lazy morons,' says Clive and he picks up his pint and takes a swig.

He's in his stride now and I'm waiting for the clarity. Since my conversation with Helen I've been in turmoil. Confused about what I'm doing. Where I'm going. Learning that Helen and Gary weren't having an affair knocked me sideways. It shook the foundations of the plan. Our plan. My plan. I needed Clive to reassure me that what we were doing was right. That I was taking the right action. The right path. Clive always puts things back in perspective.

Clive's eyes turn toward the TV screen which has just flickered into life to show the faceless silhouette and warped scales. Then he looks back to me.

'We, the electorate, are the problem,' says Clive. 'Nowadays we form our political opinions by watching Michael Moore documentaries. Or worse, Hollywood blockbusters where the All-American hero saves the day. We never ask the right questions. We watch the news and see the carnage caused by a suicide bomber in Kabul and we're told they're brainwashed and we believe it. We don't wonder how they got to the state where they are willing to do such a thing. We've become great at apathy.'

On the TV screen Libra is warning the public of the dangers of complacency.

'We go to war under the 45 minute threat and the Prime Minister holds onto power,' says Clive. 'Jean Charles de Menezes is mistakenly shot to death by the police and the Chief Commissioner gets to keep his job. Why? Because we're too lazy to hold them accountable and kick them out, that's why.'

On the TV screen Libra is advocating the virtues of taking responsibility for our actions.

'Too much is said and done in our names that will eventually come back to haunt us,' says Clive. 'We've already been attacked by suicide bombers and that won't end until we reverse the trend. And that reversal needs to start on a personal level. I mean how can we possibly hope to correct things on a national level when we don't even confront our personal problems?

'Bruv, all we are doing is shaking off the laziness, taking control of our destiny and being accountable. That's all,' says Clive.

He pauses to take a drink but he's not finished. I say nothing and wait for him to speak.

'We're in danger. And the reason we're in danger is because we have become lazy. Make no mistake about it our apathy is the greatest threat to us.

We might like to think we live in a nice and fair society, but the truth is our wealth and security has been built on centuries of war and greed. Centuries of corruption and abuse. Centuries of colonialism and genocide. Thing is, for most people if it happens far enough away then it doesn't happen at all. It's just sanitised genocide.

Problem is, it's still happening. As long as we accept politicians who take us to war under false pretences, as long as we accept a government that still rules other nations, as long as we accept a Prime Minister who is willing to invade a weaker country and rape natural resources thousands of miles away, then we endorse that war. That greed. That murder and corruption and abuse. And our freedom and security, our wealth and lifestyles, our homes and careers are all direct benefits of those policies. We might as well pull the trigger ourselves. Sanitised genocide.'

On the TV screen Libra is explaining that we are as much to blame as the politicians for the world's problems.

'It's like shopping for meat,' says Clive, 'we go to the supermarket and pick up a nice juicy steak on a polystyrene board, shrink-wrapped in cling-film. Just because we don't witness the slaughter of the animal it doesn't mean it doesn't happen.'

'Surely you're not comparing national foreign policy with what we're doing?' I ask.

'Bruv, one is just a microcosm of the other,' says Clive. 'In the same way the public turns a blind eye to bullying politicians we turn a blind eye to bullying bosses. So called mates and pillars of society who think their shit don't smell are the same people.

We're righting the wrongs done to us,' says Clive. 'That's all we're doing. Think about it: Gary, the old guy in the pub,

Bill...they all had it coming. In one way or another they have fucked you over and we are just getting them back. And this is just the beginning.'

On the TV screen Libra says: "And this is just the beginning."

'We have to stop pretending we're innocent of our government's actions and decisions and take some responsibility for our lives. But we have to start by sorting out our own shit before we can sort out the nation's. And we have to become accountable. We have to correct the wrongs done to us and the wrongs done on our behalf. Because make no mistake about it, our homes are just spoils of war.'

On the TV screen Libra says: "Our homes are just spoils of war".

'Our careers are weapons of mass destruction,' says Clive.

On the TV screen Libra says: "Our careers are weapons of mass destruction".

'These beers might as well be the blood of our faceless victims,' says Clive.

On the TV screen Libra says: "Our beers might as well be the blood of our faceless victims".

I look at Clive. Then at the screen. I look back to Clive. Then back to the screen. That voice. That eerie, doctored, distorted voice. I knew it sounded familiar. You strip away the distorted, warped sound effects and all you're left with is Clive.

Scratching the itch

It's a fucking minefield. Spending so long with one person. And it's not healthy. You get too used to each other. You know what works. It's too easy. Don't get me wrong, that doesn't make it boring. Far from it. When you're with someone for a long time that's when you're really comfortable enough to experiment. Single people can talk all they like about their experiences but until you've been in a long loving relationship you don't really relax and let yourself go.

Thing is, I'd forgotten what things were like before Helen. I'd forgotten the minefield. Now I'm back out there I never know what to expect. The things that worked with Helen, well, let's just say they're not universal.

Like talking dirty. We'd be getting it on. We'd kiss each other all over. We'd undress each other slowly. Tenderly. Gently. We'd caress and stroke. We'd, well, you see where I'm going with this. And when the time was right, when the momentum had been building, and building and building, when there was no going back sometimes I'd ask her: 'Do you want me to fuck you?'

Sometimes she'd practically beg. Sometimes she'd give me a cheeky smile. Other times she'd let her body do the talking.

I asked the same question to a girl the other night and, well, let's just say she doesn't talk dirty. No, she doesn't talk dirty, she talks sarky. When I asked her if she wanted me to fuck her she said no, that she'd prefer to clean the flat. That stopped me in my tracks and no mistake.

'I'm joking,' she qualified, 'I've just come in your mouth and you ask if I want you to fuck me? What do you think I want you to do?'

I got back with the programme after that and things were going fine. Until I opened my mouth again that is. You'd think I'd learn my lesson.

'God, you're so wet,' I told her.

'Yeah, that's because I'm thinking of Brad Pitt right now,' she said.

If there's an opposite to an aphrodisiac, that's it.

Yeah, you'd think I'd learn my lesson. But I don't.

The other problem with spending so long with one person is that you feel nothing with anyone else. The intimacy and emotions you share with a long term partner don't happen straight away and that's hard to accept when you're back out there. Everything's new. Every act is guarded. Every move is the next in a calculating game of chess.

You're not supposed to phone or text too soon after a date because you appear too eager. Likewise, leave it too long and you blow your chance. Initially you have to be all fun and leave the serious stuff for the future. But leave it too long and soon enough you get the "Where are we going?" speech.

After being in a long relationship, those kind of mind games get boring very quickly. So you go to the other extreme. You aim to feel nothing for anyone. All you want from anyone is sex. Unattached, unloving, uncomplicated sex.

But that comes with its own set of problems.

Like another night not too long ago. We were fucking for the sake of fucking. We didn't even fancy each other. At least, I didn't fancy her and she didn't seem too keen on finding out too much about me apart from how I could perform and what kind of

231

drugs I had on me. Strike that, she wasn't even interested in my performance.

This is the kind of thing Mary Whitehouse would censor. Puritans gasping behind lily-white perfectly manicured, soft, gentle hands. The kind of hands that have never done any wrong. Probably never a day's work either. Never even masturbated. Or at least that's what they would have you believe. But secretly they can't wait for the privacy of their own homes so they can strip down to suspenders and marigolds and get to work with the baby oil. They can't wait to lick each others' asses and whiff that pungent, yet erotic aroma. We spend all our lives disguising our natural, animal fragrances with deodorant and perfume and cologne and oils – all made from other animals – in order to make us more attractive to each other. But when it gets down to the nitty gritty it's the natural aroma of the nether regions that arouse and revolt, entice and repulse, excite and abhor us. The animal takes over. But then, what do you expect? You can't flick a switch and turn back millions of years of genetic engineering.

Sniffing a pussy for the first time is like your first taste of beer. You take that first mouthful of beer and you've never tasted anything so vile in your whole life. But it's compelling, it keeps drawing you back and you want it more and more. It's a Jezebel.

It's the same with pussy. You smell it before you taste it and it almost makes your eyes water. But you can't help tasting it anyway. And before you know it you're lapping away like the cat that got the cream and there's a part of you a cat couldn't scratch. Animal instinct.

Puritans, zealots, parents, all sorts of nuts can preach all they like against the evils of sex, but words can't tell your dick what it wants.

Problem is you always eventually want more than your dick.

Eventually sex alone isn't enough.

You need more.

Problem is, how do you scratch that itch?

'What do you want?' she snaps when she eventually answers her phone. I've left countless messages for her over the last few days. I've sent text messages and emails and she has replied to none of them. But I wasn't going to give up.

'Hi', I reply.

'What do you want?' she demands again.

'To apologise,' I say, 'I'm so sorry Hels. I was an idiot and I don't know what I was thinking. I'm so confused and all sorts of nonsense has been running through my mind but that's no excuse and I should have known…no, strike that, I did know that you were not with Gary,' I say.

Helen is quiet.

So am I for a few seconds but the silence is unbearable and I have to fill it.

'Please believe me, Helen, I'm so sorry,' I say again.

'It really hurt me,' she says softly.

'I know.'

'How could you possibly think I would go with the prick?'

'I don't know. I really don't know where my head was. It was a complete misunderstanding and I feel like such an arse,' I say.

'OK,' she says softly, 'well, thanks for apologising.'

'Are you ok?' I ask.

'Yeah, I guess so.'

'Are we ok?' I ask.

'Yeah,' she says, 'well, I suppose we're not ok the way we used to be ok when we were together, but we're ok as far as our new situation is concerned,' she qualifies with a bit of fun.

Our new situation. No ambiguity there.

'Fair enough,' I say. 'So what have you been up to?' I ask.

'Oh, you know, this and that. Shagging Gary mainly,' she says and starts laughing. I laugh too. It was such an idiotic thing to ever think could happen.

'How about you?' she asks, 'how have you been?'

'Oh ok, busy and bored at the same time. Nothing changes, the rest remains the same. You know!'

'Yeah, well listen, I've got to go, but thanks for calling – I really appreciate it. And we must go for a coffee soon.'

'Yeah,' I say, 'give me a call when you're free and we'll catch up.'

I hang up.

But all I want to do is talk to Helen.

Chimera

I knock gently on the half open door and say hello. I lean in and poke my head into the empty room. Not that it's completely empty. There's furniture and equipment and all that you would expect from a GP's surgery, but what I mean is Doctor Jones isn't there. His absence makes the room more than empty, like it's missing a couple of walls or the ceiling or something.

The computer hums its white noise, the clock ticks water torture style, the radiator hisses heat on the edge of hearing, but I'd hear none of these if Doctor Jones were here.

Doctor Jones is a "character". Full of life. Always ready with a quip. An endless stream of catchphrases that get repeated more than episodes of Friends. If his recycling of jokes were good for the environment he'd save the planet on his own.

I wander in and sit in the guest chair. Looking around the surgery I half read standard medical charts that are tacked to the walls: The Bones of the Human Skeleton. The Heart and its Diseases; The Organs of the Body; Lung Cancer and How to Prevent it. Charts that mean everything and nothing. Charts that are only relevant to anyone when they get ill. People with sclerosis of the liver could pass any exam on that organ. Even

234

the most uneducated sufferer of osteoporosis could deliver lectures on the structure of bones. Trust me on this, if you have a heart attack you will bore everyone who loves you with your incessant preaching on the evils of cholesterol for the rest of your life.

'Good morning!' booms Doctor Jones ending my studious interest in Human Chromosomes and Genes.

'Good morning, doctor,' I reply and in my head I trot out his next line which I've heard on every previous visit to his surgery.

'I hope you're well,' says Doctor Jones rising to my silent challenge, 'but you're probably not if you're here!' he quips and laughs at his own joke.

I sigh.

He shakes me firmly by the hand and sits opposite me in his chair. He picks up my file which was lying on his desk and starts flicking through it.

'Now then,' he says, 'what can I do for you today?'

'Well, your secretary called me to make an appointment,' I reply, 'because of a routine blood test that was carried out,' I qualify.

'Ah yes, that's right,' says Doctor Jones, 'after a fight, I believe,' he says and looks at me over the top of his glasses. In fairness, it's not a disapproving look, but more quizzical.

'That's right, doctor,' I reply.

Doctor Jones closes the file and places it on the desk.

'Normally permission must be sought to conduct blood tests,' he begins, 'but there are occasions when approval is unnecessary. One such occasion is when blood may have been accidentally passed amongst people. In such cases the potential health risk to others is key and it is essential to determine whether communicable diseases may have also been transmitted.'

Oh God I'm dying. Why else would he be telling me this?

'In the fight a number of people sustained wounds which could have transferred both bloods and diseases so it was essential that these tests were conducted.'

Hepatitis. Typhoid. AIDS. It could be anything.

'I'm just telling you this so you understand why the tests were necessary,' he says.

Ebola, Cholera, Tuberculosis.

'The good news is that no diseases were transmitted between any of the parties,' he says.

I let go an audible sigh of relief.

'But the test did throw up an interesting anomaly in your case,' he says.

Oh God! What does that mean? An interesting anomaly?

Cancer. What else could it be? You can't catch it but it shows up in blood tests.

'Don't worry,' says Doctor Jones, 'there's nothing wrong with you and you're perfectly healthy.'

So what's the anomaly? Why doesn't he just get to the point?

'Have you ever heard the term "Chimera" before?' asks Doctor Jones.

'You mean the ancient Greek mythological creature?' I ask, 'the monster with the body of a lion and the head of a goat?' I ask.

Where is he going with this? Is this some sort of a new disease? A super-bug composed of half bacteria and half virus?

'Ah! I see you know your classics,' he says.

'But no, I'm not referring to ancient monsters here, but to a medical term,' he says. 'Having said that, the condition is named after the ancient mythical beast because of its unique make-up.'

Great! I have a condition! The day just gets better.

'Although,' continues Doctor Jones, 'my use of the term "unique" is somewhat misleading,' and he starts chuckling.

At his own joke.

Again.

And then the chuckle becomes a laugh. A big belly laugh. Right now, with his big laugh, his big belly laugh, he reminds me of Dr. Hibbert on the Simpsons. I'm tempted to give him a condition.

I have a condition.

Worse than that, I have a condition I know nothing about and this guy is laughing at it.

Laughing at me.

Doctor Jones stops laughing and pulls himself together. He looks at me and clears his throat.

'The extraordinary thing about a chimera,' says Doctor Jones, 'is that it is a fusion like no other. You see every living thing has a unique set of DNA. Except for a chimera which has at least two sets.'

'How is that possible, Doctor?' I ask.

Suddenly I feel cold and I shiver. A waft of sunscreen and hash drifts past my nose.

'We need to leave,' says Clive startling me. He's standing right beside me and I didn't even know he was there.

'What?' I say to Clive, 'what are you talking about?'

'We need to leave. Now. Come on.'

Doctor Jones looks at me and clears his throat again.

'Are you ok?' asks Doctor Jones.

'Me? I'm fine,' I say, 'sorry Doctor. Please continue.'

'Don't listen to this guy,' says Clive, 'he's a quack. You know it. I know it. Come on, let's go.'

I ignore him and concentrate on what Doctor Jones is saying.

'You see, we have only recently been able to determine chimeras and we believe it explains a number of other conditions which have long perplexed medical science including Vanishing Twin Syndrome,' says Doctor Jones.

'Vanishing Twin Syndrome?' I ask.

'We're leaving now,' says Clive and he starts to lift me from the seat.

'Stop it!' I tell him. 'Doctor Jones is trying to tell me something important!'

'Er, are you sure you're ok?' asks Doctor Jones, concern etched into his voice.

'I'm fine, Doctor, honest. Please continue,' I say and I shush Clive into silence.

Doctor Jones looks at me again and then glances at Clive. Or at least, he glances in Clive's direction but seems to look past him. Through him.

'Ok,' says Doctor Jones, 'it used to be quite common for a pregnant woman to be told she was carrying twins and then told at a later date that she had only one baby. It was thought that these phantom babies may have been miscarried but the placenta remained intact to service the surviving twin. We now know that in many cases the dead twin's foetus gets absorbed into the placenta and subsequently into the surviving twin. So the surviving twin carries two sets of DNA. That surviving twin is a chimera.'

'I told you he's a quack,' says Clive grabbing my arm, 'now come on, we're leaving.'

I shrug him off.

'What are you telling me?' I ask Doctor Jones.

He sighs.

'You're a bright guy,' says Doctor Jones, 'You know what I'm telling you. You had a vanishing twin. You are a chimera.'

The Tombstone

The bar is dormouse quiet. No jukebox, no TV, no mind pureeing shrill squeaks from game machines. No banter. Just a few sad, lonely punters nursing their drinks and wondering what happened to their lives.

Clive gets the drinks in and decides we need a couple of chasers to go with the beers. I don't object. In fact, I could do with a good, stiff drink after my appointment with Doctor Jones.

Clive takes his seat opposite me and I find myself thinking: who got the drinks in?

He raises his glass and we clink and drink. He puts his pint down and wipes his mouth.

'Fuck him!' he says, 'I told you he was a quack.'

'Is he?' I say quietly. 'Is he really?'

Clive treats me to one of his stares. The one that says: careful how you tread.

I stare right back.

Clive breathes out, takes a swig of his pint and looks away. He wipes his mouth and looks back at me. A softer look this time. Brimming with understanding.

'Look bruv,' he says, 'you've known Doctor Jones is a quack for long enough. I reckon he got hit in the head too many times when he was playing rugger!'

Clive starts to chuckle at his own weak, pathetic attempt at a joke. But I don't laugh. It's not funny. If my stare were dangerous, I'd be Medusa.

Clive stops chuckling.

He clears his throat and leans forward ready to speak.

'The last time you went to Doctor Jones he prescribed Ponston for migraines and it turned out you needed glasses, as an optician found out. Before that your chest infection turned out to be a collapsed lung after three different antibiotics failed to clear it up. I know most GPs are a bit too G and don't P enough, but this guy takes the biscuit. Remember when he told Dad he was a hypochondriac and then Dad had the heart attack? All he had to do was check his bloods and he would have found out his pressure and cholesterol were through the fucking Empire State roof! The guy's a quack. You know it. I know it. Everyone fucking knows it. Jesus Christ, I reckon his own family probably go somewhere else!'

I soften. How could I not?

'I know,' I say, 'but he couldn't see you mate! How could he not see you standing right there in front of him in his office?! He looked right through you!'

Clive rolls his eyes to Heaven.

'That's because he's a quack!' he virtually screams at me. I look around the pub, conscious of not wanting to make a scene. But nobody has stirred. All the other punters are still in the same positions. Didn't even flinch. Still staring into their drinks wondering what happened to their lives.

'Ok mate, keep it down,' I say.

'Well it's hard…'

Clive continues talking but I can't hear a word because a police siren wails outside the pub. I lean in straining to hear what he's saying as the flashing blue lights flicker through the stained glass windows dappling Clive's face with colour. Mercifully the sirens stop but the blue lights keep flashing.

He's finished saying whatever it was he was saying.

240

'What was that mate?' I say, 'I couldn't hear you with the sirens.'

Clive's mouth moves again but again I can't hear him as some lads have started shouting behind us.

This is becoming irritating. The blue lights flicker across Clive's face and his mouth continues to move but I can't hear a word. Instead all I hear is indecipherable noise from behind us getting closer. Clive's mouth stops moving again and his expression changes. Becomes blank. Suddenly he looks sick.

'Are you ok?' I ask.

He looks almost transluscent. Growing more and more washed out by the second. The flashing blue lights almost shining through his skin, his face, his head until…oh my God, I can see the wall through his head! He's disappearing before my eyes. Vanishing.

'Clive!' I say, 'what's happening?'

His mouth moves, speaking to me, imploring to me, but I can't hear a thing. And this time it's not other noise blocking it out, it's that it's too weak to hear.

'Are you ok?' asks a concerned voice behind me.

'Yeah Clive, are you ok?' I echo.

His mouth moves again, but without conviction. And all the while he grows fainter and fainter.

'Sir, are you ok?' asks the voice behind me again.

I reach out to grab Clive's hand, but just before I touch it a hand lands on my shoulder.

I look around and up into the face but I can't discern who it is with the flashing blue light shining in my eyes.

'Can I help you?' I ask.

'The question is can I help you, Sir?' asks the policeman who I now see as I shield my eyes from the blue lights.

'No I'm fine thanks,' I say, 'I'm just having a pint with my brother, officer.'

'Right,' says the policeman looking at Clive. Or at least where Clive was. I see now he's disappeared again. Disturbing me more though is the fact that the whole pub seems to have disappeared. The whole thing. The bar, the tables, the chairs, the four walls and ceiling. The flock fucking wallpaper. The sad lonely patrons with their sad empty lives. Jack the moaning barman. Gone. All gone. Like it was never there.

I look down at my feet where empty Heineken cans litter a grave. My breath steams on the January air in front of me and as it clears I make out a headstone. A gravestone. Tombstone. Moonlight illuminates the epitaph – Jack 'Barman & Friend' Roberts.

I look around and I'm surrounded by graves. Clive's gone. And so has everyone else. Even Jack the barman.

I don't know how long I've been coming here but the number of empty cans tells me it's been for quite a while. I'm so cold I'm shaking uncontrollably. I can't feel my hands. My feet. My face. I can't even feel the snot that has run from my nose to my chin.

I look around 360 once more for Clive. He's not there. He was never there.

I look up at the policeman.

'Oh God, help me,' I whisper and begin to cry.

loring my voice

I'm pretty sure I cried all the way to the station in the squad car. The police officers have been very quiet. Said nothing. They took me in and I didn't resist. They haven't read me my rights. I don't think I'm under arrest. More taken in for my own protection.

At the station the same officers have a brief chat with the desk sergeant before he takes my details and I'm led to a cell. My room for the night.

The stark pastel green walls, the harsh strip lighting, the bare wooden bench, the lack of window, the impassable, imposing steel door, the cold, the cold, the cold. It's not that the cell lacks comfort, but more it's designed for discomfort. Despite that I lie down on the bench overcome with exhaustion and sleep takes me there and then.

Later, when I wake, I have no idea how long has passed. Hours? Minutes? Years? Nothing would surprise me. I would have slept forever if I hadn't been disturbed by the smell. The crippling crick in my neck wouldn't have stirred me. Nor the Arctic cold. Not even the thrumming of the old generator on the other side of the wall. But I couldn't stay sleeping in the presence of the smell.

That smell.

Sunscreen and hash.

I sit up suddenly alert and he's there at the end of the bench looking at me. Watching me.

Clive.

'Hey bruv, wassup?' he says.

'What the fuck are you doing here?' I snap.

'Well that's a nice greeting for your brother I must say,' he says laughing.

'How did you get in here?' I ask and curse myself immediately. People say stupid things all the time and I'm no different.

Clive gives me a look. A look that says 'Now don't be a silly boy – you know exactly how I got in here and I'll sit here and wait for you to work it out before we move on.'

'Oh yeah,' I say tiredly, 'for a moment there I forgot. Why don't you just leave me alone, Clive?' I plead.

Clive sighs.

'You know why I'm here, bruv,' he says. 'We have work to do and as long as that's the case I'll be around.'

'What work?' I demand.

Again Clive treats me to one of his 'who is being a silly boy?' looks.

'What have we been planning all this time?' he asks.

'I won't do it,' I say, 'I can't do it.'

'You can and you will.'

'No!' I say, 'No, no, no! I'm going to get help. I'm going to see a therapist and I'm going to get rid of you forever.'

'Yeah, right!' says Clive and he snorts a chuckle, 'you know I won't let you do that and you know you're not capable of winning a battle of wills with me.'

'But you're not real!' I scream, 'you only exist in my imagination.'

Clive's face turns stony.

Serious.

Menacing.

'I'm as real as you and always have been,' he says. 'You carry my DNA. In so many ways I'm more real than you. You're just my vehicle. I'm an Olympian trapped in a disabled body. Christ, I know what it's like to be Stephen Hawking. Yeah, I'm real. I've always been real and I've always been here. And I always will be. You can't escape me. I'm a part of you and I ain't going anywhere.'

'No!' I scream, 'You're not real! I'm going to see Doctor Jones.'

'Now don't be silly. Doctor Jones is no longer a problem,' says Clive.

'What?'

'Why do you think I was late getting to the Tombstone tonight? I've already dealt with Doctor Jones. What he knew he took with him.'

I suddenly recall an image of Doctor Jones lying face up on his office floor, a pool of his own blood expanding around his shattered skull. His eyes open. Staring. Blank. Vacant. My patient file open on his PC as Clive erases the last entry about my "condition". The hard copy already retrieved from the cabinet, the accusatory blood test results removed.

'How can you possibly think we'll get away with this?' I ask.

'We won't have to,' he replies, 'we're going to finalise the plan and that will solve everything.'

'I can't,' I say, 'I won't.'

'You have to and you will,' he says.

'I won't,' I scream.

There's a click and the screech of metal on metal as an officer slides the visor open on the door. He glances at me then his eyes do a quick scan of the cell before coming to focus on me again.

'Is everything all right in here, Sir?' he asks.

'Yes officer, fine, fine,' says Clive before I get the chance to answer. I go to speak but nothing comes out. Clive is preventing my vocal chords from working. It's like a recurring nightmare I had as a kid where I'm being chased by a shadow and I reach my front door but I don't have a key. And the shadow is getting closer and the doorbell doesn't work and the knocker is missing and when I try to knock on the door my arms move as if through molasses and make no noise on impact. And all the while the shadow gets closer and I go to scream but my voice is gone, nothing comes out and all the while the shadow gets closer and closer. And the house remains in darkness and nobody comes to the door and I can't make any noise and nobody is coming to help and the shadow gets closer.

And closer.

And closer.

'It's just I heard a lot of shouting,' says the police officer, 'a raised voice. Your raised voice, Sir.'

I go to speak but nothing comes out. Clive is in control.

'Sorry about that, officer,' he says, 'I was doing some vocal exercises and reciting my lines for a play I'm in.'

'I see,' says the officer but it's clear to see that he doesn't see at all. 'Well, there are other people in other cells, Sir, so I'd appreciate it if you kept it down.'

'Of course, officer,' says Clive, 'I'm sorry for the disturbance and I assure you it won't happen again.'

The visor slides shut and then everything goes black.

Avoiding the issue

The next time I'm aware of anything I'm sitting at a bar with a violent thumping headache and sporting a lump the size of a boiled egg on my jaw. With my tongue I can move one, two, three teeth. I taste blood.

Clive looks at me.

'Feeling better?' he asks.

I shake my head no.

'What happened?' I ask.

'You needed a nap,' he says.

And it dawns on me.

'You knocked me out?' I say.

'I suppose that's one way of looking at it,' he says, 'the important thing is that I got us out of the cop shop and set everything up. All you have to do is call her.'

I look at my mobile phone sitting on the bar in front of me.

'It's OK,' says Clive, 'you can thank me later.'

I glare at him.

'Believe me, bruv,' he says, 'this is the only way.'

'Why is this the only way?' I ask.

'You know why?' he says with exaggerated patience. 'When you're ill you need to treat the problem not the symptom. The best way to treat cancer is to remove it. Helen is your cancer and you have to remove her from your life.'

I say nothing. I stare at the phone. I lift my glass and take a drink.

Clive sighs.

'You're avoiding the issue,' he says. 'You know what you have to do. You can't put it off forever.'

I say nothing. Thing is, I know he's right. I do need to remove Helen from my life. Just not the way he has in mind. And I can't bring myself to remove her in any other way.

'Call her,' says Clive

'Not yet,' I say. 'There are a couple of things I still need to do. I'll get them done and call her at the weekend.'

I slide the phone along the bar in front of Clive and look away.

If I were a Shakespearean character I'd be Hamlet.

'You're making excuses,' says Clive. 'There's nothing important left for you to do. There's nothing important left for me to do. There's nothing important left for Libra to do. Phone her!'

He slides the mobile phone back along the bar until it sits in front of me. Taunting me. Mocking me. Making a coward of me. It's right there in front of my folded arms. All I have to do is pick it up and phone her. My arms remain folded. I hear the phone laughing. No, strike that. It's more of a snigger. Sneering. Superior. Better than me. Me and my yellow streak a mile wide.

I'm about to pick it up when Clive reaches over and grabs it. I don't know what I was going to do with it. I might have made the call. But I think I might just have launched it across the bar instead.

'I'll phone her,' says Clive and he finds her number in the phone book. I want to scream. I want to wrench it from his hand. But more than that I want to speak to Helen. Even if it is for *that* reason. I want to hear her voice. I want to make things better. We were supposed to be together forever. We were supposed to die together.

Clive puts the phone to my ear and I hear Helen's voice.

248

'Hello?' she says. It's a simple word. A greeting. But it's always uttered as a question. Just hearing her saying it lifts me. My heart soars.

'Hello?' she asks again. This time it's more of a demand.

'Hi,' I say. It's weak. Uninspiring. Says nothing.

'It's me,' I say. Pathetic. Predictable. Talking in clichés. Small talk will be the death of the language. People with nothing to say but speaking incessantly.

'Oh hi,' she says. Upbeat. Enthusiastic. Happy.

'I was going to call you later,' she says.

'You must have read my mind,' she says and laughs at her own joke. Well, not her joke. It's been with us longer than any living person and it's as funny as AIDS. But it's one of those things people say all the time like it's the wittiest and most original thing ever uttered. More filling space. That uncomfortable silence people can't live with. Show people unimaginable horror. Decapitations, rape, murder, snuff movies, mutilations, executions, disfiguring diseases, poverty, famine, bombs blowing people to smithereens and they take it in their stride. No, strike that, they lap it up. How often have people seen the footage of the plane hitting the second tower? And it never loses its magnetism. But give people silence and they can't handle it.

'Why were you going to phone me?' I ask.

'No real reason,' she says. 'Just to catch up.

There's a pause and I leave the pause alone.

'Actually, that's not quite true,' she says. 'I'd like to meet up. I need to speak with you.'

'What about?' I ask.

'I'd prefer not to talk about it on the phone,' she says. 'I want to talk face to face.'

'OK,' I say. 'It's funny, but the reason I was phoning was because I want to meet for a chat too.'

'Why don't you come round for dinner?' I say.

So Helen is coming round for dinner on Friday night. This is too easy. I could do anything. There are hundreds of odourless, colourless poisons I could add to our food. I could put arsenic in the wine. I could doctor the gas and allow us to drift off gently together. I could get a gun or any other weapon. We will be alone together in my flat and I can do anything. Except I can't. I don't have an option. The suicide of choice in the 21st century is to strap your body with explosives and blow everything to Hell.

fusion

The table is set. The Shiraz is breathing. Tracy Chapman is Talkin' Bout a Revolution on the stereo. A warm glowing ambience permeates the flat from the numerous flickering candles. Everything is in place. Table. Wine. Music. Candles. Jacket. I go to the cupboard and check the jacket. It's still there. Ready to go. I breathe a sigh. Relief.

No sign of Clive. I breathe again. Pure unadulterated relief.

The aroma of myriad foods flirts with my nostrils. I've decided to take the concept of fusion food to a new level. As a starter I've prepared a salad of smoked salmon on a bed of rhubarb and raw chillies drizzled with strawberry coulis. For the main we'll enjoy lamb stuffed with anchovies accompanied by chocolate chip wild rice and tomatoes stuffed with cabbage. And dessert is a cheeky potato brandy mousse. It all looks to be going well.

I check the table and correct Helen's napkin which has moved. And my glass. And the cutlery which seems to have slipped a little.

The doorbell rings on the dot of 7.30 and Helen greets me with a peck on the cheek and another bottle of Shiraz.

251

'Oh you shouldn't have,' I say mock admonishing her as I take the bottle and her coat. She laughs at our little in joke about the peculiar habits of people at dinner parties. The host always says not to bring anything and the guest always brings wine. And the host always expects the guest to bring wine and the guest always knows the host neither needs nor wants it but expects it nonetheless.

I offer Helen a seat and pour two glasses of the Shiraz. We clink, cheers and drink.

'So how have you been?' I ask.

'Oh you know, the same. Busy, busy, busy. All go at work and no slower at home.'

She lets go a little laugh and I do the same.

'Excuse me,' I say, 'but I just need to check on dinner.'

I go to the oven and check the lamb. Fine. All good. Should be ready by eight o'clock no question. The potato mousse seems to be firming up nicely in the fridge. Fine. The cabbage is still a little too firm for my needs. Fine. Still time. The chocolate has melted through the rice. Fine. Remove it from the heat for now and reheat it just before serving. Fine.

I check the table. My napkin has moved so I correct it. There's a smudge on Helen's dessert spoon so I polish it with the tea towel. Fine.

I return to Helen.

'Is there anything I can do?' she asks playfully. Again, the etiquette of dinner parties. The guest always offers to help and the host is always in control. The guest only asks out of politeness knowing the host will refuse. The host refuses even though they expected the guest to ask. The silly games we play.

'Now let's not be silly,' I say, 'you know everything's under control.'

The timer on the oven beeps alerting me to the fact that it is now 7.30. I check my watch and it is indeed only now 7.30. Helen is not here yet. I must have been daydreaming. I check the lamb again. Fine. And the table. I adjust the wine glasses so they sit flush on the coasters. I check the wine is open. Yes it is. Fine. I check the jacket. Fine.

No sign of Clive.

No sign of Helen. But hey, I knew she'd be a little late. She always is. Or used to be anyway.

The doorbell goes and this time Helen has brought a Rioja. I pour two glasses of wine. We clink, cheers and drink. I check dinner. Fine. I check the table. This time the candles are out of line so I adjust them. Fine.

I go back to the sofa and Helen's gone. I check my watch – 7.40. Helen is not here yet. No sign of Clive. I breathe. Relief.

OK, time to run through the plan one last time. When Helen arrives I take her into the sitting room. I take her coat and when I hang it on the coat rack I lock the door. I pour the wine and we sit and chat. I serve dinner. After dinner and a few glasses of wine I tell her what she means to me. I remind her how we promised to stay together forever. I remind her how we promised to die together. These are the kind of promises you can't break. I get the jacket. I fulfil our promises to each other. Simple.

The doorbell rings and Helen greets me with a peck on the cheek and a bottle of Valpolicella.

'I'm so sorry I'm late,' she says, 'but the traffic was a nightmare.'

I giggle.

'What?' she asks confused.

'Nothing,' I reply, 'it's just that's the kind of excuse we always used to give whenever we were late for anything.'

Helen giggles now.

'I'm telling the truth this time though,' she says. 'There were sirens everywhere. It was a real pain. I have no idea what happened but it seemed pretty big.'

'Never mind,' I say, 'you're here now.'

I pour the wine. We chink, cheers and drink.

We chat briefly. Small talk. Nothing. We both needed to speak to each other but there is a protocol to be observed. We can't just go straight into it and we need to go through the niceties first. I go and check dinner. The lamb is ready as is the cabbage so I put the starter together.

'Actually, do you mind if I put on the TV to see the news? I'll put it on mute so we still have the music,' says Helen.

'Of course,' I say, 'help yourself.'

We sit at the table and begin to eat.

As fusion food goes this rocks. The raw chillies and strawberry coulis are fantastic with the smoked salmon. Helen must have lost her appetite as she hasn't really touched her food. She's just pushing it around her plate.

'What do you think of the food?' I ask.

'Erm, it's different?' she says.

'Yeah,' I say, 'I'm experimenting with fusion food. Cool eh?'

'Er, yeah,' she says, 'thing is though, it's supposed to be eclectic but complementary at the same time. I don't think this is. Sorry.'

'Oh,' I say, 'I thought you'd enjoy it.'

I put my knife and fork down and fight to hold back tears. I think about the main. Lamb stuffed with anchovies and rice infused with chocolate – what's not to like? I decide not to let her comments affect me. She can't hurt me anymore than she already has so I decide to move on. I force a smile. I pick up my knife and fork and start to eat again.

'Oh my God!' Helen screams, 'The Queen has been assassinated!'

I look at the TV that holds Helen's attention just as the screen changes to show the Scales of Justice emblem. I hit the mute on the remote as Libra's latest tape is being played.

'To kill a serpent you must remove the head. The Queen of England is the Head of State. She might be seen as more of a figurehead these days, but make no mistake about it, she is the Head of the State of the United Kingdom. She has the power to dissolve and establish government and she has allowed her puppet of a Prime Minister to behave like a tyrant and do as he pleased even though the people have spoken out against him. Maybe the new Head of State will not make the same mistakes.'

The screen goes back to the studio and before the newsreader can say anything I turn off the TV.

'I suppose you're going to tell me sooner or later,' I say, 'but what did you want to speak to me about?'

Helen stares at me open-mouthed. She puts down her knife and fork which she's been using to chase the food around her plate. She focuses on me.

'Did you just hear the news?' she says in exasperation.

'Yes I did,' I say, 'the Queen is dead and there is nothing I can do about it. Prince Charles will be crowned King. A general election will probably take place and maybe things will change. Maybe not. I'm beyond caring,' I say. 'So what did you want to talk about?'

She picks up her glass and drains it. And all the while her glaring eyes don't leave mine. She refills her glass and takes another good swig, still eyeballing me. The look she's launching at me, well there's more warmth in the Arctic.

'Have you lost your fucking mind?!' she screams. 'The Queen is dead! Assassinated! This is huge! You can't just dismiss it because you don't care! That whole JFK thing about where you were when he was shot, well believe me this is going to be way bigger!' She stops to drain her glass.

'So do us both a favour and turn on the fucking TV!' she demands before adding, 'Please!'

'Helen,' I begin in a calm tone which betrays my inner fury, 'this is my flat and it's my TV. I invited you to dinner tonight as we need to talk. And we are going to do just that...'

'I will leave right now unless you...' Helen interrupts.

'Helen!' I snap, which brings a halt to her tirade, 'I let you finish what you had to say. Don't dare interrupt me again! At least have the courtesy to allow me to speak in my own home!'

'Sorry,' she says, 'you're right. Go on.'

'Thank you.' I compose myself again. 'We need to talk. We have both acknowledged that. We can't allow this terrible news – and I recognise that it is terrible news – to prevent us from doing what we must do. Now, I propose we continue with our evening as planned and when we have finished with what we need to do, we can catch up with the news of the Queen's assassination then. It's Sky News. They will talk about nothing else for the next week. We will find out everything later this evening and we won't miss a thing – it doesn't have to be this very minute. OK?'

She looks at me for a moment and takes another drink. She shrugs and sighs.

'Fair enough,' she says, 'I can't fault your logic.'

'Besides,' I say, 'she'll still be dead! And I know where I was when she was assassinated. Do you?'

In spite of herself she lets go a little chuckle.

255

'Don't you think it's a little early to take the piss even for you?' she says.

'Nope! Now, ladies first. What did you want to talk to me about?'

She pauses and looks at the screen again. She drains her glass again and refills it, topping me up in the process.

'This is really hard for me to say,' she says, 'and I've played it out in my head a thousand times and I still haven't got it right. There are a couple of things I need to say so please be patient with me and let me finish.'

She takes a deep breath followed by a good drink of wine.

'OK, the first thing you need to know is that I still love you and I want to give it another go.'

Together forever

The words seem to hang in the air: 'I still love you and I want to give it another go.' I knew words could take your breath away but I'm truly winded. I've been punched in the stomach before so hard I can't breathe. I've had knocks to the kidneys that have left me crumpled and kicks in the balls that have paralysed. But this news combines all three times infinity. And it's the best I've felt for years. Did she really just say that?

'The second thing though is that for this to happen I want you to get counselling. I think you're severely depressed and need help.'

This wasn't part of the plan. This wasn't how it was supposed to go. I've got my jacket ready.

'I know I'm not easy to live with so I'll see someone too. I want us both to really try.'

We were supposed to die together. I've got my jacket.

'I've been thinking about this for a while and I think it's the right thing to do. Even after what you said on Christmas Day,' says Helen.

I top up the glasses. Numb and dumb. I drain my glass.

'Are you going to say anything?' she asks.

257

'You really want to get back together?' I ask.

'Yes,' she says, 'I really do.' And she smiles.

'I can't believe it,' I say and look away. This was not the plan. I've got my jacket. We were supposed to die together.

'Of course, I appreciate this is all a bit much to take in right now,' she says, 'so if you want time to think about it then that's fine too.'

This was not the plan. We were supposed to stay together forever. We were supposed to die together. And she wants us to be together now. This changes everything. In a good way.

I smile back at her.

'Of course I want to get back together,' I say and I lean over and kiss her. I breathe Helen in. Her sweet perfume. Her conditioned, fresh hair. Her soft skin. A combination of fruits and flowers. Herbs and spices. Fresh. Nice.

Then.

Sunscreen and hash.

'What the Hell are you doing?' says Clive startling me from the kiss.

'Don't listen to a word she says, you fucking moron! She's an inveterate liar and will end up hurting you again! Stick to the plan!'

'No!' I wail, 'Go away! Leave me alone!'

'What?' says Helen, 'I thought you wanted to get back together!?'

'No, Helen, not you. You don't understand! Please don't go anywhere. I'll be back in a minute,' and I drag Clive to the bathroom. I lock the door.

'Clive, please leave me alone,' I plead, 'Helen wants to get back together. We can make it work.'

'You reckon?' says Clive. 'From prison? Don't forget, bruv, you've left a trail of destruction in your wake and a number of victims. This isn't Hollywood. You don't get to walk away from shit like that in real life.'

'I know and I'll take whatever punishment is to be handed out for those crimes but I've got to try to give this a go.'

There's a knock on the bathroom door.

'Are you ok in there?' asks Helen. 'What's going on?'

'I'm fine honey,' I say. 'I'll be out in a minute. Just please wait for me in the sitting room.'

I wait to hear her shuffle away.

'Clive, I'm going back out there and I'm going to enjoy my first evening back with Helen. I've been given another chance. I've got to take it.'

'What you've got to do is put on that jacket and finish this thing,' says Clive. And once again he takes control of my body and much as I struggle against him I find myself in the hall opening the cupboard and putting on the jacket.

I go back to the sitting room where Helen is looking confused. Concerned. Worried.

'What's wrong?' she asks. 'And why are you wearing a jacket all of a sudden?'

I go to speak but I have no control of my voice.

Clive opens the jacket showing off the home-made explosives and detonator. Helen gasps and covers her face with both hands. She looks up again as if trying to disbelieve her eyes.

'We were supposed to be together forever,' says Clive stroking the detonator. 'We were supposed to die together.'

'We can be together forever,' says Helen, tears forming in her eyes. Her voice shaking. Cracking. 'Just please take off the jacket and talk to me.'

'It's too late for talk,' says Clive. 'You should have thought about that months ago!' he says jabbing a finger at her. With one hand on the detonator and the other gesturing at Helen, he seems to lose focus on me and I'm able to free myself from his grip. I launch at him slamming him into the wall before stamping at the back of his knees bringing him to the ground in a crumpled heap. I hold him face down and pin his arms behind his back and sit on him.

'Now listen to me,' I say, 'we're getting back together and there's nothing you can do to stop that. Do you understand?' I ask.

Clive says nothing. He tries to shake me off but my grip is firm. I push his arm up his back to the point of dislocation, his face becoming a contorted grimace.

'Do you understand?' I ask again.

Clive nods his head yes. He's growing fainter under me.

'Leave. Us. Alone.' I say and Clive becomes transluscent before vanishing completely.

He's gone.

Again.

I breathe. Unadulterated relief.

'Helen, I'm going to go and get help first thing in the morning,' I say.

She nods at me. Tears streaming down her face. I sit back against the wall totally exhausted.

'What just happened?' she asks.

'I'm not sure,' I lie. 'All I know is that I need help and I'm going to get it.'

'OK,' she whispers. 'Are we going to be ok?' she asks.

I look around the room. Clive is gone. I take a good sniff of the air. No sunscreen or hash.

'Yeah,' I say smiling, 'we're going to be fine.'

I breathe. Unadulterated relief.

I laugh and Helen laughs too. I get up and take off the jacket. I go to her and hug her tight. Firm. Never wanting to let go. Never going to let go again. And I wouldn't except for my mobile phone ringing. I don't recognise the number.

'I'll ignore it,' I say.

'No it's fine,' says Helen, 'answer it.'

'Hello?' I answer.

'Hello, Detective Campbell here,' says the voice on the other end of the line, 'I wonder if I could trouble you for some information about the night Bill was attacked.'

'Of course,' I say, 'I'd be glad to help.'

'It's to do with your timings. You said that you got to the Spirit Lounge at about 9.30pm but on the CCTV footage you don't get there until just gone 11pm. Can you explain that?'

Fuck.

Think, think, think!

'Have you checked that the time was correct on the footage, Detective Campbell?' I ask.

'Yes, we've checked all of that and it was correct on the night,' he replies. And he leaves it hanging there. Waiting for me to hang myself.

Can't think.

Help.

What do I do?

'You're fucked now matey!' says Clive at my ear. 'The fuzz are onto you and it won't be long before they know all your dirty little secrets and you'll be sent to prison for the rest of your life.'

I'm paralysed. Clive has control. His hand moves toward the detonator.

'What are you doing?' screams Helen.

Clive's hand closes around the detonator ready to press the button.

'Are you there, Sir?' asks Detective Campbell, 'can you explain the anomaly?'

Tears run down my face as I turn to Helen.

'I'm sorry,' I say.

'You two were meant to die together!' yells Clive.

'You two?!' screams Helen.

'Don't listen to him, Helen,' I say. And just when I'm about to explain about Clive. About my twin. My condition. Chimera. Just as I'm about to make Helen see sense and tell her I'll get help to get rid of him. Just as I'm about to beg for her forgiveness and patience and understanding, the world flashes sideways in a blur and I find myself in a crumpled heap. And between me and the floor is Clive. He punched me but it didn't quite work out the way he thought it would and I've landed on top of him.

And now he's grabbing for me again. Except he's not grabbing for me. He's reaching for the detonator which he dropped in the fall. And now I'm reaching for the detonator too. And Helen is reaching for the detonator.

We were supposed to die together.

We will die together.

Does it have to be now?

Three hands land on the detonator at the same time.

Made in the USA
Middletown, DE
18 December 2015